SANBUSAKU

TOKYO TRILOGY

Alex Kahney

First published in Japan in 2011
This edition first published in Great Britain in 2024

Copyright © Alex Kahney, 2011, 2024
All rights reserved.
ISBN-9798321791745

"Every good storyteller nowadays starts with the end, and then goes on to the beginning, and concludes with the middle. That is the new method."
—Oscar Wilde, *The Devoted Friend*

"I'm making my own maxims."
—Adrian Roots, *In conversation*

Many grateful thanks to William Miller at PaPa's for much splendid help and advice

Jyakuten: Hamartia

1

"Cash-based society" is one of Japan's epithets. Cash is primarily used in transactions, not credit or debit cards or checks. Even salaries are paid cash in many cases, and companies use cash to count their assets and pay their men and women. Companies reckon their success in terms of how much cash they have. Very few bars and restaurants accept credit cards, although most retail shops do—at least in the cities.

Japanese people pay their domestic utilities bills in cash, at the counters of banks or convenience stores. Payer and payee alike trust cash: there is no arguing with those ten thousand, five thousand and one thousand yen notes, which are carried around by people young and old in wallets full as thick as a paperback book. Most Japanese adults like to have over twenty thousand yen on them at all times; some, three or four hundred thousand. That is four thousand U.S. dollars. Many Japanese say they feel bare and insecure without carrying at least a certain amount of cash, say five thousand yen (fifty dollars). Furthermore, they mostly dislike borrowing and are cautious not to overspend: hence credit cards are infrequently used or even owned. High school sweethearts take part-time night jobs and start saving up for their marriage until they can afford to pay for it in cash, perhaps a decade later. Those credit cards that are in use average two-to-four purchases a month and must be paid off in full with each monthly bill—that is the rule. Despite the Japanese preference for using cash, however as might be supposed, the majority of Japanese do not have great amounts of spare money to spend freely—basic living costs are too high for that, especially in the cities. Food and drink are dear, rent is high, nights out are expensive; travel costs a lot.

But it is considered normal to want and try to obtain as much money as you can get in Japan. If you say that you are not interested in gaining money, or that life contains more important things that money cannot buy, the average Japanese person will look at you strangely. In one respect, that doubtful person is right of course—for what can we do without money? The great majority of us are enslaved by getting enough of it to live on, and everything we want to see or do remains barred from us without it. But this is not the only reason that Japanese consider working hard in order to get money to be quite a natural and even a good endeavor. Above this, there is something else: In Japan, the average person is affluent but no one is really rich. Therefore there are no models of rapacity, acquisition and wastage, privilege and over-feeding for those who are not as well off to witness and resent. There are no insular moneyed barons hiding in towery castles or top-floor offices from which they commit dirty tricks, take advantage of poorer persons or just laughingly live it up unscrupulously. In Japan, money is not sullied.

If you will listen, I am going to tell you what happened to me when I went to Japan: an incredible story with cash, Japanese money, somewhere at its heart. This is not to say that I went to Japan specifically to make money or to get rich, as many other Japan-bound visiting workers do—although I did become rich, very rich; it is more that by using money—that is, its tokens of banknotes and coins and not its surrogates such as credit cards, bank transfers or standing orders and the like—meant, these monetary exchanges, that I was literally in charge, personally present and able to inspect and oversee where all my funds came and went. This enabled me very clearly to compare the cost of whatever I was buying or paying for against what I had done, and the time I had spent, in earning the cash that I was handing over in exchange for that entity. And this does not mean that while in Japan I was becoming stingy or an unmoving money-minded capitalist—on the contrary, I spent money hand over fist—it was that being intimately knowledgeable of how much I was spending simply could not be helped; it was a consequence of having no standing orders, credit loans, interest charges, bank costs, monthly repayments, percentage points, statement sheets, current balances and all the abstract representations of assets and revenues to worry about—just cash. And not an hour went by, it seemed, in that thronging commercial center, Tokyo, when I was not either acquiring or disbursing cash.

It was late October 1993 when I came to Japan to start my new job at Nimsan Science. I arrived at Narita Airport on a Saturday afternoon—all flights into Tokyo from Europe land in mid-afternoon—and after some confusion over my visa, which was resolved by the intervention of my new colleague from Nimsan, Dr. Gunji, who was waiting in the terminal to greet me and managed to explain to the customs officers who I was—(that is, Nimsan's new-boy)—I was permitted at last to enter into the country. This experience, as a matter of fact, my very first interaction with Japanese people on Japanese soil, was, as quite often happens when someone makes a transgression into untold new avenues in his or her life, such as I was doing on that warm and beautiful afternoon—was gifted with prognostic indications.

This I could hardly have known on that day, back then, but my struggles to explain that I was a new employee flying into Tokyo to start work at the head offices of Nimsan, one of Japan's biggest pharmaceutical manufacturers, to those uncomprehending immigration officials, and their attempts, in turn, to get through to me that my visa which I was brandishing toward them was not a visa at all, but actually an application form to obtain a visa, all written in Japanese, together with the fact of my finally being allowed to enter the country instead of being turned back to London, following some words from Dr. Gunji, provided me with some miraculously well-timed insights into Japan's society that I would soon, over the months ahead, come to observe and grow quite used to on a broader scale. Because what transpired in that bare-walled little interview room set off beside the now-deserted passport malls was that I, a foreigner, or *gaijin* (remember that word!), who had arrived to start work at a Japanese company without having the required visa, was waived through, regardless of this deficiency, because a research doctor, a senior at a big Japanese company, put in a good word for me, and this was accepted as a valid reason partly because of whom this person represented in society, but also on the grounds that I, as a guest, a guest not only of the company I was about to join but, in a sense, of the nation as a whole, would have been seen as unspeakably inhospitably treated had I been deported after being taken into the company's hands; and furthermore, no less, because of the fact that I was simply *gaijin*, which entitled me, in those days, as I was to find out, to an almost charmed life in many day-to-day ways, for reasons that belong to the Japanese way of thinking, (which I shall enlarge upon passim), these factors were sufficient to see me through and inside safely.

There was also some more about Japanese life revealed in this precursory drama, as I was to discover later. Namely, that comprehensive, full and unambiguous communication is all but impossible between *gaijin* and Japanese. This simplistic-sounding statement, which is rooted in more complex foundations, but will be borne out by endless trial to anyone who enters Japan for the first time having grown up elsewhere abroad, is what I have come to know in the years that have elapsed since that first day when I landed at Narita Airport. A few days previously, I had received in the post back at home a letter from Japan inviting me to join Nimsan at my earliest convenience, as well as an official document purporting to be, in the words of that letter, a work visa permit. So then after arriving at Narita I had discovered that not only was this assertion not correct—was a miscommunication on the behalf of the secretary at Nimsan—but also that the customs officers themselves were not able to make me understand this miscommunication (all they could get across was that I did not have a visa, when I assuredly did have one, I thought), and then that, as I was starting to accept that I would have to go all the way back home, when upon the arrival of Dr. Gunji I could be allowed to go through customs into Japan to start work after all, was to herald, all this, to my tired and completely baffled consciousness the beginning of a new life of coping with never-ending incomplete comprehension and of going by the nose. In this odd way, I picked up the pattern of my life-to-come in Japan within an hour of setting foot in this unique and ineffable land.

    I was in Japan. Everywhere to be seen were ranks of Japanese people. Although literally obvious that Japan must be full of Japanese people, for myself to appear there and be recognizably out of place was an amazing oddity—pleasurably odd. I had gone from a place where people were of all shapes, colors and sizes to a place where uniformity was apparent, not just at a superficial glance, but really so, (so far as I could make out, and not even wishing to believe it), styles of dress included. Except, it seemed, for myself. There were no fat people, no bald people, no beards of flame-orange or white. No one was gangly tall, no one was even ugly. There were just neatly trim bodies and shiny healthy straight black hair, in two styles: long on women and short and tidy on men. Everyone was well dressed, in western styles—uniforms or suits-and-ties predominated. And how did I look? Longish curled brown hair, denim shoulder bag, jeans, home-made T-shirt with "The Damned" decaled in Gothic lettering, and holding a guitar case. This was my first impression of being in Japan: It was as though my uniqueness, till then known only to myself, was made manifest by body-metamorphosis. I positively stood out. I imagined that this put me in a fine position, and I was to be quite often justified in this, in ways both that I had assumed and also sometimes surprising, in the months ahead. As I wandered through the airport toward the exit carrying my belongings, keeping up with Dr. Gunji, who marched ahead, I had made an intuited recognition: I had already fallen in love with Japan.

It took about an hour and a half to drive in Dr. Gunji's car from the airport to the dormitory where I was to live for the immediate future. Gunji was a pocket-sized muscular energetic man of about fifty with an ever-present smile and good cheerful face. His short hair was going through a revolutionary outbreak of white strands appearing all over and multiplying. He had big prominent cheekbones and brow with sticking out ears, and so along with his broad physique appeared to be made of an assemblage of lumps. En route as we drove along the freeway, Gunji explained that he had promised the customs inspectors at the airport that Nimsan's company personnel department would hastily apply to obtain a visa for me first thing on Monday, and that in the meantime while I waited a few weeks for the application to be processed it was imperative to business that I commenced my duties forthwith. Gunji himself had declared responsibility for my conduct, which was enough to carry the argument through successfully.

I sat listening to Gunji's commentary while looking out across the city as we sped along the freeway, past blue bays, steel bridges, train tracks and lorries by the hundred; office blocks getting taller and taller and compressed tighter and tighter together as we made our way farther into the mega-city. At one point, over to the left in the distance, Disneyland suddenly appeared, a shock to see the fake castle and roller coaster rides over by the shore at parallel to the freeway. Then following this glimpse, which turned and revolved like an axis projected on a point between us with hedges, trees and trucks hurtling past my eyes, onwards and gone along the road. And for miles and miles, following along the edge of the traffic lane the whole way, recognizably Japanese shrubs and trees, in lobular and symmetrical shapes, a signature reminder that I was in the Land of the Rising Sun, something that airplane transport hides from the traveler going anywhere till he or she leaves the airport at destination and looks around from on the ground—evidence that you are where you set off to go, somewhere you had only hitherto seen in pictures.

I was in Japan! I was twenty-three years old, not long out of university, and had fallen luckily into a job at Nimsan that an older friend of the family, Gary Gosling, had arranged on my behalf during the summer just gone. Gaz was a scientist at a London university laboratory, engaged in research into organic chemical synthesis, building and characterizing compounds and investigating their potential as pharmaceutical molecules. Some of his research had been conducted in collaboration with chemists from Nimsan Science U.K., Japanese Nimsan's main European operation, and at one point he had even been invited to Tokyo to make a presentation on his findings. After a few days of doing this and touring the research facilities, meeting other investigators, he had decided to stay on for a whole month in Nimsan's Tokyo laboratories sharing advice and research ideas with his Japanese fellow scientists.

It was during that stay that Gaz had met the American David Gallienne, one of the technical editors at the Research Communications Department based in Nimsan's head office. During one night over beers and *sake* and Japanese finger snacks, this editor, Gallienne, had told Gaz that, in secret, he was intending to leave Nimsan and return back to his home in New York. Nothing more was said about this aimless remark, which was not considered at all important by my friend, but somehow however it flitted about in his mind like a blush cage bird. Hence already it was surmised by Gaz, in a yet-unknown way, that a connection of fate was made by the throwaway statement. Some weeks subsequent to that night, after Gaz had returned from Japan to London, when he and I happened to be talking about nothing remotely connected to Japan, but rather that I was thinking about leaving my job, which I had begun immediately after leaving university without putting much thought into the matter, the flighty cage bird descended with full stop on its perch: Gaz said, "I can get you a job in Japan."

"Japan? You mean working with your friends at… whatever that company was called?"

"That's right—at Nimsan. There's going to be a vacancy coming up, in the Communications Department. If I put in a good word for you, the job's yours."

"What, just like that, you can get me a job? How? You don't work for Nimsan. How can you influence them to give me any job?"

"Because," replied Gaz, smiling at the sound of his words, "In Japan, personal connections and recommendations, from people in esteemed positions—such as the one that I hold in Nimsan's eyes, for example—count for more than any university education or amount of relevant work experience that you can cram onto an eight-page-long résumé."

I made my mind up on the spot and told Gaz that I would love to go to Japan. But, I added, it is something that naturally enough I had never even thought about before. When Gaz asked me what else was I thinking of doing if I quit my current job, the answer was a pre-formed vague snippet of an ambition to go to Europe, Amsterdam perhaps, and live on my wits doing painting and writing.

"And if you did that and went to Amsterdam, how would you make money to live on?" asked Gaz.

"I don't need money," I replied. "Well not much. Just enough to feed myself, that's all."

Gaz laughed. "And what will you do when the weather turns icy cold and it drizzles endlessly for weeks or months? You can't protect yourself from that using your canvases as a blanket! Nor can you eat sheets of poetry for food. What a ridiculous idea you have there. This job in Japan I can get you will provide you with housing and four million yen a year. That's almost thirty thousand pounds. Think about it, you will be able to afford essentially whatever you want to buy. You can save most of your wage packet and still have enough to acquire anything you want. They'll provide you with your own room in a dormitory, which is more-or-less a hotel, for you to stay in at virtually no cost. Compared with being a student living on two thousand pounds a year, as you've been doing for the last three years, you'll be practically a tycoon."

I thought about thirty thousand pounds a year, and Japanese girls.

"Gaz? When can you get me the job?"

"I'll arrange it for you. You'll be there in a couple months. You'd better get your poems and paintings out the way now."

No good poems and not a single painting were ever made. I left my job and spent the time reading at home and trying not to think about whether Gaz's promise would come true. I did not want to spoil the outcome by wishing too hard. Gaz on the other hand was awfully confident and never once even hinted that he did not know what he was doing. And indeed he was quite right and kept to his word. At first I had an interview with some Japanese people from Nimsan who were on a visit to Nimsan U.K. and had made discussions with Gaz over research proposals and some interesting compounds that were going to be patented. While in Gaz's lab, they asked whether the young man who had expressed an interest in replacing David Gallienne, who had by then already left Head Office and returned to New York, was still resolved to go to Japan, and when Gaz said yes and phoned me to come and meet them, I put on a tie from Dad's wardrobe and was at the lab in under thirty minutes.

Dr. Gunji's car pulled up outside the dorm just as the afternoon light was starting to go. A blue evening tint was beginning to mix in, cooling colors. The static air pinched with cold on autumn afternoons tugs a barometer in my stomach—I could almost cry. I felt glad that the atmosphere so remindful of my childhood in the Shropshire countryside could be felt the same across the world in Asia's greatest city. The dormitory was thankfully nothing like I had imagined it, seeing mental pictures of bunk beds and pillow-fights and Tom Brown's schooldays. Actually it was just like an international business hotel complete with a rotary drive and downstairs lobby area, although at four stories high not overly big. Staying here was going to be just like living in a student campus residence at university again! A few hundred yards down the road, I had glimpsed Nimsan Co. as we drove past. Devoid of visible activity, a lone security guard could be seen sleepily occupying his hut at the entrance gates, which were blocked by a low vehicle-barrier that meant "We're closed." In the brief chance that I had to survey the place, I saw several big windowless buildings within the complex—and then we were round the corner out of sight of Nimsan.

As Gunji was lifting my trusty old acoustic guitar and my suitcase out of the car boot, refusing to allow me to help, a young Japanese man wearing glasses, baggy gray exercise pants and white T-shirt came out of the dormitory and approached us. He spoke to Gunji, mentioning my name transformed into Japanese accentuation, I could hear, and then turned to me and with an abundance of reservation and bashfulness, seemingly not knowing whether to shake my hand or bow, so that I started becoming awkward as well, introduced himself as Itoh.

"Pleased to meet you," I said. "Tommy Parker, at your service." I say that the fellow called himself Itoh, because over time I re-learned that that was his name—he was to be my neighbor occupying the next room to mine in the dormitory and had been requested by the company bosses to look after me for the first few weeks. At the time of our introduction, however, I had forgotten his name within a split second of hearing it despite earnestly trying to remember the appellation. This was going to be tougher than I thought—I was going to meet a lot of people in the next few days and weeks, without being equipped with any reference means to serve as a mnemonic in recalling any of their names. How can you remember lots of new names when they are meaningless sounds?

While we are on the subject of names, perhaps I should say something about my own, Thomas Parker—better known as Tommy. I had been given the name in part as an "amusing" reference to Elvis the King's famous road manager, Colonel Tom Parker, because my Mom was a fan of Presley from her teeny-bopper years, and, upon earning the name Parker by marriage, when I was born she could not resist the temptation to "honor" me with such an appellation associated with rock 'n' roll's finest son. The name Thomas was also in my family lineage, popping up among uncles, great grandfathers and distant relatives then and there throughout history. However, I hated it. It reminded me and everyone else in school and onwards of the matron in the Tom and Jerry cartoons whose legs were only ever seen. And I and was not going to go around as Tom Parker either. People would say where's your cigar or where's Elvis? Tommy on the other hand was great. It was British, spirited, valorous and remindful of medals and a flashing victory V. I could see myself in a tin hat launching a fist full of hand grenades while jumping into a German machine-gun nest shouting, "Eat pineapple, Fritz!" Thus I had used and been called Tommy by everyone since as long as I could remember.

Dr. Gunji, Itoh and I went inside and I was shown my room on the third floor (that is, counting the ground floor as the first, and going up two flights)—wherein there was just a small single bed and a few white built-in closets and drawers, shiny dark veneer "floorboards," and cream-white wallpaper that on close inspection was wattled with a mesh of tiny squares, the reckoning of the sheer millions of which expanding over the four walls could probably drive me mad. The room, its clean dustless bed and pristine surfaces gave the impression of having never been touched. A virgin room. I liked it! I noticed that it was already night-time outside. The view from the solitary window looked frontward over the driveway and onto the lamp-lit darkened street, where cars droned past with their front lights feeling the road. Although night had fallen, everything outside the window was made visible, by one means or other artificially lit: shining or reflecting like the sun and the moon. I checked the time—just about six o'clock and dark already. Calendar time in Japan is set so that even in midsummer the sun goes to bed by six o'clock. (A-ha!—The Land of the Rising Sun.) Not long after Gunji and Itoh left me alone I got on the bed and suddenly went to sleep. I was in Tokyo, where each night millions and millions of watts flood along power lines to lamps of neon and tungsten, festivities reign, and crowds heave, and there was I on my bed, out like a light.

The next day, Sunday, I awoke early with a rejuvenated mix of excitement and refreshment from sleeping off the crushing jet lag that had sedated me the day before. My bare room, concealing in functional drawers my few clothes that I had brought with me in the suitcase and put away the night before, pleased me a lot. It was cosy and agreeable to sleep in—my own room. Furthermore, and this was something that particularly mattered to me, the room contained no unwanted bearing of incorporeal presence after the light went off, or at least had not done so on the first night, the most important test. This implied that I could look forward to sleeping there soundly—good news! Outside the window a lovely clear autumn day was being prepared; the sun had climbed the horizon's fence, birds carried twigs in their beaks telling ants to build a barn of sky. How blue it was! Dark at the point looked, flaring out white like the eye itself. It was time to see Tokyo. I had already studied my guidebook and street maps extensively and had some idea of the most important places to visit and see first. It amused me to note that Tokyo was sectioned into twenty-three wards, or districts, because the street number of my home I had left behind was number twenty-three, and here I was in my new abode far, far away, in the City of Twenty-Three. Twenty-three had always been my favorite and lucky number, and I was twenty-three years old too, completing the comfortable feeling I had that I was in luck moving to Japan.

I walked a few minutes to the nearest Metro station and bought a ticket. Pricey! The train arrived, and was almost empty with all passengers-that-there-were being able to sit not having to stand, so I settled down on one of the long sofas that distended longitudinally down each side of the carriage, which in its red velvet cloth looked so clean that it had just come off the clothesline. As I sat there and looked around me, I began to notice something else: a new sensation to go in the living-in-Japan cabinet. Everyone, it seemed, was either asleep or looking at me. Directly across, a man of about sixty years was apparently studying my face, in a way that did not betray curiosity exactly, and was not overly intrusive either, although he did not glance away whenever I looked up. His expression gave me no clues at all as to what he might be thinking as he looked at me. I assumed that it was something xenophobic about foreigners coming to live in Japan and how the country was going downhill as a result, or perhaps it was a rueful meditation on young people and how disrespectful they are nowadays. In any case something along those lines. Little did I know that over a short period of time I would soon begin to see that assuming what is going on in a Japanese person's mind is an exercise in getting it wrong.

I checked around me with quick periscopes and confirmed that quite a few people were indeed openly regarding me—those who were awake that is. Most were not. One young woman was so deeply asleep that she had rolled, head back and eyes shut, with black hair spread out on the quilted breast of her coat, and was gasping deep snores on her neighbor's shoulder, a male stranger who was simply a passenger that made a good pillow. For his part, he sat and read his book without flinching. A moment later, when we came to a halt at a station, I saw that the young woman in the coat, as well as a man who had also looked, up till that point, as though he were fast asleep in his seat, came awake, stood up and calmly stepped off the train, disappearing onto the platform. Neither of the two exhibited any appearance of having got off at the wrong stop.

This observation merited further investigation, so I made a visual note of where all the other sleeping passengers on the train were positioned, and each time we stopped after that I monitored their movements. Sure enough, at each station some of the sleepers roused themselves and unhurriedly exited the carriage, seemingly at the right stop for them. Was this some kind of recuperative micro sleep they had timed not to last more than the length of their journey? Had they all somehow perfected their body clocks? I could not think that any of the passengers had really been asleep. Were they pretending to be asleep? A moment later, something else happened which stimulated my interest. At the next station, the passengers at either end of the bench opposite mine, which could seat about ten people all squeezed together, got off, the two of them jumping out of the most proximal doors, and as soon as they stood up and vacated their places, the people who had been sitting next to them both moved over onto the empty places at either end—one shuffling left and one right simultaneously. Then they nodded off. This exchange would probably not have quite so attracted my curiosity if the process were not repeated whenever those two end seats—as well as the equivalent end seats on all the other benches in the carriage including the one I was sitting on, I observed, were relinquished. The nearest person would quickly budge over to take the still-warm position. Those really were the prized seats! Little did I know as I watched all this that what I was seeing going on in that train were several manifestations indicative of the worm of frustration that pushes away under the subsoil beneath Japan's sunny tended garden of appearances.

That Sunday, I planned to go to the Ebisu district first then walk from there to Shibuya and take another short train ride to Shinjuku, to experience some of Tokyo's major hubs of activity. At the first of those stops, once I was outside Ebisu station I observed in the main square adjacent to the exits a street performance of sorts, starring a highly unusual obese Japanese man, one of the first overweight persons I had seen since setting foot in Japan, who had long black hair and overflowing beard and wore white robes, chanting and meditating into a microphone surrounded by a group of female dancers in white veils and some mad headgear, floppy-eared elephant masks with long trunks hanging over the wearers' noses. Their dance motions, get-ups and pachyderm masks had an Indian-gods look about them. The fat man squinted and seemed almost blind while chanting into the mic over and over again, *shōko-shōko-shōko-shōko*. Since two schoolgirls standing next to me were laughing delightedly and pointing at the absurd group, I asked them what the spectacle was. One of the girls, whose name I learned was Keiko, could speak English and informed me that the man was the leader of a religious cult called Om, named after the sound of one of their mantras, and that the word the man kept repeatedly singing into the mic was his own name Shōko. The girls found him very ridiculous and comical. I stood and watched the show for a bit longer then left Keiko and her friend laughing at the funny fat man, and started walking in the direction of Shibuya.

At Shibuya, the afternoon crowds of people were overwhelming, brimming over the sidewalks and lining the curbs, filling every avenue and space. Colors shelled at me, penetrating to the backs of my eyes. Of the day's peepshow, suits were much that I remember, and pink shades on girls—pink striped border T-shirts and socks pulled up above the knee, like adolescents still attending kindergarten. I was dumbfounded by the never-ending numbers of cute girls. In all the crowds that filled every space both out in the open promenades and thronging the interiors of shops, it seemed that every girl was pretty. And the fashions they wore displayed remarkable invention. Among thousands, tens of thousands perhaps, every girl I saw stood out distinct.

I went to look for a large multistory import bookshop that I had read about in my Tokyo guide, and found it crammed with people, leafing through volumes at the stands and populating the square stairwells perpetually going round such as peoploids in an Escher woodcut. It was quite suffocating getting out of there, I was reminded of the stone steps in narrow castle keeps back in England: coiled anticlockwise going down to favor right-handed swordsmen protecting the towers from invaders rushing up.

Out on the street again the throngs were increasing. Who could keep count of the numbers? Hundreds, maybe thousands passed on each side of the road in a minute, streamed in and out of shops and burrowed down side streets. The result of observing and following the commotion and tumult was to embrace in the mind a common credo that everyone out there had someplace exciting to get to that was worth the press of fighting through the crowds. I became quite enthralled by it, passing through this way and that. The abundance of goods for sale, as well, was amply fit for the profusions of shoppers. So many commodities were on offer that the shop entrances spilled them in packing boxes out onto and continuously with the road. Shop staff too were to be seen standing some distance out and beyond the limits demarcating their stores: many with loudspeakers in hand, barking the songs of their trade, and encouraging and supervising the flow of customers into and out of the shop entrances, which bustled chaotically. Everywhere I looked, yellow neon lights were in front of me. Electrical equipment and flashy goods, high-fashion stores, department stores with long window displays, branches of the coffee shop chains, all overflowed with patrons. Noise amounted to a high clamor of constant pitch above which only the loudest or nearest sounds could be heard, such as interlocked cars parping each other and people's conversations as they span past. I noted how many young people smoked—in fact nearly everyone seemed to be puffing away, walking by with a cigarette burning in one hand and their partner's hand in the other. I also noticed that whereas I swapped looks with nearly every other girl who walked past me, those who were accompanied with their boyfriends modestly kept their glances turned toward their beaux and did not make eyes at me.

I was getting hungry and could no longer stand apart from these people I was hiding among: I would have to order food. Suddenly, however, as this resolution sank in, it seemed as though all the lunch outlets, restaurants and fast-food joints that I had been seeing and walking past earlier in the morning inexplicably disappeared. Where were those big windows behind which people casually chatted, smoked and relaxed while eating or finishing off a snack and a nice cup of coffee? Furthermore, what were all these inadmissible and shut-looking abodes that passed for cafes, no doubt catering for long-standing and elderly local customers only, with signs all put in Japanese, that had here-and-there taken the place of those welcoming fast food emporiums I needed?

I approached one of the said venues and peered into the dark smoked window. A menu resided on the inside of the pane, with pictures of what I now know to be *soba*—Japanese buckwheat noodles—with various different provisions fried in batter and thrown on as toppings. It all looked good, and I was in Japan to experience life from a Japanese insider's point of view, so I pushed open the door and paraded into the establishment. An old woman who by all appearances looked not to have ever heard of rheumatism or of fatigue rushed over and was at my side within an instant, pulling me toward a table and repeating the shop-owners' coin-word, meaning welcome: "*irasshaimase*," in chorus with a waiter and not only the waiter the cook too, whose head struck out from round a curtain at the back to join in the cajolery. So I was seated and with much youthful blushing and hand waving to show my ignorance of the Japanese language, I pointed out my order on the menu, which was identical to the one displayed in the window, illustrated with pictures of the bill of fayre. I picked a *soba* with *ebi tempura*—noodles with battered prawns, which I could identify from crisp pink calcified twin tails protruding from two sandy brown rolls. Then I waited as the order was enacted.

   In front of me on the table was a chalice containing wooden chopsticks packed in paper sheaths. I took out one set, snapped the two conjoined sticks apart, and attempted to load them amid my fingers, sneakily copying the man on the table in front who was sitting faced toward me, who provided a fine model of technique. He hardly noticed me watching him; he had his head down almost on top of his bowl and was rifling noodles in at a great rate, making almighty slapping and gargling noises with each ingurgitation. He also snorted mucusy snot back upwards into his nose during pauses as he ate—he appeared to have no table manners whatsoever. From him I observed, in the intervals when his utensils were kept still for a brief pause and his hand hovered over his bowl, that the lower stick had to go between the thumb and middle finger, while the upper stick moved up and down clamping under the action of the pointer digit: top and bottom like the jaws themselves inverted. My food arrived and I set about it with the balsa-wooden chopsticks, finding the noodles very easy to lift and much more so than I had done with the slippery ivory-made chopsticks that I had always failed to utilize in Chinese restaurants back at home in England. Even the short-length fragments of single noodles straddling in the basketwork on the bottom of my bowl as I finished were collected up and gratefully eaten. I supped my soup (*miso* soup), which had a slightly fishy nuance and a piece of soggy seaweed floating on top. I considered the meal quite good but lacking any vigorous sapors. I also was not sure whether I was still hungry. But this was my first full day in Japan; my taste buds were resolutely attuned to my hitherto diet of bread– or potatoes-with-what have you. Within a couple of months I would be wishing to eat nothing else but subtly extraordinary Japanese and Asian food, and was turning my nose up at the fulsome tastes of salt, fat and chocolate which overpower western cuisines.

   Back outside on the milling avenue the swarms continued strolling past. I took a step in among them and started back toward the station, Shibuya. Walking behind all these people, I started to become frustrated at the slowness with which we were moving. Progress beyond the persons in front was practically impossible: on one side was the wall of shops, and people coming the other way brushed past continuously on the other. Try overtaking on a busy conveyance like that! I was stuck behind people going at a snail's pace a fraction of my normal walking speed—it was quite antagonistic. Furthermore, people going the other way often shouldered me or swiped me with their shopping bags, or abruptly stopped themselves from colliding into me by looking up at the final second, then very irritatingly crossing right in front of the angle I had charted ahead to avoid them before they were looking. This happened several times. It became a guessing game each time, to predict which way these human obstacles would go past me, left or right. And every time, I got it wrong. Not a word was said by anyone who impeded me like this, nor in fact any indication of contrition made even such as a change of facial expression. Each time, after causing me to lurch to a halt, they just kept on going. It was peculiar behavior like which I had not before seen. I began thinking that the Japanese were very odd, whereas before I arrived in Japan I had not entertained any prejudicial thoughts other than that people are much the same everywhere. It was starting to look like I might have to append that decree with "except in Japan."

I made my way to and through the crush of the station and bought a ticket to Shinjuku, a six-minute train ride of three stops up the line. Shinjuku station turned out to be even more crowded than the one I had just left. About a dozen railway lines converge on its platforms, and with trains arriving on each platform every two or three minutes, with maybe ten carriages per train all loaded with, let us say, forty seated passengers plus five multiplied by five equals twenty-five more in each door area (one hundred people at four sets of doors per carriage) and two rows of people standing the length of the carriage knocking knees with those seated, which is another forty people, making a total of a hundred eighty people per carriage or one thousand eight hundred per trainload; and if they all get off at once (which is precisely what seemed to happen at Shinjuku), then over twenty thousand people must tramp along this station's complement of platforms every few minutes! Multiply by sixty and you arrive at over a million passengers coming into the station every few hours. Compare this with the First World War German mass army that overran eastern France in August 1914's "Battle of the Frontiers": the timetabled troops of the German Schlieffen Plan were brought to combat in a mere five hundred fifty trains to the French border daily for about ten days; in Shinjuku station, five hundred fifty trains arrive every three hours.

At one point as I was making my way round and round the vast underground burrow beneath Shinjuku's train tracks, trying to find my way out of the station's complexity, and had just stopped for a moment to take a bearing, a Japanese man in a charcoal suit approached me and, hardly even looking up as he spoke, asked me in unclear English for what sounded like telephone cards. I waved my hands to say that I did not know what he was after and he quickly made off, leaving me to make a connection: I had momentarily before just seen small numbers of groups of Middle Eastern men in tracksuits standing around in ones and twos in the station, prominently soliciting attention, and evidently doing a line of business with the huge flow of crowds passing along. "So selling some kind of homemade forged telephone cards is what they're up to," I told myself. I carried on walking, and the next similar huckster I saw I accosted and was right. I bought ten telephone cards from him for one thousand yen: I handed over the cash and he slipped the ten credit card-sized plastic inserts with a bright picture of Mt. Fuji in springtime on the top from out of a large chunk he was carrying, then backed off and continued smiling at the crowds. Hence the first object that I bought in Japan was an illegal counterfeit phone card.

Outside the labyrinthine station standing in the daylight at last, the main drag of Shinjuku was, as I found out, lined with more multistory department stores with great video screens halfway up their facades; like totem poles, the skies fractured by neon bulbs, and further uncountable multitudes of shoppers teeming about on the ground in all directions. I hardly saw any foreign people anywhere in among these throngs, either at Shinjuku or Shibuya earlier in the day. Those fellow foreigners whom I did pass often nodded or winked in acknowledgment, or if we found ourselves stopping side by side waiting to cross a road we exchanged where-are-you-froms. I probably saw less than ten foreigners or foreign couples all day. Some foreign men were with Japanese women; I would not see a Japanese man with a foreign woman all year. I spent the remainder of the afternoon idly walking about and pondering and reflecting the myriad sights. I should say here something about my musings during my perambulations. Apart from Japan's many novelties, there was also much that looked the same as in England, only was done

17

differently. When I discovered differences between what I observed in Japan compared with what I was used to in England, and the differences were inexplicable, I exercised myself with trying to work out what were the causes: I cannot promise that my conclusions were always on the right lines.

    The same melancholy which I always feel pointing me out in October afternoons pressed me into remembering to call home, so I determined to try out one of my phone cards. The first two phone boxes I saw, positioned side by side with the line of basket-fronted shopper bicycles and mopeds that cluttered every sidewalk almost touching the telephone box doors, were occupied. I stood around waiting for five minutes then got impatient at the two people inside twittering away like they could not survive without talking to anyone for an hour even if they tried, and furthermore realized that I was not the first and only person waiting for them to stop either, because others were already loitering around the doors, I set off in search of another box. The next two twinned cubicles I came across were also populated, and so I saw it manifested that I would have to wait.

    Finding a phone box where no one else was apparently waiting, I parked myself next to the door and listened as the young man went on and on about something, making plans to meet the person on the other end of the line later on that very day in all probability, his bright voice dulled behind the glass. When at last I was able to go in—the exiting person walking out the door without seeing me and letting it slam in my face—I found that although my counterfeit phone card was accepted and I was able to dial, I could not get a ringing tone, just the irritating engaged signal. (That is, it was what signifies engaged on every telephone I had used before.) I knew that it was early Sunday morning back home and unlikely that Dad was on the phone at all, and definitely not for all the time I kept trying. Not knowing what to do, I banged the phone down and went looking around for another telephone box, the first one I saw being by chance different to the others I had observed to date, gray as opposed to lime green, and distinguished inside with a menu card that said International Calls with instructions in English. A-ha! This was quite an interesting development: Therefore most phones were wired for domestic calls only and Tokyo with all its semblance of cosmopolitan modernism had little market for public telephoning outside the country.

I called Dad and told him all about Japan and how I was nearly refused entry at the airport but not to worry and how exciting Tokyo was. He listened in and made a few laughs with all the happiness he held for me in whatever I did as boldly audible as ever, even though he would have been sad and missing his son gone so far away. He told me he loved me and I do not know whether I said it back, maybe I said you too or just laughed, a kid I was. I next called Mom and her too told all about Japan. "It's great here," I said. "There doesn't seem anything at all to worry about, from what I can see, and tomorrow I will start at my new job so I'll meet lots of new people." At that moment, my telephone card, which had been ticking off credits on the L.E.D. screen at a rate of seconds, clocked to zero all the way from ninety-nine and flicked out with a beep, the telephone abruptly going dead. I put the used card in the handy garbage can next to the telephone for recycling—the exquisite lack of littering or any such carelessness everywhere to be seen in Tokyo had already compelled me to be very fastidious as well—and then stepped out of the cubicle onto the street.

I was in a little side-road just off Shinjuku's main drag, standing opposite the entrance to a coffee shop. It was already coming on to evening and lighting dazzled everywhere. I walked up toward the wide road I had left, where a continuous flow of fabulously dressed fashionable shoppers milled past left and right. I could already see that the road had been powerfully lit, but as I entered the thoroughfare I was amazed at the volume of light that hit me. All of the buildings lining both sides of the wide avenue were covered up to nine or ten stories high with beetling ramparts of electric light, as covered as the four-square floodlights that fill football stadiums with silver, an intensity of shine marking the outline face of each building out against the evening sky, which unable to compete had given in to night. Glass of red, sea of green and Moon white rose in banks of encrusted crystals for a mile in front of me, flashing and sweeping in preprogrammed movements. Brand names for beer and cigarettes stepped up on the rooftops, soundless video screens showed adverts and pop artists dancing, Japanese logograms urged me something in red, pregnant with meaning.

That night when I got back to the dormitory I drank a few tins of beer out the vending machine in the lobby, while sitting searching the channels

19

on the TV in the common area. There was something highly satisfactory and civilized about having a beer vending machine on the premises, I thought, doing a quiet business round the clock. Presently I got up and went to soak myself in the Jacuzzi room. After me, one or two of the men who lived in the dormitory came in, bathed, and got out during the period while I was sitting there: I could feel their awareness of me, the new foreigner whom they must have been informed about, concentrating onto me but no one said a word in my direction, and for my part I kept looking away from them too. If we were going to have commerce, they should approach me with some kind of welcome I thought. Japanese beer was very good I noted, my remaining tin which I had opened in front of the TV faithfully accompanying me to the bath. No one else who had sat around that sunken square of hot water was drinking; it was probably not allowed or not done. Dr. Gunji had mentioned various conditions of stay at the dormitory, which were more-or-less stricter rules than I could imagine the same number of twenty-three-year-olds back at home thinking of obeying. For a start, I knew in advance before I arrived that the dormitory was closed-off to all women visitors. I had also since learned that, furthermore, residents were supposed to clean their rooms every weekend, not make any noise, choose their meals from a menu posted up a month in advance (to help the cook get the right amount of ingredients in), indicate when they were going to be away (a month in advance), and carefully sort their trash into separate packages containing newspapers and magazines, combustibles or plastics for recycling.

After finishing my beer and toweling myself, I was in no frame of mind for lying down and going to sleep at not even half past nine yet. Japanese TV seemed to be just celebrities sitting in their studio sets shouting and out-laughing each other on every channel, which was of no interest whatsoever. TV did not appear to represent Japan very much. So I determined to have a walk around my local area to see if there was anything of curiosity nearby. I knew from my earlier walks to and from the station and from looking at my street map that I was living in a quiet corner of the city's sprawl, not far from the endless miles of docks that stretched along Tokyo's industrial waterfront within the Tokyo Bay, which went south to Kawasaki City and beyond that to Yokohama in a seamless conurbation housing thirty million people. Near to me, however, were not many shops and domiciles, just the giant factory and labs of Nimsan Co., Ltd. and several other smaller company warehouses and depots all dark and closed for the weekend. I got dressed, picked up a couple more cans of beer from the vending machine and walked outside into the cool night.

Insect noises kept it down. Traffic had ceased. I walked along the short driveway to the main road and made a left turn, opening a can of beer and taking a swill for good measure. The sound of the night-time insects, unfamiliar to my ears, was a wonderful mystery; the low chirruping seemed to occupy a plane going in a disc around my knees. Every sense-receptor in my body was keen with a certain excitement, a liberty not altogether but partially made available by simply not having to be on the alert in case of malefactors or drunkards or macho teenagers up to no good in the shadows ahead—which was what I was more accustomed to confronting in urban areas at night. Utter peace reigned; the lack of antisocial vibrations could be felt by their absence all around. I crossed the empty street and made my way toward the entrance to a well-lit shopping road, or walking bazaar, which had a sign arching over it proclaiming, I supposed, the name of the bazaar. It was quite like the banner over the gates of the filmic OK Corral or Boot Hill. As I got there, I saw that the road was lined on both sides with shops which were all closed for the night except for a Lawsons convenience store inside which one or two people were standing at magazine stands reading away beside the windows. Hanging tautly between the tops of the lampposts the full length of the road, which was narrow and went straight ahead for a few hundred yards before rounding a bend, were garlands of red paper lanterns with white letters on the side, each lit by a bulb within—two lines of plump tomatoes stretching away above. Piped along the road, in addition, was weird crackly Japanese music played on a *koto*, a plunking Japanese stringed instrument familiar from the soundtracks of many samurai films or TV documentaries featuring oriental traditional culture, playing out above my head at a liltingly agreeable volume from speakers also dangling from the lampposts all the way along the deserted street. What a charming place! I walked the full length, listening to the strange broadcast which smoothly went into the zither movie theme from *The Third Man* at one point, quite a tasteful transformation and respite from the earlier stuff, I thought.

Arriving at the end of the bazaar, having passed not more than one person coming the opposite way, I went under the banner which was identical to that at the start of the musical lit street and emerged into another, dark and empty urban road. I continued on my walk for a while, stopping to look at surprising features and oddities here and there, such as well-kept clean public toilets abundantly provided on every other street corner, and the peculiar sight of a man standing waiting to cross a road at a red pedestrian light, even though not a car had been past yet or seemed likely to come along all night. I watched as the light finally went to green, and he continued plodding on his way. Other fine details and features struck my attention and kept me amused. Next to one of the abundant public conveniences I saw was a tiny square of neatly cut grass with a low ankle-high railing going round: A park, a public green area—except no greater than six-by-six feet in area! Were people to sit there enjoying the sun, picnicking on a summer's day? If so, they would have to do it one at a time.

Continuing my walk, I also noticed there were no litterbins anywhere. Thus the remarkable cleanliness of the huge city was an exercise of mass will, whereas the filth, grime, litter and vandalism of London's streets, to take one example, were due to a lack of any such willpower despite all the bins provided everywhere.

Eventually I came across the foot of an unbalancingly steep set of steps going up and up to a shrine, a *pi*-shaped red wooden gate arching over the threshold at the top. I walked up and investigated, all was quiet with no one around. No barrier or lock was put in the way of anyone entering the ground, which was a pavement leading from the gateway at the top of the stairs to a richly carved edifice crowned by a curving Japanese roof darkly silhouetted on the glowing but blank night sky. I looked around and observed the details of the scene: a red thunder-god statue was imprisoned inside the shrine, visible through slit windowlets; several small trees bordering the pavement walk bore an orchard of paper scrolls bound with ribbons in their branches; a couple of sub-shrines with squatting Buddha-like statues and offerings of dry flowers were set on white podiums near to the main building. All was still and peaceful—a glass office skyscraper in the distance joined the scene as I had one last look then turned and made my way back down the soaring stairs and onto the road again.

Once back on the ground, however, I could not be sure of the direction from whence I had come. I was fairly tipsy from drinking four or five tins of Japanese beer (blimey they were strong!) but moreover I did not have any signal, topographical, or astral guidance to indicate where I was. That is, I can usually tell which way I am going by noting the stars, which I will always absorb myself in looking at if they are out, but on that night could not be seen; I was absolutely unfamiliar with every building on every block extending in every direction; and not a road sign, bill poster, shop name, or company logo that I could see meant a thing to me. I was surrounded by here squiggly, there slashed, and yonder paint-daubed or lit-up Sino-Japanese characters, the *kanji*, and the feeling was slightly unnerving like being a spy behind enemy lines. No one at all was around; it was getting late on a thermometer-plunging October Sunday night in a non-residential area. Everywhere was locked up and empty, and the brows of shopfronts were thrown under shadows from the street lamps. And I had to start on my new job the next morning, must be punctual!

I tried to work out which way was home. When I first saw the steps going up to the shrine, they were on my left, so by going right (I thought) I must make the correct start. But, when I set off in that direction, I immediately knew that I had not seen any of the buildings and road ahead before. Or had I? It was difficult to tell. Maybe I was more drunk than I thought, what with still being jet-lagged in all probability as well as having just jumped out of a hot bathtub prior to venturing out, in addition to consuming beer for dinner. On the way to where I was, I had paid attention to where I was going, aware that I could get lost, and had roughly kept in a straight line at all times so that I might go back by simply turning round. But when I had tried to do that, I found that "straight ahead" was more often either slightly staggered to the right or slightly to the left in a series of parallel choices which would soon clock up to going way out of course in a geometric scale of additive errors. And on top of this, I found that upon giving the streets my full attentiveness, it became clear that even those that appeared to be straight were in fact not so over a greater distance. I could not peer down any road for more than a block before it was crossed by more roads or curved round a corner. I was quite closed in.

Going back in the direction I was most convinced seemed the right move, however, I saw a saving sight in the distance: a train moving off on a viaduct bridging above the level of the street. I could either get a train back to my local station or follow the railway line on foot; I could not have been more than the distance between one or two stations from my own. I relaxed my fear of being lost and made my way toward the black bridge on which the train had passed. When I got there I saw once again the skyscraper that had been visible from the shrine I had visited, and by reconstructing the relative positions of the various points could be sure which way to follow the railway. So I set off home. At first the road I walked followed directly under the line, but then and there I had to divert from its as-the-crow-flies directness whenever it flew over blocks of buildings in my way. Going round these obstacles and keeping my eye on following and trying to rejoin the course of the railway track demonstrably confirmed my initial finding that the streets were a warren of fanned-out crescents and diagonals with no basis of regularity whatsoever. On several occasions, imagining that I could reach a tall building visible in the near distance ahead by setting off down the street that went in that direction, I found myself turned far off the scent by the road's wending course and that by taking each subsequent side-road branching off in the direction nearest my intended destination, this happened again and again so that I could not make any progress. Occasionally I was sidetracked so far away from the railway line I was trying to follow that I lost all sight of it and thought I had lost it—lost a big noisy raised iron construction going over rooftops. This was in part not only due to the confusion of the roads on the ground level but also the railway itself snaking about up above as well. What madness had produced this serpentine whorl?

After about thirty minutes' walking I began to see signs of familiarity: a twenty-four-hour shop I had passed earlier and knew to be near the dorm, then finally the tops of the Nimsan buildings themselves. At this point I changed course from following the railway and went off toward Nimsan, entering the gates of a dark unlit park in between us. I could see the other end of the park, or rather the lighted buildings beyond it, and hoped that there was another exit over there somewhere. I was getting tired now as the beer's effects diminished and I just simply wanted a good night's sleep before my big day ahead. As I got to about the center of the park, however, I began to feel a suspicious inkling of the children's play equipment I had vaguely looked at with little thought when I first went in. Taking a better look though, I found that the slides, climbing frames, see-saws and swings were nothing of the sort. What were the black sticks and unlit shapes all round me? I stopped in my tracks. All was silence. Taking a step up to the nearest object and looking closely, I made a discovery that threw a pint of cold water down my back: I was in a cemetery surrounded by grave markers pointing fingers into the dark heavens. Only there were no crosses or statues of angels—just flat wooden sticks like narrow planks. A-ha, I thought: Japanese are not Christians. Each memorial was inscribed with a name, presumably, or epitaph written vertically down it. Some granite mausoleums with flowers in vases placed on top also stood around; these had given me the impression of play rides. The atmosphere was not friendly: The whole place was filled with a whispering resentment ordering me to flee. Quickly I made my way toward the other end of the place and left. I would find out later from several people at Nimsan that the cemetery was believed to be haunted.

2

At dawn the next morning I awoke very early—far too early to get up and stay agile throughout the ensuing day—but although I tried I could not go back to sleep. I was in a state of excitement and suspense caused by not having any idea what to expect in my first day as a Nimsan employee. I washed myself in the basin in the corner of my spotless room and inspected my chin as to whether shaving was necessary. Nope, the rugged look would be bound to have a more striking effect on the all the beautiful girls I was imagining populating the office. There again, would I be even working in an office? I could be given a bay in some large open area resembling a telephone pool, with neighbors clustered in groups of four on a grid plan. Nonetheless I had a picture of my new workplace that I had formed in my mind, and had visited it so often that it had taken on its own reality: a small office with four walls, containing four desks on which as-yet faceless people sat beavering away reading over mountains of documents, the place decorated with perhaps nothing more than a lonesome chrome circular clock poised above the door....

At just after eight o'clock there was a preordained knock on my door from Mr. Itoh. I opened it and was glad to see that he too was not wearing anything special for the occasion such as a suit and tie, just a T-shirt again, and jeans. I myself wore a white shirt tucked into navy dyed Levi 501s that were not denim, some other cotton. As far as I was concerned, that was real smart-wear just a degree short of suiting up, which I had only done three times in my life: one time each for the two interviews leading to this and my former job, and once when I appeared in a magistrates court to surrender my driver's license after being stopped and breathalyzed by the police one Sunday morning heading off to play park football after a night out. (I had been pronounced still over the maximum alcohol limit and banned from getting behind the wheel for a year as punishment.) So, those were the only times I had worn a suit before—on trial in an office and in a courtroom.

Itoh and I went down and ate breakfast in the dormitory canteen on the ground floor. The whole building had come alive in vivid contrast to the desolate quiet of the two weekend days preceding; young Japanese men were emerging from the line of doors which were opening and closing in regular turns all along the corridors. The canteen area was doing a swift turnover of breakfasters with people generally wolfing their bowl of rice, throwing a cup of hot green tea down their necks and hurrying off, banging trays onto the rack on the way out. I was introduced to a couple guys whose names I jettisoned instantly; they were super friendly and interested to ask me questions. Smiles came to Japanese young men as frequently as they were not on the faces of British people my age—I was much endeared by the openness; it gave me an outlet to be the same. I had never known that I wanted to be more open. Itoh and I and our two new companions made the short walk down the road to Nimsan passing a variety of different local small businesses, workshops and factories in the area as we went. The locale was very much a light-industrial area.

The working week was reared up and back on its feet: cars rolled past on the road in two conga lines crossing town; two or three dozen schoolgirls in navy uniforms like starched formalwear for a morning wedding service came by us in the opposite direction, walking in pairs and groups; noise of machinery and forklift trucks, lorries reversing and calls exchanged between workers hovered on the air. With a grating screech someone on a bicycle braked and briskly swung past me on the sidewalk, making me jump reflexively. The other guys just laughed at my startled expression and explained that in Japan, people cycled on the pavement not the road. You've got to watch out they added! We moved on. Amid all the traffic and heavy plant noise was the loud raucous cawing of big birds—I saw one as it landed almost at my feet, a fearfully massive jetty raven of a fowl with kukri bill: it plucked a squeezy-bottle from out a white plastic garbage bag and with one flap levitated into a tree gnashing it, cawing. I then noticed more of these great crows hanging around on trees and electricity pylons, making cynical commentary on us people below going to work. Within an instant later I saw another, different type of creature: perched in the middle of the sidewalk, a two inch-long, leaf-green insect—a praying mantis. The group of us stood round it and inspected it. Miraculously detailed with wraparound eyeshades and sparring-matcher's raised fists, it was the first time I had set eyes on a praying mantis. I wondered what might happen if one of those big crows saw it. Fisticuffs?

We walked on, and next encountered a section of the sidewalk narrowed off by cone bollards, a crater dug into the sidewalk was being tampered with by workmen in rubber boots. On either end of the cordoned-off temporary causeway stood a guard in blue uniform with white riband and matching construction helmet waving pedestrians along with a red baton alive with colored lights. It seemed so odd to have not just one but two guardians of safety at such an innocuous and blatantly perspicuous shallow crater. We stepped onwards. In the open space before one warehouse or motor pool, I observed as we passed the big truck-sized open doors giving access to it, were ten or so older people in beige overalls standing in formation and doing stretching exercises in not-bad unison. A speaker hanging over their heads played scratchy martial music with a soothing but sinister male voice counting *ichi, ni, san, shi, ichi, ni, san, shi, ichi, ni, san, shi* to which the troupe's motions were conducted. Slowly, left and right they arched over and creaked, touching the ground with an outstretched arm. To my astonishment, one of the men had a lit cigarette in his mouth as he bent over. This somewhat surreal vision was of only momentary note, however, because less than a minute later our little group turned into the main entrance gate of Nimsan Co., Ltd., and its full spectacle of activity took over my attentions.

The security guard I had seen almost asleep at his post on Saturday afternoon was now standing halfway between his guard hut and the gate, exhorting us and a few other last-minute arrivals into the complex with a gesture of tapping his wristwatch and of bowing good morning combined. At the precise moment we were through the gate, a siren sounding not unlike the type used to warn of a coming Luftwaffe air raid in archive films of the wartime London Blitz heralded that it was eight-thirty, time for work to start. Half a dozen people wearing white lab coats ran around ahead of us in the grounds, dwarfed by huge buildings, and vanished down corners and into glass front doors. Mr. Itoh signaled that we too should be quick so we increased pace toward one of the great buildings. A few more people also dashed about, then in an instant the external vista was deserted. I took a look around as we made our way into the complex. There were five great-big main buildings to be seen, all light-greenish in color and windowless, some of which had silvered fume exhaust chimneys running down their walls. Who knows what chemicals, reactions, laboratory animals, poisons, sterile areas, fumes, glassware, installations and the like were housed inside these cordoned-off places!

We arrived at a small one-story building and were met by the familiar face of Dr. Gunji, to whom I was handed over by my new friends, who promptly dispersed into their respective work areas. Gunji and I entered the one-story building, which proved to be a changing room, and I was shown my locker space and given my uniform: a gray two-piece boiler suit. I had been given prior warning about this practice by my friend Gaz Gosling—everyone at Nimsan wore a uniform. Transformed, I followed Gunji, who was very cheerful to see me and asked me about my weekend, across an open space with a mown grass soccer pitch and volleyball nets, into my building—Building Number Twenty-Three. (Good, I thought, my lucky number.) This was a two-story edifice, long like an aircraft hangar. We went up a flight of steps and through an unmistakably office-y door with a square frosted glass window into a large extended workspace taking up what looked like the entire upper floor.

The instant we went in I felt a stir of people looking at me, working at the same time on the one hand and looking at me on the other. Everyone wore the same uniform as mine. The office manager, a tall skinny fellow whose name (I was about to learn) was Dr. Zen, came over and greeted me. He was slightly nervous and, as with all the new people I had met in the previous two days, smiled freely in a way that I appreciated. I gave him my best bow, very awkward it was, and he, Gunji and I all had a good laugh about it. I was next ushered around to meet more people, whose names all went the usual way down my memory chute. I vaguely noted who was supposed to be important in the office hierarchy, that is by the order I was shown them and where they sat, what they said to me and such like. Everywhere I looked around I caught glimpses of people looking up at me and talking about me among themselves. There were quite a few girls in the room, they all looked very cute. It was exciting, my first day in the office in this strange friendly land. I was shown to my corner and there first set eyes on my fellow editors, two women: one American and one Japanese. They stood up—the American was very tall, quite a giantess; the Japanese very small, a midget. "This is Loretta Martin," said Gunji "She's the chief editor of Medical Communications; and this is Toda, an editor like you."

"Hi," I said to them both. When Loretta answered with a deadpan Hullo, however, I was surprised by the deep, toneless expression, considering I was a new arrival. Could she not be a bit more friendly? She was about forty-five with mannish facial features emphasized by a man's short haircut showing the ear. As she finished saying hello she went and sat down, looking bored as though to say, Well gosh I'm glad that's over. Toda-san was a bit nicer, however, asking me about my flight and impressions of Japan so far. Then she too went and sat down, sharing a desk face-to-face with Loretta. They could be seen in the background talking about me as I was whisked off by Dr. Gunji and Dr. Zen to continue my round of introductions.

The morning went quickly with a brief orientation run-through about the company and the incoming visitation of an oversized bulk of a fellow with an amazingly big head and face, from the accounts department, asking me a range of personal details about myself in order to set up a bank account on my behalf. At the end of this interview, he stood up, not so much overweight with fat but just a wall of mass and strength, and said: "Well I think that's all I need from you. In this case, you needn't have to worry about having to provide a sample *hanko* impression to set up an account with Saruda Bank; with them it is not necessary for customers to have a *hanko*. They're a new bank with many foreign customers."

"I don't understand," I said. "What's a *hanko*?"

"*Hanko* is a stamp," replied the man from accounts. He reached into the inner pocket of his gray boiler suit and took out a mini felt bag, opened it, and showed me a small cylindrical ivory object like a piece of blackboard chalk, with his name inscribed in *kanji* intricately carved in reverse on the end, which was smudged red with ink. The overall appearance of it was remindful of a lit cigarette. "See—that's my name, 'Ōmori,'" he continued. "In Japan, everyone has *hanko*, each one handmade and unique. It is to identify you, same as your signature. When you set up a bank account, for example, you normally need to put a *hanko* imprint on your application form. Then whenever you go into your bank to make a cash withdrawal, you need to display to the teller your *hanko* mark. Nowadays, however, with ATMs and more modern banking, some banks are not insisting on their customers having a *hanko*—especially foreign customers, who don't have *hanko*."

"What happens if one guy steals someone else's *hanko*?" I asked. "Can he or she then go into a bank and withdraw all that person's money?" The accounts manager shrugged, either to mean that he did not know or supposed so. He looked surprised by my question all the same. "I'd like to get a *hanko* carved with my name," I added. "It looks like a great thing to have in Japan, just as a souvenir even if I don't need to have one."

At that moment the long lone note of the same siren that I had heard at eight-thirty in the morning rose up in simultaneous soundings from several directions I could hear outside. Dr. Zen, who was sitting next to me, indicated that this was the lunchtime announcement, and as he did so I could hear people on the move in the corridor running past the office. We went out and I saw that the entire workforce was on its feet and traversing in different directions here and there. Outside the building, Zen and I made our way toward the Nimsan canteen amid an army of men and women in gray uniforms, mostly traveling to the same destination as we were going. Once again we crossed the big central open area inclosing the soccer pitch, which had come alive with what looked like one but must surely have been two identically clad gray teams having a kick-around, and around the periphery of which more people played volleyball or practised whacking baseballs into a large green net. Further observation of the scene of activity revealed even more sporting going on elsewhere: on the roof of what looked like and was confirmed by Dr. Zen to be a sports hall, surrounded by a barrier of more green netting, were several sets of doubles partners playing tennis; down a track alongside the far wall of the sports hall some people were firing arrows from longbows at big round concentric targets about fifty yards distant— this was Japanese archery. Others still threw baseballs back and forth to each other, catching the white dots with a far-off smack in brown leather gloves. It seemed as though the whole campus was running around, playing sports and exercising.

Zen and I eventually arrived at the canteen where a line of Nimsan workers had made a long queue up the stairs and inside the second floor. When we got to the top, which was surprisingly very quick considering the numbers waiting in front of us, I saw the familiar sight of canteens everywhere: a stack of trays to take, stainless steel conveyor runners to slide them on past glass counters of hot wares in recessed containers under steaming lids. However, although the set-up was familiar, the food was all new to me: broad stringy noodles in a thin soya stew, thick sloppy curry-like stuff with rice, and peeled egg, carrot and unrecognizable vegetables cut and shaped in cubic slabs, all simmering in a broth. I chose the slabs, which Zen explained to me was called *oden*. Then amid the

31

kitchen crashing noises, slamming metal clangor and hundred tongues at work filling the hall with a pond of vocal acoustics, we went in search of a space to sit in the rows of tables filling the canteen. In front of my eyes as I went along hoisting my tray was a mosaic of identical, cute girls' faces all set off by black hair and gray Nimsan two-piece overalls. How was I going to distinguish any individuals out of that morass? I was the only person in the entire complex, nay whole locale in which the complex was set, and possibly within the nearest ten square miles, who was not Japanese! When Dr. Zen and I sat down over our repasts, I pointed a thumb in the direction of all the people sitting near to us and remarked that everyone looked so similar.

"Only to you they might, but in my eyes they don't," said Dr. Zen. "In my opinion, foreign people all look very likely the same." He laughed, but he clearly meant what he said.

"But that can't be possible," I replied. "In my country, everyone has a different hair color and facial features, there are different body sizes from the very tall and broad to the very small; and people all dress according to an almost infinite range of individual tastes and styles. Whereas, here, everyone has black hair, Japanese features, slim body build, not too tall, and dresses pretty smartly—mostly in a dark suit or ranks of the same uniform."

Dr. Zen laughed and found this very amusing. "It's quite the contrary from my point of view," he said. "There is not one person in this whole canteen who looks remotely like anyone else as far as I can see." He made a quick rotary survey of all the people, then added: "I think that I probably know nearly everyone in here, at least by sight if not in person. I expect that I know just about everyone's names as well. That's Japanese style. In a company, everyone knows each other. On the other hand, I have terrible trouble in recognizing foreigners' faces and telling them apart. For us Japanese it is the other way round as in your situation—we think that all foreigners look the same." With this he carried on laughing.

I next asked Dr. Zen about all the sports activities I had witnessed at Nimsan and was told how popular it was for the workers to have such amenities on site. Furthermore, I learned that the company had a "social club" in the evenings where workers could eat dinner and drink beers and *sake* cheaply, a no-cost pop-in barbershop for those monthly trims (one style only—a "seventy-thirty" for men—that is, a short-back-and-sides parted seventy percent across the crown), a sick-room with nurses, a weightlifting gym, basketball and probably any sport that could fit inside the sports hall, and two gigantic hot-spring baths, one for men and one for women, in which the tired troops could soak at the end of a long day camped in the office, lab or factory. I asked Zen whether I could play soccer with the guys I had seen and he said certainly, he would ask on my behalf.

After Japanese lunch, which was starting to make a good impression on my taste buds, I was handed over to Loretta and Ms. Toda to receive instruction in my new occupation, Medical Editor. At this pow-wow they ran through all the different types of materials that we would have to deal with—Loretta doing all the talking while Toda sat still, both of them sitting across from me at a table piled with papers—and I mostly listened and tried to take it all in. Basically, we edited English manuscripts reporting experiments involving the different drugs manufactured by Nimsan, mostly animal toxicity and teratogenicity experiments, mostly chillingly cruel by the sound of it, mostly repetitive, protocol based, for the record. These reports were either archived for Nimsan's internal use, sent to foreign subsidiaries, used as part of patent applications, or entered the company's annual general report, a huge tome of several hundred pages which was published in both Japanese and English versions, the latter mostly for the benefit of overseas subsidiaries as well as associated other companies. Some of the materials that came to our department for checking were original research reports intended for scientifico-biomedical journals; other texts were advertising or educational materials or promotional stuff for the company.

After this talk was completed, I sat at my desk and went about marking-up a few easy examples of simple experimental reports, which no doubt had been selected in advance as appropriate for my beginner's handiwork, with some corrections and deletions I made in red pen. The English was quite primitive so I tarted it up. I was very satisfied with my desk of robust old wood and gray metal, pushed out into a position of minor but not inconsiderable importance with a good view of everyone. The desk drawers were well stocked with pens, a roll of Sellotape and paperclips in a little tray. As well as a stapler. All mine! The afternoon passed in a flash. When the siren signaled five-thirty I had displaced a small top-section of my pile of A4 leaves, via the top of my desk in front of me, where my pen awaited to dispatch each page in red slashes, and each sheet dropped into my out-tray. To check on my progress we had agreed that Loretta was to inspect my editions for quality assurance prior to their being returned to the original authors: the study directors and laboratory heads occupying the many scientific research departments of Nimsan Co., Ltd. Thus at the end of my first day I took my tray of completed reports over to Loretta's desk, and she indicated by a hand motion where I was to put it without uttering a word to me. Apparently she was concentrating on her own editing, so I did not disturb her further and went over to Dr. Zen, who asked me how was the work. "Fine," I said. "Nothing too complicated."

"Good," he replied. "Let's go to the social club and drink." We walked over to the canteen area, which doubled as a saloon bar in the evenings, escorted amid another large-scale exodus of people, all on their way home, bidding each other goodnight with much nodding, bowing and excitable chin-wagging. My impression of this workplace was much like my impression of Japan all over—so far—confirming what I had gathered—of a combined society whose members stood together. Once we were inside the social club, which was situated on the floor one level above the canteen, and were ensconced at our table, Dr. Zen ordered beer and snacks including *sashimi*, raw fish, which I regarded with much interest. "You eat that raw?" I asked him.

"Yes. Why don't you try it. You have to dip it in soy sauce to taste the fish."

I followed Dr. Zen's demonstration and sampled *sashimi*, and very delicious it was. Almost certainly the most delicious food I had eaten, not that my normal diet up to that time had been *cordon bleu* or anything. As I munched, a part of my mind was strangely astonished in a disorienting way: Could nutrition be a higher experience than simply relieving hunger? I did not dwell on the problem for very long, because beer arrived, but something like a conclusion was gestating. Dr. Zen poured one of the two big bottles that had been set on our table into our tumblers and we held the glasses up, I having rapidly learned that in Japan I should watch what happens first then follow suit. "*Kampai*," said Zen.

"*Kampai*," said I. We quaffed the beers, which were wonderfully cold and complementary of the snacks. As soon as I emptied my glass, Zen refilled it, leaving his empty. Thus I poured him one too. And another and another….

The next morning after getting changed into my boiler suit I entered the office at eight-thirty sharp. Already the place was alive with activity, with much running around and loud talk. I noticed that all the women always ran everywhere, so that whenever they got up they were off in a thrice, bounding between tables. It was all part of the busy-act. Also whenever anyone appeared to be receiving instructions they acknowledged each direction with a military-style "*Hai*!" to show that they had got it. All that was lacking was a salute—although there was more than enough bowing going on to compensate for that. I observed much of this showbiz as the forenoon developed, with private amusement, it was all very enjoyable and somewhat fascinating to watch, this alien behavior. Japanese mannerisms and customary deportment were not intuitive and off-hand, or easygoing, but rather ceremonial.

During the early part of the morning, a few more people came by to "see me," it felt; I was apparently drawing considerable attention from all over the company, mostly for being young and British and flamboyant and, after being spotted in the social club the previous night, available for entertainment and drinks more than likely. Loretta sat looking peeved about something with her back turned as much toward me as she could, the body language was clear enough. I noticed that she was fundamentally averse to my habit of unobtrusively humming and singing in the office—a low tune which had spontaneously emptied out my vocal cords at one point during the morning set off a primal dance of territorial marking behavior and warning signals from her corner. So I was to be quiet was I? Amid all the bustle and blabber going on all round us. I was extremely tempted to keep it up and taunt her for a while, but I let it pass. I continued working quietly on my pile of papers, getting through them one by one by one. I started checking the clock often. The initial enthusiasm and excitement of being in a new place was fast declining and becoming replaced by ennui at the contents of all the papers before me, all of which had to be done quickly since Loretta and Toda had finished theirs.

Then in midmorning, the door near to me opened and Dr. Zen walked in. Bizarrely, he was wearing a white surgical mask held over nose and mouth by two elastic strings hooked on the ears. When he sat down, two or three people in quick succession went over and talked to him; none appeared at all put out by the manifestation of the mask. For Zen's part, he talked away back to them as though nothing was amiss, the movements of his lips underneath causing the mask to wriggle about. I turned to Toda-san and said what on Earth's that Dr. Zen's wearing?—and learned that such masks are to stop the wearer from spreading cold bugs around the staff. "If he has a cold, why doesn't he just take the day off?" I asked. No answer. (In Japan, sick days are taken off from the individual's small total of paid leave days.) I was getting bored and there was something I had wanted to do since arriving in Tokyo—see Mt. Fuji which I had found out was visible sixty miles away only on very clear days such as the one outside that morning. I got up and exited the office; no one noticed me. I needed to find a tall building with a view so went off on a walk across the soccer pitch.

Outside, the campus was deserted except for the odd person in a lab coat who emerged from this or that door of one of the huge buildings and ran off in the direction of another. I walked over to the biggest building that I could see and went inside. Shiny floors and low fluorescent lights as well as hushed quiet greeted me within. The entrance floor hummed. I summoned an elevator and got inside, pressing the top button: Floor seventeen. The car slowly coursed up the shaft—no one else got in as I ascended. Up on seventeen I stepped out into a setting of more shiny floors and low lighting. Two young women in white lab coats walked down the corridor going away from me and disappeared into a room. The sulfuric/furry odor and general appearance of the place were of chemical laboratories and caged rodents behind closed doors. On my right was an exit door leading to stairwells going up and down, so I carried on upwards and a moment later was out on the roof, a notable wind which was not present on the ground breezing about.

I peered over the perimeter wall. The view of the city around Nimsan presented a long, wide-screen vista of endless numbers of buildings with countless shapes and heights filling the plane below and ahead for twenty miles all round. Most buildings were cream-white apartment blocks, with some gray or brown or yellowy, overwhelmingly new looking and modern with tiny far-off balconies and flights of exterior stairwells visible. There was no antique architecture, stone, marble or historic masonry to be seen, anywhere, with the exception perhaps of occasional temple rooftops whose antiquity I was not able to assess. Even they looked contemporary. There was no sign of dilapidation in view, nor was there even a suggestion of a slum-quarter—and nowhere appeared exclusive either: I saw no hilltops adorned with villas of the rich. There was only sheer immensity of un-reckonable regularity. On all buildings, concrete or metal sheet facades were most common—not very many were built of brick it seemed. The impression of every structure was functional and plain, but not grim by any means. Businesslike. As I viewed the city, a shinkansen bullet train snaked among the buildings in the near distance, enhancing the futuristic prospect.

At the far edge of my radius of vision much taller office towers and skyscrapers rose up both individually and in hugging groups over the horizon. I could make out where I knew myself to be on the map in relation to the high-rise turrets of Shinjuku and Shibuya over in the distance, and thereby got an idea of the size of the city. Huge. Tokyo Tower, a replica of the Eiffel Tower in vivid scampi orange and white, was also prominent in the distance. Built on the top of a short hill, it was possible to see the full length of Tokyo Tower rather than having its base of four girdered podiums being lost amid the city's topography. The average height of Tokyo's apartment buildings, at least in the nearby town sector, was apparently eight or nine stories. Not a break could be seen among all the rooftops; the entire area was built up with no parks or lakes or any open spaces that I could see, apart from around the several temples whose massive dark roofs were visible at various locations: near to these alone were treetops and breathing space apparently. The density of the living wards was inconceivable, not like London, even in the city center, which appears mostly green with trees and open parks, squares and cemeteries when viewed from an equivalent height. I continued my investigation and strode across the rooftop to the far, south-facing side.

Right until I reached the opposite perimeter, all I could see above the enclosing wall was blue sky; but just when I got to the edge Mt. Fuji came into view, a spectacle of wonder lurking close-by the city, neighbored away by a fence of low blue intervening mountains. It was so enormous, a decapitated wedge, white with snow and flat-topped crater, that it was hard to believe that on most days of the year—all except ten or twenty perhaps, very clear days—the mountain may not be seen for obscuring intermediary mists, fogs and clouds. I stood and looked at it for a good ten minutes, in rapturous contemplation: it was a mountain from Mars or the moon, with details of slender rivulets cut into the snow starting from the cropped peak down the near sides. It had the appearance that no air was up there at the top, just rarefied planetary space. The mass of cluttering buildings filling the valley in front of my scope of view to a distant blur going away toward the bank of foothills which were themselves not an inconsiderable mountain range, about halfway to Mt. Fuji from where I stood, say forty miles distant, were reduced to littleness and lowness by the mountain's hulking rhomboid dome standing placidly beyond. The farthest buildings that I could make out at the edge of the city, perhaps a forty-minute train ride away, were just specks.

Back in the office, after re-sneaking in and quietly settling in my seat, hoping that no one had noticed my absence, which had clocked up to over half an hour no less, I was pretending to be poring over a manuscript when my previous day's work was dumped back on my desk by Loretta, who was already nearly returned back at her own desk by the time I looked up to see who had been over. I picked up the papers and viewed them. She had gone over my red-pen corrections with a pencil, re-correcting most of them and canceling out others. There were also many more that I had missed on each page. She was thorough but also impeccably correct. Some of the things that I had missed were now obvious. Furthermore, with an eagle eye commas, semicolons, closing brackets at the end of long parenthetical sentences and lists and such like were all inserted in their rightful places using punctiliously neat editorial symbols and printed letters, whereas I had made a mass of untidy crossings out and joined-up scrawls. I would have to improve my next lot of documents or I could see that there would be trouble from Ms. Martin, who was already making it obvious that she loathed me! For example, when it clouded over, darkened, and started to rain after lunch and I remarked out loud, in her direction, by way of making conversation with her, "How can the weather be so pleasant one minute and chucking it down the next, eh, Loretta?"

—she replied curtly: "Because you have no imagination." This was about the fourth time in one and a half days that my attempts to be civil toward Loretta Martin were not only rebuffed, but done so in a way deliberately designed to show me her contempt. I considered what to do about it. She was a big person, hardly feminine at all, with ungentle movements and malign facial grimaces which she made in response to any little thing she did not like, such as the contents of a badly written science report or being told to do something by Dr. Zen and others in the office. From her overall appearance, she could have been a male transvestite for all I knew. Nearly everything she said to anyone at all was accompanied with a strong hint of malice: sarcasm, negativity, impatience.

I observed Loretta secretively. Should I ignore her acrimonious remarks toward me or tell her to go fuck herself? Getting on with her looked out of the question. She was hardly nice to anyone, but at least minimally respectful to people she dealt with for the most part. She reserved her open hostility for me alone. The only person she showed any real decency toward was Ms. Toda: they seemed to be quite friendly, going to lunch together and working harmoniously. The problem between her and myself was that I was a flippant youth, or appeared to be, whereas she was the very opposite: sober, uptight and businesslike. I openly admitted that I could not care less about work *per se*, although I always did my best to do a good job and on time. I wanted to do it as a necessity and awaited the end of each day to run outside and play around. Loretta did not see things like that. For her, when in the office one must be a "professional"—a word that she used very often and was starting to get on my wick. It sounded so phony; I thought "What is the point in lying about your attitude to doing these daily tasks?" Loretta also deeply cared about seeing that work ran smoothly from one to the next person in the production line, whereas I did my bit as conscientiously as I could then passed it back and forgot it. Loretta was of the opinion that double checks and chasing up were the way to do things properly. Everything about her was curt and distant: the way she talked to people in person and on the phone, her written notes and memos. I, on the other hand, wanted to be friendly; people could come to me and ask for something and the answer was always "Sure." To Loretta, this was as irresponsible as anyone could get, and she showed me so with glares and scowls. Her work must be scheduled and prioritized; she would have to check her diary and give an accurate date as to when the materials might be done and ready, including an extra day in store in case something went wrong and the deadline could not be achieved. The way she organized things was against human nature—never in my life had I known any reasonable person to get upset really if I did not return them something exactly on time. And when was I late anyway? I could guess how long something might take with a quick on-the-spot estimate, why bother with all the time-is-money type nonsense. It was just not me to act like that and I was damned if I were going to pretend to be a commercialized stooge just to please a pen-pusher like Loretta. Of course, from her point of view I was therefore a pain in the butt to her. How dare I come along and not toe the line the way she wanted, after all her years of hard work blah blah building up this empire *et cetera et cetera* making things here run like clockwork and so on and so on. This was her department and she did not want it changed, and I represented a change just by being there, and I was not going to change either! We were at odds and were never going to see eye to eye.

As the days of the first week passed, I decided that the best course of action was simply not to volunteer saying anything to Loretta, even Hello, and just do my work in a separate sphere. The problem of course was that she was the senior editor in the department and was going to be checking my work for the next few months till I was familiar with it all, varied and detailed as a good deal of it was. I was also obliged to go to her and ask for assistance whenever I could not understand something, which was a daily occurrence. This was the most unpleasant task of all: going up to the ogre and saying excuse me, then having her make me wait till she was ready to finish what she was doing, as well as show me her annoyance at being disturbed at it, before exercising her might as the senior person who had been in the department X number of years and making a pronouncement on what I should do. Once this was done I was to enact something to signify the making of an apology for my inadequacy and scuttle off.

The position I was in was a stalemate: I had no intention of leaving the company after traveling all that distance to get there, and besides was enjoying every part of my new life except when it came to dealing with Loretta. Furthermore, the company was providing me with accommodation and I had no job to go to back at home. I could not leave quickly even if I wanted. On the other hand, I could not go to anyone higher up at the company and protest that this woman was making life difficult for me—they would probably laugh their head off. I could not contest her skills and knowledge of the job either, since they exceeded mine. If I involved Dr. Zen, I appreciated, he might speak to her to try to find out what was going on between us, and she would produce exhibits of my work and declare it substandard. Since she and I were the only native English speakers in the department capable of divining what quality the work we produced really was, it would be her word against mine. And she was the senior editor with the long track record. Therefore I had to be careful not to get myself into a harmful situation regarding my interests and prospects in Japan. I was stuck with Loretta!

It occurred to me as the week wore on and things persistently got worse that Loretta of course knew very well and exploited my position. I tried to remember the name of the person who had worked in the Communications Department before my succession and had gone back to New York. I asked Toda-san what his name was: David Gallienne. That night I was to meet the men of Nimsan Football Club, who trained every Friday from six o'clock on the soccer pitch. Before doing so, I could ask whether Dr. Zen was in favor of a couple beers in the social club after work ended at five-thirty, and try to find out about David Gallienne and how he had got on with the staff in the department and the circumstances in which he parted with the company. So that evening, with Zen perfectly eager to wind down the week with a few bottles of beer, we arrived in the social club and made our way to a table.

I started by telling him about how I felt toward my job, stating which parts were most interesting and that some of the work was quite involved scientifically speaking, to put him at ease that I was just innocently reporting on my progress with no such thing of a complaint to make, then I tested him by alluding to Loretta and stating that occasionally she could be quite difficult to work with, what with her being so attached to her duties all the time and it thus being inopportune to disrupt her concentration with my calls for help and guidance. I carefully watched his face and listened well for clues in his words. If he were expecting any trouble, he would make some outward sign like a flinch or responsive eye movement at the same second that I encroached on associative words such as "Loretta" and "Martin."

"Loretta-san is an excellent editor, very dedicated and experienced," was Zen's reply. He seemed all very calm. "You should listen to her advice. She has more than ten years behind her in the office." So, Loretta had been to Zen behind my back I thought. Complaining about me. Dr.

Zen's feeling on the matter was that since I was new I would require time to adjust, that was all. He did not want any trouble from pesky foreigners, who were more prone to resist obeying orders than Japanese. I pushed him a bit further, albeit evincing the impression of carefree ingenuousness on my part.

"Loretta can be a bit awkward at times, don't you think?" I suggested. "I mean, she has not been over-friendly to me since my arrival." Zen gave me a look that showed that this was all new to him, that she was not remarkably inimical to anyone as far as he knew. His reaction was that of a fairly unobservant man too insensitive to notice such matters going on nearby to him. Obviously Loretta had always been courteous toward the boss all right. "Well I'm beginning to find her quite insufferable," I ventured. "Today for instance, I inadvertently picked up some work she had printed out in addition to my own manuscript off the top of the printer; I noticed this within an instant and handed her sheets to her just as she herself had converged on the printer to pick her papers up. She plucked them from my hand with a look as if to say, 'Give me that and how dare you waste my time by not checking what you're doing.' Her face was burning with hatred you know. Then earlier on, when I went over to her and asked…." I stopped talking because Zen was looking away and not listening, drumming a hand on the table.

When I had finished he said: "You can ignore Loretta. This is a workplace. It's just business. You can do that."

"Why should I ignore her?" I said. "I didn't come all this way to Japan to work with a person like that. I'm not really that saintly-patient I'll have you know, nor quite as peaceable as I look. The next time she tries to insult me, I've got a good mind to kick her ass."

"You're young," chuckled Dr. Zen. "Pay no attention to her and stay working with us. You have good potential for a career here. Don't listen to Loretta, just do what she says and ignore any other thing she does." Although I was irate and letting it out after a pent-up week, Zen's true words tunneled in as an unplugged washbasin whirlpool on my skull—suddenly my indignation was gone with a guttural up-belch.

So I agreed: "All right, I'll just ignore her and carry on with what I'm doing. Can I change the subject now? I'd like to know what happened with my predecessor, David Gallienne? Did he have any trouble while he was working here?"

"Oh he was awful," said Zen. "He could not do anything right. We had to fire him—he went back to New York."

I drank my glass of beer and said that I had to go to football training.

While waiting on the pitch for training to commence, standing in my boots and shorts and track jacket as the guys turned up one by one, I nodding to each new arrival, by chance I mentioned to one of the first people who spoke to me, a wiry little fellow with punch-permed hair that was dyed brown-reddish and whose name was P-chan, that I would have to take it easy for the first few weeks at the club because some time before, I had turned my ankle during a game, and that was on top of a previous injury to the same ankle that had not fully healed, resulting in extensive ligament damage and entailing myself hobbling around on crutches for a while. I told P-chan that since the second injury, nearly a year before, my ankle had not been fully right; it was still naggingly a bit swollen and spongy to the touch. P-chan, who spoke hardly any English but got the point, then indicated that I should lift the ankle in question and stand wading bird-fashion on the other foot, while he held his right palm out toward the damaged ligament and whispered some kind of what seemed like a spell, for about a minute, as I tried to hold my balance. Then he stopped and we both jogged off toward the group of players who had by then multiplied to a squad of around twenty or so, kicking footballs around the green floodlit surface.

Football training consisted of a few stretching exercises for ten minutes followed by some ball kicking and training games such as knocking the ball wide of the park and running on to the box to receive a curling cross from the winger placed near the corner flag; two touches only were allowed in front of goal: one to control the ball if necessary and one to shoot past the keeper. These and other such exercises were well organized and a lot of fun. Training ended with a mini-soccer game using half the pitch. I had been introduced to the guys in the team at circle in the beginning of the session. The team's members were mostly all from the factory, youngsters like myself, with unmistakably sporty, short-nosed faces that showed adventurous courage rather than trappings of noble leadership and deliberation, which are signified usually by a longer snout. The Nimsan F.C. boys were so small and thin, some of them looked like little children. They messed around with each other and laughed at almost anything that someone who stepped forward and said, usually a joke about one or other of their number as far as I could make out.

Besides the coach—Hiro—and the players, there were two female "managers" who were involved with the team somehow; they stood in tracksuits observing the training session and afterwards joined us in the *izakaya* bar where we all went for drinks. *Izakaya* are Japanese inns. Normally their patrons are seated at western-style tables on moppable tile floors, but nearly as often the inns have *tatami* mat flooring and are no-shoes venues. Shoes are slipped off and put in drawers by the entrance. The *izakaya* we went to that night was of this latter type. About a dozen of us went in and sat down on thin wine-red cushions laid on the floor mats around a low table. Big foaming mugs of beer were brought over and everyone set upon them, thirsty from running around. Straight away after we started drinking, though, Hiro the coach got down to business and asked me what would I like my squad number in the team to be. "Twenty-three," was my reply. "It's my lucky number," I added, "and also my age, and furthermore it is the street number of my home back in England." Hiro consulted a clipboard of papers that he had drawn from his bag, checked whether the number was available, and confirmed that twenty-three was not taken. This would from then on be my shirt number.

With this done, everyone leaned in toward me and asked questions via Hiro, the only person seemingly able to speak any good English except the big person from accounts whom I had already met on my first day, Ōmori "Ken," who was goalkeeper. He shyly said very little, just knocked back drinks and grinned at the laughs going round the table. Everyone smoked, and drank like fish: most switched to *sake* or *shochu* after one or two beers. *Sake* was delivered hot from a metal teapot held with a towel over the handle. I drank a tumblerful: it was perfumed with a powerful reek of volatile alcohol fumes, quite palatable though and clearly strong enough to knock out even someone the size of our goalkeeper. *Shochu* is a similar drink, but less flavorous. It tastes like a dull neutral organic solution such as weakly diluted acetone might, by the smell. To enjoy it, it is mixed with ice tea or mineral water and fruit juice. These cocktails also are deadly brews disguised as innocuous refreshment.

Going round the table one at a time, everyone introduced me his or her name. Then I was entreated to recollect them all starting from the first. I did badly—the whole group found this hilarious. After an hour or so everyone was getting too drunk to concentrate on one subject—me—for long, and I presently found myself talking to my neighbor as did the rest of the team in respective pairs. I was having a whale of a time trying to make myself understood and extracting any information about Japan that I could with the poor fellow. He told me something that I often heard from the Japanese, about their unhurried sense of patience and aptitude for waiting their turn and till they had accumulated the requisite means: he was on a waiting list for a car park space to become available outside his house and estimated that that would take another two years, at the going rate, but in the meantime, anyway, he was still saving up the cash to buy his car, and all being well these two endpoints would coincide in two years' time. One could not buy a car in Japan without first having a registered parking space, he added.

At some point in the evening, the goalkeeper from accounts, Ken, who was sitting across from me on the opposite side of the long narrow table, next to Hiro, with whom he was in conversation, broke off and leaned over to me. "I made you this," he said. I looked down into his hand and saw that it was holding out a *hanko* name stamp. On the end of it was carved in neat letters a quarter of an inch tall, YMMOT. "Each individual letter of your name is symmetrical—the same backward as forward," he said. "So it was very easy to get right." I thanked him for it and studied it. The letters had been carved out of the end by a knife or cutting tool, carefully and perfectly. I thought as I looked at the miniature relief that perhaps I had not expressed my gratitude enough, because I loved it, a precious thoughtful present. I thanked him again. Apart from Hiro, no one else noticed Ken giving me the *hanko*—the timing was as unobtrusive and considerate as the gift was welcome. My reception by these youngsters of Nimsan F.C., who did menial office tasks or manual loading and cleaning work on the pharmaceutical factory floor for a living, was so unexpectedly warm and open. That night I did not even pay for the countless drinks and dinner I had consumed; my new friends would not hear of collecting money from me. I had been in Japan for a week and was overwhelmed by the civilization I had entered, where the items of coexistence had been honed to a common law by all the citizens. Where were the trouble-makers, violent sociopaths, urinators, drunks, loudmouths, push-ins, and intimidating elements that hang round among late-night crowds back in the nation I had left? Why had I not heard a police car or ambulance siren once, despite the great numbers of people, amounting to the millions, out on foot in Tokyo's hundreds of brightly lit mini entertainment centers that nucleate in the vicinity of every underground or urban commuter train station, all night long?

After finishing the drinks, walking home spinning with alcohol, I vowed that I was determined to settle-into this country, which felt like a refuge that had been waiting for me since I had been buffeted and bruised through my teens and adolescence back in England, and I was not going to let my life be spoiled by anything or, in particular, anyone now that I had found my new home.

3

When I awoke, none too worse for wear despite having drained myriad drinks of a variety of different malts and formulations, I got up and wondered how to spend my first full weekend in Tokyo. By good fortune, I had arrived at Nimsan just before month's end and had been paid for one week's work on the previous day. This had been in cash enclosed in a Nimsan envelope, since my bank account was still being set up by Ken Ōmori. Because of the payment, not only did I not have to go without money for the first few weeks, as I had thought might happen, but also I could straight away buy something that I had had in mind right from the time when Gaz Gosling had told me how much salary I could have, working for Nimsan: a mountain bike. Slinging my trusty shoulder bag containing a good book into place, I locked my room and went downstairs to discuss a breakfast of grilled sardine with a dollop of mashed horseradish plus rice and *miso* soup. The expression for breakfast in Japanese is "morning rice," dinner is "evening rice," and in fact any intervening meal is colloquially called "*gohan*"—rice. And that is exactly what is eaten. In the canteen, a big pop-open thermal vat of rice with a plastic spoon on the side was ever-present at the entrance, no matter what the main menu—and also a big pail of *miso* soup with a ladle. When going in, the first thing I had to do was get a bowl of rice and a bowl of *miso* on my tray, then approach the chef behind the counter and sniff around what he had prepared. Regardless of the main course, be it fish, omelet, croquette, fried oyster, whatever, the same two staples complemented it: *miso* soup and rice. They went with anything.

After breakfast, I traveled a couple train stops to Oimachi, a nearby local center, where there was a branch of Marui fashion department store. In the sportswear section I found precisely what I wanted to see: a bicycles corner. I asked the young assistant, who spoke passable English and was quick and helpful, about a Marin bike—U.S.-made, the best mountain bikes of all—and after he took it down from where it was dangling hooked up on the wall, the boy (or so he looked, he was so small and thin) was apparently quite surprised when I indicated that I would take it right there and then without any indecision and further shopping around. In fact, he almost gulped when I said it. He made some mechanical adjustments and tightened up a few nuts and bolts, and after

I paid, he brought the bike down in the elevator with me, brave enough to ask where I was from when we were out of the shop-floor environment. Once we were outside the store, he gave me a quick lesson on how to use the brakes, as though I had never seen a bicycle before in my life, then I thanked him and was pedaling off down the road. Although it was supposedly illegal to cycle on the road, I did not want to cycle on the sidewalk and have to look out for every pedestrian and countless other obstacles. Cycling on the road was what I was used to in London, and I reckoned that if I were stopped by the police I could try to talk my way out of any trouble by claiming ignorance of the custom in Japan.

I was not going to take any chances in getting lost again, even with my pocket map on me, and followed a course always in sight of the railway. The new bike was fantastic, all shiny and working with obeisant well-oiled shifts when I clicked the gear changers with either thumb. As the cold air went about my head and ears, this was real freedom! I started by taking a thirty-minute cycle to Ginza with its opulent department stores and from there went a short distance to the moat-rimmed grounds of the Imperial Palace. This latter was somewhat of a disappointment since not much could be seen of the royal buildings behind the massive stone-gray ramparts, and the tourist such as I must remain forever kept away by the wide duck– and swan-swum waters ringing the periphery. From there, next I cycled up to Nihonbashi—"Japan Bridge"—and had a look round that locale. All was commerce and motion, cars and taxis jamming the roads, sidewalks lined with people. The crowds were not as voluminous as those I had observed the previous weekend in Shibuya and Shinjuku, however. They were more like the thickness of crowds to be encountered on a weekend stroll in the center of any European capital city. The Nihonbashi itself was an unremarkable road-bridge spanning a shallow canal, save for its iron blackwatch-fog Victorian lampposts and an exquisite bronze statue of a dragon stuck on either end as decoration. Perhaps the bridge was once a grand archway remindful of its counterparts crossing the Seine, the Thames and the Danube; I found it dwarfed by a concrete-clad motorway flyover passing over bridge, canal and all. My next journey was across the city to Asakusa, where I spent the day looking at the temples (and the girls, many wearing kimono) and ate an excellent ice cream—green tea flavor.

Sanbusaku Tokyo Trilogy

As the afternoon wore on I resolved to make my way to Roppongi, the drinking-entertainment area frequented by *gaijin* such as myself come every weekend. From where I was situated in Asakusa, Roppongi was a forty-minute cycle away. En route, after passing back across Ginza and from there on traveling via a notably quiet area (dotted on my pocket map with diplomatic missions and embassies), I took note of something that, conspicuous as it was, although I tried to glimpse it again on many later occasions when I happened to pass through the same area on my bike I never did find again: an extraordinary and incredible sight—a rigged, Captain Kidd galleon, full size, sitting on top of an office block with its planked prow resembling a golden hatching henbird high up in the sky.

Not long later, arriving in Roppongi, I parked up my bike and tethered it gunslinger-like to a railing, and spurred into the first "saloon" I saw, a tiny pub where the annular ring of a bar in the middle had just enough room all round it to squeeze in high-stools almost backed against the enclosing walls, and therein drank a few beers aching to converse with someone apart from the Australian barman who was brisk and responded to my talk in stopping starts between doing rounds of his territory-of-the-taps that was across the dark tabletop. Apart from the two of us, there was no one else in the pub. Soon, however, a young Japanese woman came in and sat down on a stool near to me, so I scooted over and engaged her in chit-chat. She was full of smiles and flirtation and we immediately started laughing and making merry with an infinity of conversation to cover. Unfortunately, she was there to meet her friend who soon arrived, and as they made their reunion I said Ta-rah and made my way out of the bar. Exposed to the cold air waiting beyond the door, it was night outside—darkness plunges in Japan—and the street was milling with people. Pink and assorted-color neon had been put on and showcased the town. I stood at a crossing of the road that was lined with yellow taxis and got talking to an American guy of about my age, Pete, a broad chunky fellow wearing a big sporty track-and-field trainer top that expanded him even wider than he was already. I explained that I was new to Tokyo and asked him some good places to go. He said come on and we took a short walk into a narrow entrance at the foot of a slender building and got into the elevator. The inside of the said car was hardly any bigger than a coffin for the fattest man in the world, and was plain-white not walled with mirrors as elevators in England are, making it feel all the more enclosed. Everywhere I went in Japan was small, cramped, and concise. The twin doors opened and we found ourselves already standing inside another bar about the size of a living room, as though a curtain lifted, with a band playing and much noise. People sat around on the floor watching the musicians and shouting to each other over the beat.

We bought beers and Pete explained the best places to go in Roppongi, drawing a map. Motown Bar was the place to meet girls, Gas Panic for dancing till late, and so on. Pete clearly knew Roppongi, I thought—I should stay friends with him. He had been in Tokyo for nearly a year, working in an American bank. We drank some more beers and talked away while the band kicked up a pub ruckus. Nearly everyone in the bar was not Japanese, so it was surprising to me when a Japanese guy got up from the audience, with much encouragement and clapping and whistling from the morass, walked onto the stage and put a guitar on, an old well-used Les Paul Custom in spangly gold. He spoke over the mic in a heavy acquired U.S. accent, something like Aw shucks fellas OK this one is called Roadrunner one two three four and went into playing the song with the band, performing a fine solo on the beautifully toned and heavy-sustaining electric ax. After this song, Pete and I jumped up and went back down the spaceless elevator onto the open streets where a people-stampede herded past in clumps, mostly drunk and cheerful, some inebriated and being helped along. Cute Japanese girls in sexy outfits were everywhere and I was more than interested to get talking to any one of them. As we paced down Roppongi Street, we were distracted by a commotion outside one of the open bars so drifted over to investigate what it was.

What we saw was the most comical scrap there could be—a Hollywood fight from the silent film era. Two very drunk Japanese middle-aged men in suits with their jackets taken off were slugging it out while many passers-by stood around watching in amusement, smiling and laughing at them. One of these two broilers was swaying on his feet holding a bunch of car keys in one hand over his head, and swearing something in slurred language, then tried to make toward a car parked in the street, when the other guy rugby-tackled him, sending him clattering onto the car hood. They wrestled together with the assailant attempting to confiscate the keys, when the one intent on driving broke free and lurched toward the car once more with the key pointed at the near door, and was again beset by his friend, both of them falling to the ground and rolling on the road. The crowd whooped it up with merriment at the loony showcase. Not a punch was exchanged in the melee, just holding and grappling and expression, a pantomime.

We walked on. Next, Pete took me to Motown Bar, which was much larger than the previous two places I had visited and packed full of drinkers out-shouting each other amid a din of rock and dance music played by a DJ raised on a podium shielded with a blue glass windscreen. DJs always amused me by their inane chatter over the microphone, which must take a lot of doing, and their indifference to music which they play indiscriminately and usually turn down in order to talk over the best parts of anything good they chance to put on, such as the guitar solo: for this reason I always eschewed radio as well. Inside the bar toward the back, past hot crowds of bodies, were some people known to Pete, and after introducing me to them he got talking away to one bunch and left me with two of the girls, both Americans, who indulged me with conversation about what we were all doing in Japan and such things. A short while later, the girls and I were joined by another straggler who limbed over to us holding an identical beer to the ones we were clutching, an uncapped bottle of Budweiser, and joined us to talk—a man who was remarkable in the oddest, unsought way, an oddity that had been conferred on him out of the blue: he was the exact double of the president of the United States, Bill Clinton. Utterly, indistinguishably, the same facial features, same puff-cheeked smile, same woolly white hair. We all laughed as it was immediately pointed out by one of us and he acquiesced with a despairing assent. He told us that he had been asked to play the president's part in a movie and was about to accept the role but changed his mind when he had learned he was required to wear a bulletproof vest while filming.

The night had gone in a flash and it was soon almost midnight; I had drunk ten or more bottles of beer at between five hundred and a thousand yen apiece: maybe a hundred dollars' worth. I was drunk enough to fall about on anyone, with loud talk and an exaggerating tendency toward showing off; hence I was earning so-much, was playing for such and such a great football team, was one of the crowned heads of Europe for all the truth I was telling. I was also making a beeline for all girls I spotted, and was hardly making much of a good impression on any of these heart's-desires since I was drunker than all of them. To this I was not aware in the slightest, and meandered among my targets undaunted. The loud music and thick atmosphere with many people smoking were combining to weary me of the Motown Bar, so without saying a word to Pete and my other new friends, who were still at the back end of the room intensely exchanging inaudible shouts to each other, I decamped.

I walked a block down the street, which was half empty compared with when the night was young, although populated with a sprinkling of bar workers who were distributing leaflets and hustling customers into their lairs. I saw that there were dwindled numbers of drunks-wearing-suits and large groups of six or more people out and about; those had all gone home to sleep it off. Most people I passed walked in ones and twos and were more composed than seen to be reeling about on the sidewalk—they must have been the all-night survivors off to late-hour haunts. I tried to find somewhere inviting to go, where young people were having a party in a less deafening establishment than Motown. As I turned one corner, having been stopped and directed to such-and-such a nightclub by one of its staff posted for the purpose of recruiting clientele out on the street, I found myself suddenly walking in the midst of a squad of about ten male U.S. Army soldiers out on leave-take—they were in mufti—jeans and sportswear but their shaved haircuts were unmistakable. They immediately responded to my joining in with them by all facing me, a mean-looking gang. One with just a round dome of cropped hair at the top and none elsewhere on his head spoke in my direction, affecting a cissy walk toward me: "Gee, my hair used to be at least *three times* as long as yours!" Compared with the hostile orphans and damaged abuse-victims I had faced growing up in the vicinity of my hometown, however, this fellow lacked the psychotic ferocity to come across as any threat to cause me genuine alarm, big and many-accompanied as he was. I reversed off without saying anything back and hopped out of sight round the corner. I made a very brisk walk but not a run back up to the main street; in my experience, this is the time when a gang either catches you and beats the shit out of you, or they are not going to come at all.

No one followed me and I made it back to the well-lit main street intact. Once there, somehow it was a surprise that the area looked exactly the same as I had left it moments before and that it continued to exist as though nothing had just happened—people walked by regardless of my presence and not caring that someone had tried to provoke a fight with me. I calmed down and my mind called off the alert. I had not been afraid, and that had shown on my face as I bid my goodbyes to the gang. However, after I got away I became bothered by how those people had encroached on me like that, in this city that I had claimed as my new home. The night was infected by the incident—I became aware of how the types of people going about had changed and become ugly to look at. A demographic alteration had been underway throughout the evening. Any Japanese men who could be seen at this later time wore bright-white penguin shirts along with black coats, and had their hair greased back flat and shiny in the poseur manner of teddy boys. They were Roppongi's nightly vampires. Women wore long boots and showed their thighs. I noticed puke in doorways. The majority of the people parading the street were tall skinny young white men with the same harsh skinhead haircuts as those I had just come up against on my way to the nightclub. The happy atmosphere going the rounds earlier on had vanished.

I went into a bar that was crowded and as noisy as Motown inside, with dance tunes pealing from wall to wall. I was still very drunk and soon found myself switching from holding a bottle of cold beer while observing the patrons from the edge of the dance area that was pretty much the entire floor in the venue apart from the bar, to being among the dancers moving my body and swinging my arms and feet to the music. I soon shifted and approached some girls—one a foreigner with blonde hair tied in two wide Norse-maid's plaits, and a couple of Japanese—who were dancing away within arm's reach, and had been looking at me. "Hello," I said to one of the Japanese girls, all of us becoming entwined dancing in a huddle, I still holding my beer. And: "Who are you?" She told me her name which I forgot and then her hand gently pushed me toward the foreign girl, explaining that she was their English teacher and that today was the last time they were going to see her because she was leaving the school and that was why the three of them were all on the town having a final night out together. I was quite squashed up against the petite slender teacher, whose body was as soft as wool. We tried speaking for a moment on the dancefloor until she, who I could just hear was an American called Gill, took my hand and said we should go outside to get to know each other since the bar was too loud.

Out in the cold air we went down a smelly alley and sat in a dark and empty back doorway of some or other establishment or restaurant. Gill was drunk, more than I was, and spoke complainingly with lip-slurring about her year in Japan and how she was dying to leave the country and go back home. She disparaged "the Japanese"—or perhaps it was just Japanese men—or at any rate some of her students—as being nothing but boring robots with no interests except working till late in the office all the time, and supplemented this lamentation by going over various other gripes of a similar nature. I laughed at most of the statements, and when I got close to her on the doorstep, she reacted to my motivations by ravenously kissing my mouth. She also pulled up her T-shirt and showed me her breasts, not minding at all who might walk past. They were so surprising to be there in front of my eyes, her small, full tits, that it took me a second before I could think how to respond. I went to put a hand up on them (what else could I do?), then they were just as quickly back covered up under her reorganized T-shirt. Gill continued talking and next let me know how Japanese men could not maintain an erection—a somewhat arguable thing to say of a race whose population was around a hundred twenty million in 1993. I wondered how many of her male students she had unsuccessfully tried to lure in order to have reached that conclusion.

After we had talked for about ten minutes perched on our doorstep, Gill was up on her feet again and we went back onto the main street and stopped a cab. We had tacitly, mutually decided to go back to her apartment that she said was a twenty-minute drive away. We jumped in and the taxi door, on an automated lever, clunked closed. Gill continued talking to me en route and I listened while taking-in the seemingly endless streets of lights and nightly activity outside the cab window both at the same time. I have always thought that there is nothing quite like being driven to-somewhere after having imbibed a lot of alcohol—that is, having become aware that my safety is dependent on the sobriety of the driver, who is in opposition in that respect to me—and this always makes me quite serene for some reason. Like being a child passenger in Dad's car again.

As we drove along, I had no idea whatsoever where we were going. When we got there, Gill's apartment, which was on an upper floor in a block of flats, was so small inside that I was amazed. I did not know, at the time, that apartments the size of hers housed a large proportion of most single Tokyoites as well as countless hundreds of thousands or perhaps even millions of couples and small families in an unreckonable colony of similar buildings all over the city. Gill's apartment made me think I was entering the inside of an igloo. The door opened onto a square concrete step on which one person could just stand using both feet, while I tried to slip my shoes off and leave them thereon among several pairs of Gill's limp footwear. Right next to the door, compacted into a kind of hallway, was the kitchen area, a doll's-size low sink with a few plates and cutlery standing up on a plastic drying rack. I supposed that there was nowhere such as a drawer to put these utensils in afterwards, once they had dried, and so they were continuously recycled between use, the washing-up bowl, and from there back onto the rack again—a roundtrip not exceeding two armlengths, it seemed, in Gill's cramped little living space.

Beyond the kitchen was a choice between two small plastic-and-glass folding doors, one leading to a miniature bathroom (actually, just a bath beyond the door, not a bath-room) and one going to a living area that consisted by way of furniture of a few big-sized flat cushions on *tatami*-mat flooring, a litter bin with some magazines disposed inside it, a low table with a small cubic TV against one wall and next to that a folded camp-bed. The far side of the room was occupied by the sliding doors of a unit wardrobe—I could see some of Gill's clothes hanging on a rail inside. The room was just about long and wide enough for a person to lie down across, feet nearly touching one side and head just short of the other, I guessed. Gill unfolded the bed and we both jumped in. The apartment was no exception to the rule of apartments that curiously they are always much colder than the air temperature outside, and we were both freezing. We clung to each other in her tight sleeping bag to warm up and I rubbed her back and arms to create some calorific heat by the friction. We were both laughing about it.

We kissed deeply in the low light and shadowy bed we had made, and I eased off both her clothes and mine, a routine of sorts that the male normally does this important obligation and duty. Straight above us and below the floor, to the left and right and diagonally away upwards at the sky and soaring down to the street in a bees-nest of identical cubes, other tenants lay similarly in a regular formation of synchronized repeated living rooms and beds. What a strange thing is privacy, in a metropolis! Even all our fellow block-dwellers' heads were most probably oriented in the same way: the layout of the room suggested only one place to put down a bed, that is, consistent with the longer floor dimension, leaving a choice of two ends for the pillow; but in Japan one never lies with one's head facing to the north, alleviating one option—that direction of supineness is reserved for the dead in their graves and bad luck for those who live.

After we had made out, I lay on my back cuddling Gill on my shoulder. It was early morning and a magician's outstretched cloak of light was abracadabring up through the curtains. I had been in Japan for exactly a week and was thankful to know that at least in Roppongi, the foreigners' entertainment area in Tokyo, there was somewhere to find such companions as Gill, who was due to fly back to her home in Kentucky two days later. On the other hand, I was firmly uninterested in the bars and the majority of people I had seen the previous night, and recalled all the meaningless talk I had exchanged with women I had been chasing in Motown Bar: Japanese, Australians, Americans. My novel friend Pete, for sure, had been quite amiable and shown me around, presented me to his circle of mates, but as I lay in Gill's sleeping-bag recalling what he and I had said the night before, there was nothing apart from being in Tokyo that we shared in common. My goodness, Pete liked "any music, classic rock"! Those words are sadly my anti-shibboleth of friendship. I was already lonely. Gill had been the one person with whom I had unreservedly connected all night. She was willful and pushy and a show-off, all great characteristics in my book. What I needed was a normal representative Japanese girlfriend, and I told myself not to go back to visiting the foreigners' entertainment hub, Roppongi—an oasis of outsideness—again.

The following Monday I went into the office early and started work. Soon Loretta came skulking in, tightly not offering an "*Ohayo gozaimasu*," the customary morning greeting, to anyone—least of all to me. She kept her eyes pointed in directions other than at my table, and went and sat down at hers not ten feet away. She looked ferocious and in a bad mood as always. I carried on reading my report, an account of a study conducted in mice given an antihypertensive medication for such and such a reason. As I was about done with it, however, all of a sudden, much like as in a cowboy movie, the shadows of two heads fell onto the top of my desk, and I panned up to see the disproportionately un-level figures of the twin gunfighters Loretta and Toda standing there. Instead of a pair of six-shooters, Loretta held out a pile of papers pointed at my head. Both she and Toda looked brimming with fury. Ms. Toda volunteered first. "Parker-san" (I hated being called that—I was Tommy) "Parker-san, we are very angry at your work."

"Why is that then?"

"Look at all these corrections I have had to make," said Loretta, taking over from Toda. She held out a manuscript I had marked up to the best of my ability on the preceding Friday—it was overdaubed in her pencil marks. "You don't like editing do you?" she accused me.

"Not really," I responded. "I can think of better things to do."

"Well to be an editor here you have to be *passionate* about it," she continued. "You have to have an eye for spotting errors and corrections on the page, and be absolutely thorough in eliminating them. If there is something you don't understand, look it up in the library. And finally, you have to proofread line by line over what you've done, prior to returning the manuscript to the client."

Loretta liked referring to the people who handed us their written work to check as our "clients" although they all worked for the same company as we did. Because she was making this set of demands with a raised voice, and since she and Toda were invading my desk standing there with hands on hips and angry faces, Dr. Zen came over to see what was happening. As he arrived on the scene, Loretta continued in a telling-teacher vein: "And in this office we do not sing nor make personal telephone calls or go round with no shoes on—that is not professional." I could not do anything but sit at my desk looking up at these two people who had by then been joined by Dr. Zen, my sock-only feet feeling very vulnerable under my desk. I thought that if I stood up at that minute Loretta would see my moving toward her as a come-on for a fight and probably try physically to attack me.

Zen attempted to calm both Loretta and Toda down by asking what

57

was going on. They immediately went into the same protests at once. Clearly Loretta had been winding Toda up against me and done a good job of it, no doubt armed with examples of my recent work-efforts to instruct her of my ineptitude. Toda herself was not able to make much of an assessment of what I did, being Japanese with English as a second language. She mostly did checking to see that our changes were properly incorporated into each draft and mediated between our department and our "clients" to see that their needs were met. She was just a goody-goody siding with her friend. I thought of a good name for her as they both poured their complaints out at Zen: Toady.

I perceived that this might be a good chance for me to defend myself and spoke up to our communal manager, Dr. Zen. "I don't think my work is so bad. It is true that I don't have much knowledge of the science side, but I can speak and write English well enough. I thought that I did quite a good job on all these reports." This produced a heated chorus from Loretta and Toady, which Zen hushed up with arm motions.

"Have you done Dr. Kawahara's animal toxicity study report yet, which I gave you on Friday?" said Loretta to me, knowing that I could not have.

"No," I said. "But you said that you didn't need it back till this week."

"Tomorrow I need it. I have to send it back to Dr. Kawahara by Wednesday."

"Okay," I said. "I'll do it right after these manuscripts that I'm checking now." Sensing that an air of cooperation had re-formed in the atmosphere, Dr. Zen stepped in and pronounced that we were all back on track and that work should continue. He shooed Loretta and Toady back to their desks and went off back to his own; I got on with my work, fuming at Loretta's effrontery toward me. This lovely little scene that had just been enacted was a mini microcosm of office life, I thought, of bosses and underlings and their resentments and maneuvers to compete and win over each other, all for a small share of the proceeds that is an allowance known as a salary. And this ruthless nastiness and contempt toward each other person sitting at the very next desk day by day must be always concealed by a fine façade of courtesy and decency in the workplace, so that I was prevented above all from saying something that I would have very much liked to such as Hey Loretta, why don't you kiss my ass? or from poking my finger in her eye, which I am certain would have immediately ended her aiming all this trouble at me. But alas I was not able to do such a thing, was I? Who would have heard of it?

The afternoon passed-by slowly and boringly, with me becoming increasingly unable to bear reading any more reports. The manuscript I had promised to do for Loretta sat in my in-tray as a reminder of her; I knew that I would have to finish off my first lot of papers by the end of the afternoon so that I could get started on Loretta's when I came in the next morning. Round about four o'clock, however, I looked up to see the stone face of the very same person looking down on me from high above, as she had silently come over to my desk. "I'm ready for the Dr. Kawahara report now," she said. "Have you finished it yet?"

"I haven't started," I replied. "You want it tomorrow, remember. We agreed that this morning."

Loretta was livid. "I wanted it ready first thing in the morning, but since I've finished what I was doing early, I've come to get it now. What have you been doing all day?" She raised the words "all day" to a great volume to show her pronounced annoyance. Then before I could answer, she stormed off to Dr. Zen's desk and made a complaint. I just sat where I was. The two of them came over, Loretta still protesting about this that and the other, I could not hear what exactly.

Dr. Zen looked very bothered by this latest disturbance as he asked me what was going on. I explained what had happened and how it compared with what we had agreed would happen. Loretta burst in again with further protests about scheduling and timetabling. Zen, confused, said that I should hand the work in on time and that I should do it now.

"It will take hours," I said, "and it's gone four o'clock already."

"Then you will have to stay behind till it's done," said Zen, about to walk off.

"I don't want to stay behind."

"You have to. Business is priority." I looked at Loretta, who was fuming with anger toward me. I remembered what Dr. Zen had said about ignoring the things she does and getting on with the work. A moment passed. So I agreed to do the report that day and Loretta went off without saying another word, as though this were not a token concession on my part but something that I had to do with no choice in the matter. In the end I stayed in the empty office till late at night working on the report, finally putting it on Loretta's tidied empty desk at almost eleven o'clock, switching off the lights in the office, and closing up shop.

During that night, back in my dormitory room, I had time to go over the day's occurrences in my mind and saw that Loretta had worked it all out in advance, had set me a trap. She was clearly trying to get rid of me by making me resign from the company just in order to get away from her, or by having me fired if she could paint a picture of me as of no use to the senior managers. She had done this before as well, I realized, to my precurrer David Gallienne: she had implanted in Dr. Zen's mind that Gallienne's work was poor and in the end got him pushed out. Loretta was like a Bluebeard, serially disposing of people who got in her way. Her way toward what? Running the department in a manner that suited her set-up, a steady workflow that she could control and do automatically and get paid a lot for doing. All this hardship that she was causing me was just for that one nugatory little end. Therefore I would have to counter her ploys with some scheming of my own and get her the boot instead. I had a think about it as I lay on my bed in the quietly sleeping dormitory.

The next day I requested a lunchtime meeting with Zen, and we went off to the canteen together when the siren called out to announce that it was noon. Over our two hot bowls of noodles submerged in a tasty soup, I made an earnest apology to Zen for the previous day's inexpedience suffered by him, to which he responded by waving it off in a manful way that meant oh it was nothing. Then I slowly explained my side of the story, as I saw it, and he listened sympathetically. Included in this chronicle was an account of how I had bravely put everything right by staying behind late to finish the report in time for Loretta's demanding deadline, synchronizing the tale so that Zen could be allowed to dwell on a consideration of the excessively late hour to which I had been detained in the course of carrying out this selfless feat. I also mentioned that it was according to Dr. Zen's advice that I had wordlessly and uncomplainingly absorbed her challenges to my composure and been able to see the best course of action to take in order to resolve the dispute. Finally I rounded up my speech by intimating with quiet suggestive allusions on how Loretta had extended the targets of her rudeness to include Dr. Zen himself, reminding him of the faces she pulled whenever she spoke to everyone and how she had no remorse about kicking up a fuss in the office which, I touched upon with barely noticeable hints, was supposed to be flourishing under the calmly stable leadership of Dr. Zen himself.

Zen appeared to be absorbing all this with a look of consideration after each point I made—the appeal seemed to be doing its work.

When we arrived back at the office, Zen called a meeting with Loretta and myself and announced that for the purposes of improving efficiency in the department, work would thenceforward be split into two sets of projects: those that were to be handled by Loretta and those that I should do, with no overlap required. This was an excellent solution I thought; Loretta was revolted but could do nothing to reverse the decision. It was the beginning of the end of her rule. The two of us trudged back to our desks in silence. I spent the afternoon chatting to the young women in the office—Yuri, Tomoko and Seri-chan—who were full of interesting talk about Japan and lots of jocularity. They were a goldmine of information about my new homeland. They told me why people eat noodles with so much slurping noise—to suck up more soup and improve the flavor—and they also acted as though they believed that if people wanted to eat like that, hunched over their bowls as though not using their hands at all, why shouldn't they? This attitude typified their general outlook I found. Indeed the lack of a strict table etiquette, propensity for blindly walking into each other, the rush to claim a precious seat on public transport, spitting in the street, chain smoking, and other seemingly undignified public behavior that I saw exhibited by Japanese people daily, were not really self-centeredness but rather a side product, part of a kind of wider courtesy-in-reverse, elaborated by Japanese society. For, instead of being meticulously polite and conscientious so as not to irk each other, their system was that each person turned a blind eye to every other one and ignored their conduct to the greatest possible degree, and let them do as they pleased: by so much that they sometimes could not even see one another, and collided. The Japanese do not raise complaints. What more benign and perfect manners can there be? Let each person do what he or she wants. And this in turn led to the Japanese' very enduring tolerance and open-mindedness, which as far as I could tell seemed extended to almost anyone's idiosyncrasies and eccentricities. Fat people "liked their food" and "were well fed" or "looked happy"; lazy ones were "not used to exercise"; and so forth; I never heard them utter harsh criticisms or caustic remarks, the livery of envy in other cultures. Their outlook was always gentle, every time. "*Kiyotsukete,*" meaning "Take care," or more accurately "Take good care of yourself," was an exhortation I heard exchanged continuously, as often as I ever heard "Fuck off" in England. "*O-tsukare sama*" was another phrase used in all kinds of situations, exchanged by friends or strangers: "You must be tired."

I also found out why I was always being stared at by people on the train. When I asked the office women why this was so, I received the straight answer: "Because you are handsome." The Japanese also all seemed convinced of the given-ness of reincarnation, which they accepted very naturally. This came across from the indifferent way they imparted the fact, and was responsible, I supposed, for their ultra-easygoing nonchalance toward facing death, either their own or anyone else's. In this respect, suicide was often a natural way out of life's difficulties from the Japanese point of view and was invariably committed for reasons that to me seemed very trifling. Company executives whose business was going bad were often in the news having topped themselves, for instance. Along with their wives. The ornamental ritual of *hara-kiri*, in former days done with a ceremonial sword leaned onto so that it plunged into the sacrificer's stomach, was long since replaced by usually jumping in front of an express train as the preferred means. But there is still in Japan a romantic attachment to the act of suicide, a sort of nobility, viewed in the context of the culture. Suicide is not done in manic depression and desperate anguish so much as in imitation of the balletic self-murder of Romeo and Juliet. In any case the Japanese do not generally regard death, natural, accidental or auto-inflicted, with the shivers and misgivings of grief and dismal eternity that westerners associate with it. One of my Nimsan colleagues whose elderly Mother died, when I offered him my condolences, laughed them off with the reply "She was old. One person dies, another is born—it's natural." Even his astonishing cheerfulness, I discovered, was a Japanese custom—to put the best face on, which is a smile. Thus one morning when I went into the washroom and trespassed on someone busy retching vomit into the sink—hung-over I suspect—he span round to me with a beaming grin and dashed out the door. The Japanese always seemed to see the funny side: on one occasion when I was cycling along a busy main street I observed the embolic presence of a car facing the wrong way down the oncoming lane holding up a backlog of blaring traffic, just as a purposeful policeman strode over to investigate what was going on, a pad of violation chits in hand—and the man who was driving the car was raising his hands quizzically toward the cop and *laughing*.

Other mysteries the office women explained were more mundane, such as the underlying reason why a person I had spotted cycling along one-handed, holding an umbrella up with the free hand, was going to such lengths to keep dry in an insubstantial drizzle: the rain in Tokyo is so acidic from pollution that it erodes the very hair from the citizens' heads, and thus they protect themselves with a bat-release of umbrellas as soon as the skies begin to open. Everything the office women told me concerning strange sights and marvels to be seen in Japan was perfectly logical once explained. In fact, Japanese logic often proved more basic—that is, I believe, correct—than western logic, which, when analyzed, seemed founded on broadly accepted convention rather than on first principles. An example of this, which in itself is of little consequence, but illustrates the point, is the way addresses are written on envelopes. In the West the convention is to start with the addressee's house-number and street, then town, county, and the rest going upwards in scale from small to large;—in Japan, conversely, the regional area comes first, then the town, ward, block, and other elements finally culminating in the house number: a logical way to direct the postman to the right place. Also the currency, the yen, a central preoccupation of life in Japan, is inherently logical: just the one unit. Why must we have pounds and pence, or dollars and cents, when the yen single-handedly covers the price of the cheapest items, which cost a few yen, right up to the most expensive properties in the thousands of millions or more.

Another wider example was the layout of station railway-line platforms in Tokyo. Once or twice when I had boarded a train not knowing that it was a limited-stop express service that went flying past my intended station at great velocity, I alighted at the first subsequent stop and stood on the other side of the platform waiting for the next train to take me back. On boarding this, however, I soon found myself going somewhere else altogether and was completely lost. My assumption had been that the two tracks served by a railway platform both must be the same line: one is for trains coming from one direction and one for those from the other. But such a set-up is just conventional and not consistent with logic. It is better to use each platform so that both sides have tracks running approximately in the same direction at a fork, since passengers changing trains normally keep going like that. Japanese railway lines are aligned in this manner, aiding the vast numbers of passengers changing trains from having to go up and down stairs and across bridges to find their connection. Furthermore, local-area maps hung on the walls within every underground station had in the top right corner a compass pointer showing which way was due north, but this could be directed at any angle on the map including straight down, rather than always directly up, strictly dictating the map's layout:—this alternative schema was to assist persons looking at the map so that they only need remember simple directions such as "At the exit, turn right, then left" instead of having to invert the map in their minds as is necessary with maps that conventionally have north at the top but whereas the station exits actually face any other directions.

Yuri, Tomoko and Seri-chan also told me much about Japanese history and culture. From them I heard that the cause of the immense overcrowding not only in Japan but all over Asia was down to the staple foodstuff in the region, rice, the water-logged crop that never fails to grow. That is, whereas the early hominids of Europe, Africa and the Americas were culled and decimated by starvation whenever the wheat harvest was poor, the people of Asia—the region known as the "Rice Belt"—never had to go without food and therefore flourished into the millions and billions. The dependence on rice diet, and the manner in which this staple is gathered—by mucking in and wading among the fruits—also may have had another effect on the early evolution of Japanese culture: the development of the group mentality. For, if everyone in the village has to collaborate on fetching food, which grows wild, with no especial opportunity for landowners to emerge, or foremen to take command, and all of the villagers then eat that same food, which is the same every day, it seems likely that a society of cooperative individuals with no ranking elite must emerge. In Japan, it is well known that the needs of the group—the work group, the school group, any conglomeration of people—always take precedence over those of the individual. This notion is deeply ingrained in the Japanese mindset, and underlies, I believe, much of the Japanese (and wider Oriental) reputation for wisdom, because of their willingness to suspend the temptation to satisfy their own needs and instead to investigate what is best for everyone, which always appears as level-headed self-denial. At any rate, there is usually one extra step in their approach to taking action, placed somewhere between seeing an opportunity and just grabbing it for themselves. Hence some of Japanese people's baffling strangeness can be comprehended in terms of their tendency to ignore each other, that is, anonymous strangers, completely, as I have mentioned, unless, and only unless, the other person is known to them and hence a member of their group, in which case he or she is deemed fair game for excessive intrusion over, mind control, restriction to conformity, and nose-poking into their business.

The office women also looked at each other in fright when I told them about my adventure in the cemetery on my first night-out exploring the local area around my Nimsan dormitory. They said that the cemetery was famously haunted and that Japanese ghosts are not benign—they remain on Earth looking for vengeance or to see an injustice righted. Japanese ghosts are angry. On the whole, I found, Japanese young people were remarkably sophisticated. They were knowledgeable about good things such as fine cookery, paintings, classic films and books, or at least interested in such entities, and pleasantly unaffected by competitive forms of "cool" and machismo that tend to retard and infantilize western (or British) youths who may be touched by these influencing factors far into adulthood. Japanese people's inclination toward preferring better things was strongly intuitive in them and suggestive of an ability to make a truly unbiased survey of what is on offer—hence they were exercising free thinking. They never favored mediocrity or rubbish on the grounds that such things were safe and harmless and had mass popularity. When conversing, I found them always to listen attentively without interrupting with their own unrelated contribution—the hallmark of politeness. They were also curious to take note of recommendations and tips on what to look out for and try; I could see in them none of the arrogant attitude of people who comport themselves as though they already know everything. Nor were the Japanese naïve in any way—they could absorb new insights into their native point of view and consider them from there. I was impressed by their open minds. Having a healthy curiosity seemed to be a national characteristic, not just representative of a few well brought-up lucky souls. I never found any exception to this generality in any walk of Japanese life.

4

I started spending any office time that I could spare in-between work projects learning Japanese. I had brought a Japanese textbook along from home but had yet to look at it till up to that point. When I had a break, I quietly opened the book and started going through the pages. I found that the rudiments of Japanese language are fairly simple and contain many grammatical differences to English. There are forty-six basic sounds, pronounced *a* ("hat"), *i* ("kit"), *u* ("do"), *e* ("get") and *o* ("cot") and a set of corresponding syllables which rhyme with these exactly—*ka, ki, ku, ke, ko, sa, shi, su, se, so, ta, chi, tsu, te, to, na, ni, nu, ne, no, ha, hi, hu* (or *fu*), *he, ho, ma, mi, mu, me, mo, ra, ri, ru, re* and *ro* as well as *ya, yu* and *yo* (*yi* and *ye* are not necessary because they can be formed from combining other syllables), *wa* and *wo* (*wi, wu* and *we* are also not necessary) and the consonant *n* which is pronounced as a dead "n" grunt (sometimes with an *m*-like component) like saying "can" without the "ca" part. When *n* precedes the syllables beginning with "n" and "m," a double "n" sound is formed as in Ben-Nevis or Tom-Mix. Similar double consonants can also be formed with "k," "s" and "t" syllables, for example in words such as *kek-kon* (marriage), *is-sho* (together) and *nat-to* (fermented soy beans). The syllables starting with "k," "s" and "t" furthermore can be respectively "softened" to the pronunciations "g" (*ga, gi, gu, ge, go*), "z" (*za, ji, zu, ze, zo*) and "d" (*da,* [no "di"], *dsu, de, do*). The syllables starting with "h" can be softened in two ways: so as to start with both "b" and "p" sounds (*ba, bi, bu, be, bo; pa, pi, pu, pe, po*). The consonant "p" can also be double pronounced; for example "Nippon" is said with a distinct break: Nip-pon. This total of seventy separate syllables, all spoken with equal length of intonation like verbal bytes, may be combined in various ways to make every Japanese word. Tokyo for example is *to-u-ki-yo-u* said quickly. As I read my textbook, sitting at my desk hiding it from Loretta, who would surely tell teacher if she saw me not at work, I checked and made myself convinced that the same applies to all the words that I knew at the time: *sushi, futon, sumo* ("*su-mo-u*"), and so forth. Nimsan is *ni-m-sa-n*—that is, the *n* sound cannot help but being an "m" when between *ni* and *sa* whereas after *sa* it becomes a comfortably rolled off "n." In Japanese, "n" and "m" at the end of a syllable are more-or-less the same; this also applies to "r" and "l" sounds, which are notoriously difficult for

Japanese to distinguish, because Japanese "r" (as in *ra, ri, ru, re, ro*) is rolled off the palate somewhere between the differentiated "r" and "l" of English.

Each of the forty-six basic syllables is inscribed represented by a symbol in the Japanese phonetic alphabet; when those that can be softened, are, a small diacritic point similar to a double quotation mark is written next to the symbol on the above right. In the case of *ha*, attended by the same mark it becomes *ba*; to make *pa* a small circular diacritic is utilized in the same place above right. To represent double consonants except *nn*, another small mark is written to the bottom left of the doubled sound—that is, when Japanese is written across the page from left to right. It can also be written down the page in Chinese-fashion; in this case the descending columns are read starting from the right and going left. There are not one but two sets of symbols representing the phonetic alphabet to learn, one for when the sounds are used to write Japanese language and one to represent the same sounds, which comprise more-or-less the entire range of the Japanese person's spoken vocal capability, when they are applied to inditing foreign names or products and objects. Hence London is written in the second of the two alphabets as *ro-n-do-n*. Beer is *bi-i-ru*.

Apart from these two alphabets there are the complex *kanji*, the daunting square-shaped characters derived from Chinese, representing nouns, verbs and adjectives that number into tens of thousands. Each must be learned on its own. Japanese children start memorizing them at elementary school and are still mastering them by the time they graduate from high school at eighteen. There are also rules on how the *kanji* should be written, the order of each stroke and the direction in which each stroke of the *kanji* is inscribed on paper. As a rule, the *kanji* are drawn from top to bottom and left to right. They consist entirely of straight lines (strokes); there are no curves or dots. Vertical lines are made with a downwards slash, horizontal ones inked from left to right; diagonals always downward irrespective of whether slanting to the left or right. Square shapes begin with the left border drawn with a downward stroke, then the top drawn in from left to right and down the right side. Finally the bottom of the square is drawn from left to right: a total of three strokes. In *kanji*, or motifs of *kanji*, that have a vertical stroke that extends above the top and past the bottom of the other elements, as a rule that stroke is written last: the stroke is the axis that pins the character on the page.

Although these orthographic rules struck me as very restrictive when I first read about them, telling people how they must write in their own hand, (and also when I heard that the whole set-up was devised so as to facilitate right-handers, with lefties not even considered and in many cases being taught to take up the pen with their unnatural right hand), upon reflection I realized that the stroke order was positively the only means of making it possible for people to remember the thousands of *kanji*—by repetitive exercise. Moreover, the directions of each stroke, when grasped according to the laws of Japanese calligraphy, had their own intricate logic as the pen-nib scratched and swung from side to side down the characters. Written quickly the *kanji* take on their own form of joined-up writing just like alphabet letters, and the Japanese can guess much about a person's heart and soul from looking at his or her handwriting.

Although I decided not to bother trying to learn *kanji* too much, knowing that it takes even Japanese natives in full-time education a dozen years to memorize by rote just the basics, I at any rate took an interest in them. I quickly discovered that far from being all written differently, they are composed of many of the same elements and motifs repeated, squeezed into halves and quarters in the same way that heraldic charges fit on shields. Furthermore, many *kanji* are pictograms, especially those denoting elemental or natural particulars which were probably the ones that were conceived of first: *yama*, "mountain," is three upright lines on a flat one, symbolic of peaks in a range; *hi*, "sun," is a square "disc" with a horizontal stroke through the middle representing a sun-spot. *Kanji* for "tree" is a boy-scout's representation of a conical pine with a trunk and two down-sloping branches; that for "woods" is two of these trees but more slender, packed side to side; that for "forest" is the same two flattened to half their height with one more on top. Other *kanji* are more beautiful and complex—*ai*, "love," is a heart (four strokes indicative of the heart's chambers), above which is a roof, above which is rain: love protects the heart. *Kanji* for "tiger," *tora*, is an abstract pattern of slashed strokes puzzlingly highly reminiscent of the shock and danger of encountering a wild Asian tiger in jungle—a work of art.

By keeping to the primary building materials of the language, and after learning the first few rules and memorizing a bit of vocabulary, I was ready to advance. To parse Japanese sentences, the verb is placed at the end, whereas in English it comes near the beginning or at least always precedes the accusative portion: English is an analytic language, whereas Japanese is synthetic—word order is not strictly defined. For this reason, I started to discover, the act of thinking itself, when performed either in Japanese or in English, is reversed—hence right from the beginnings of language-comprehension an oppositional variance exists between western and Japanese cognitive rationalization. There is no future tense in Japanese either—future and present are expressed the same. It is as though wilful projections and plans for making change are not really conceived. Other fundamental differences could at once be seen when comparing English and Japanese, such as the lack of plural forms and low usage of pronouns in the latter tongue, as well as an absence of articles equivalent to English's "a" and "the," contributing to a certain vagueness and imprecision in Japanese. Think this: in English, "dog," "dogs," "a dog," and "the dog" all imply quite different nuances, while in Japanese there is only the word "dog" to suffice for all situations. "I gave food to dog" versus "I gave food to the dog, to a dog, the dogs, some dogs...." Because there are no articles and pronouns, conversations naturally tend to stick to what is already mutually known, preferably about subjects that are right under the conversationalists' noses so that they can both see them and point. The Japanese rarely talk about abstractions. Japanese is not a suitable medium for stating terms, instructions and demands, for polemic and debate; it is suited to prior agreement and group convention. In this way, daily misunderstanding among the Japanese themselves is rife. Because of the Japanese language, they are quite unable to explain what they mean, and this is even worse for them when they try to communicate with foreigners: because they can never capture what they really want to say, the Japanese people have acquired an international reputation for incomprehensibleness and lunacy.

One difference in particular between Japanese and English will illustrate how Japanese is best suited to prior agreement and like-minded thinking. In English there are semantically distinct subjective and objective lexemes, (and it follows that there are separate concepts, because what can we conceptualize without words?), for adjectival terms that describe perceptions, sensations, emotions, judgments, situations, predicaments, and so on: amazing is different to amazed—and the same applies to scary and scared, painful and in pain, dangerous and in danger, and all the rest. In Japanese there is only one word phrased for both—the outward cause and its inward effect share the same expression. "*Itai*" stands for both "painful" (or "looks painful") and "I have felt pain." This means that in Japanese, since, to take another example, "embarrassing" and "embarrassed" are mentioned identically ("*hazukashii*"), everything that is embarrassing must cause embarrassment equally in all comers, implying universality. English speakers might not all agree on finding the same things embarrassing. "I'm a bit embarrassed," indeed, is an English euphemism for "I've got no money on me"—something which has never personally made me feel embarrassed on all the many occasions, only sorry.

On the whole, however, as I started to pick things up, I found that with its easy pronunciation and straightforward grammatical rules I could get ahead with learning a bit of Japanese relatively easily over the weeks I spent studying it at my desk in Nimsan, practising my sentences and phrases on the women in the department. During my first month in Japan, I was absorbing novelties of acculturation ranging from the assorted flashes of day-to-day differences to other encounters that were quite marvelous, such as my completely healed left ankle which had been miraculously cured within a very short time after the secret spell woven by my friend P-chan from the soccer team, I know-not-how, and I was learning new words at the rapid rate at which a newborn baby comes to adapt to life outside the womb. I was thoroughly enjoying my new existence whenever I was not confronting Loretta, which was every time we passed each other by. There was to be a reckoning with her coming right up at any moment.

One morning when Loretta was off sick, after I had been at Nimsan for about a month, Toady asked me to check one of Loretta's manuscripts which was supposed to go back to a research doctor in the Bioequivalence Testing labs on that day. Toady had taken to making impatient demands of me whenever she spoke to me; she was thoroughly indoctrinated into siding with Loretta. Her treatment of me was just as aggravating as Loretta's especially since I had quite liked Toady at first and observed in her a kindred spirit of sorts. She was throwing my offer of friendship back in my face, fanatically preferring Loretta's brand of "professionalism" and viewing me as not conforming. She was just a dim-witted sycophant without enough intelligence to judge me for herself based on my general bearing or to reckon on who was going to win the ongoing battle between Loretta and me. I received and read through the manuscript and saw nothing amiss, and gave it back to Toady. Then I went on with my Japanese study, quietly humming a tune to myself, free from the Evil Eye of Loretta for the day.

Early the next morning I had a series of glimpses of Loretta restored to fitness for work: coming into the office by the door at the far end of the room, wearing a long black coat on top of her Nimsan uniform; then a snapshot-look at her standing side-on to me next to her desk without the coat; and later talking to Dr. Zen over at his corner of the office. These still-life vistas of her movements remain in my memory such as telephoto lens-captured images of a spy or suspect under surveillance. A short while after these, I looked up again and saw her determinedly marching straight at my desk—her face an iron mask of hate. Toady came running along behind her—with exactly the same expression! "What is this!" screamed Loretta. I say that she screamed because she did exactly that—not just raised her voice but used the maximum volume of her vocal cords. I looked at what she was showing me: the manuscript I had checked over the day before and given to Toady.

Toady spoke: "I doubted whether you could do such a good job in the short time that you took to check the manuscript, so I kept it back for Martin-san"—her name for Loretta—"to do properly. And now it is late; as you know, it was supposed to go back to the client"—Toady was using the same words as Loretta as well as copying her facial expressions—"yesterday."

Loretta could hardly wait for Toady to finish so that she could continue: "Not only is the manuscript late, but poorly done as well. Look at this"—She pointed to various crossings-out and editing marks that she had made on the pages. I vaguely looked. "You missed all this and this, and this," she fumed.

"Well I thought you had already done it, so I just read it over briefly," I offered. I was playing along, hoping that the pair of them would go away.

Then, Toady added: "We are going to have a meeting with Dr. Zen to discuss what we should do with you and decide what kind of work you can do, because your competence as an editor is too low for this office.

And we do not have time to teach you how to do the work here." Her face was a mixture of unconcealed loathing for me and of gloating self-satisfaction at having voiced an opinion that was bound to impress Loretta, her idol in the work-world. However, for my part I was not going to allow any such thing as she was proposing to go ahead, a trial and analysis of my capability in which I was to sit quietly and be interrogated and persecuted by these two pains in the ass.

So I looked at them and said: "No," in an even voice only just loud enough for Toady and Loretta to hear and no one else. I was sitting right underneath them, they both standing in front of my desk—Loretta as big as a policeman. "No," I said, "we are not having any fucking meeting and the two of you can now piss off." They both froze as my words lit the short fuse to their inner heads. Then suddenly Loretta, a Maenad released by this revelatory anarchic transgression of all office rules of verbal conduct, was upon me with her hands clawing at my neck, her hard fingertips invasive probes with lacerating cutters. The white ceiling went down or did I fall on the back of my chair/Loretta was over the desk and on top of me on the office floor, fighting to get at me. I squeezed her wrists and diverted her struggling hands from my throat with all my power, which exceeded hers. But still she was on me, her weight considerable and intention to defeat me relentless. Her short hair was in my face, she was a werewolf or beast trying to devour me! Then just as quickly as she had sprung on top of me, she blasted-off by power of flight up into the air; I saw that the whole office was standing around us in a ring and that several people had pulled her up. I lay on my back in the open looking up at the long striplights embedded in the white panels above, an upside down pavement on the moon. The sight of Dr. Zen and all Loretta's colleagues looking in shocked amazement toward her restored her to her normal self and she walked out attended by a group of those who had arrested her, who were all at once agitatedly inquiring of her what had started the brawl. I got up and was surrounded by Yuri and Seri-chan and several of the other female staff, whose faces were urging for meaning and concern over my injuries, looking at the cuts and scratches along and under my cheeks. I was burning hot and my movements rapid and heightened, blood still pumping bioreactive escape factors around inside me, engorging limb muscles and disallowing all thought but to get out. Gradually I too calmed down and became myself again. Zen urgently wanted to know what had happened, and I said that Loretta had come over and attacked me over some piece of work I had done. Gasps of amazement ensued from all who heard and comprehended. I repeated the tale. Order was restored and the office middle-ranking captains and sergeants rounded everyone back to their seats. I accompanied Zen to his desk and narrated to him a report of how Loretta had gone insane and leapt at me after I was made to look at a piece of work that I had done for her when she was off sick. I said that Ms. Toda and Loretta had mentioned something about wanting to have a meeting regarding division of duties and that when I indicated that no, I did not think such a step was necessary, that was when Loretta had lost all control. She was plainly unhinged I added.

I knew that that was to be the last I would see of Loretta. How could she herself think to come back? Furthermore, in Dr. Zen's mind it must be obvious that she should be fired if she did not disappear on her own accord. So I had successfully utilized two unwavering facts about Japanese life against Loretta to usurp her: first, that full comprehension across the cultural and linguistic divide between Japanese and foreigners is never the case, and second, that in the Japanese mind, where approximation reigns and precise terms are banished, general appearance can sway any mere spoken terms used to describe what has happened, no matter how accurate and factual they are. Therefore neither Zen nor anyone else in Nimsan including Toady could ascertain how much the exact words I had used to provoke Loretta might have done so—they only saw Loretta appear to jump me. Nor could Loretta ever sufficiently explain her side of the story, since no one would fully comprehend her anyway. If she did try to defend herself in order to save her position, her judges would only hear that I had uttered something-or-other to her and that in her opinion that was good reason to go crazy. And they had all seen what she did right there in the office—that would take some explaining away!

Loretta did not reappear that day and resigned on the next, so Dr. Zen told me. A week later, Toady requested to be moved into another department, and after she left I hardly saw her again, except occasionally when her head bobbed up amid the sea of Nimsan uniforms in transit between the buildings at lunchtimes and home time. On those occasions when we passed each other by, she tried to smile at me in an awkward way that meant she was embarrassed about what had happened to me under the tyranny of her former General and when she herself shared some of the executive power. Since the war was over and she was a civilian again, she wanted forgiveness and to forget former times and events—so her demeanor communicated to me. As for myself, I cannot say that I felt like pardoning her or making up—she was just another person to get in my way in life, as people have and, I dare say, always will come along and try to do.

In the meantime, as the autumn went by, without Loretta being around, the atmosphere in the office changed from being flavored by the friction of dealing with her, to having no essence at all. Every morning as I made the short walk from my dormitory to the office, I became less and less willing to enter the Nimsan gates and begin another day of drudgery, sitting at my desk for hours on end, something I had never done before ever, even in earliest childhood or at school, looking at the constant flow of documents, articles, letters, contracts, and whatever else I was given to do starting from half-eight in the morning through to evening when the siren went off for close of affairs. All day long I found myself checking the clock on the wall. How slowly the hands changed their postures! I just wanted to get outside. I made several daily excursions out of the office, usually in the afternoons, to walk around and check out the buildings within Nimsan's complex, which was considerably expansive, or to go and drink a tin of cold green tea from out the vending machine, or just get some air. I was stifled and oppressed by ennui. The documents were so unbearably boring, I could hardly stand to read a whole paragraph at a time without wanting to get up and walk out.

I wondered what were the other people in the office doing, that allowed them to stay at their posts for all those hours day in and day out, except for at lunchtimes when they filed out, and for a brief sorting of exchanges and movements when they all came back, prior to settling down for more work. Within the office space, no one ever budged—each just sat at his or her place with head bent down, apparently intently concentrating on the task at hand. Some people had been doing this for years, some for decades. Dr. Zen himself had been a bureaucrat in one departmental office or other at Nimsan since long before I was born. The chances were, that at the same time as everything I could ever remember, going back to my youngest recollections, Zen was simultaneously sitting at his desk in his office, as immortally enthroned as Olympian Zeus. I pictured him directing all my previous actions from his pedestal as though I were his champion Heracles, performing my penance of twelve labors on Earth prior to being manifestly brought to dwell eternally at his side.

Few things can be more unhappy to look at than the faces of people trudging en route to work. Their expressions range from the perfectly blank to hangdog to sullen and fed up. The pace of a legion of white-collar workers after being offloaded by trains and public transport and moving on-foot toward an office district or big company such as Nimsan is slower than a geriatric shuffles—thus is the manpower's reluctance to get to its destination. Once inside the office, however, things are not quite as bad for these working people, or at least an investigator might be led to believe as much by interviewing a sample of them at their desks. For instance, I would often get up from my post at Nimsan bored almost into a sleep and go and disturb Yuri or Tomoko or Seri-chan in search of some amusement, and more often than not when I did, not wanting to be distracted, they would say to me, "Don't you have any work to do?" or "I'm busy now, please don't disturb" or some other such cliché to get rid of me. But the dreadful meaning of those utterances!

When I got talking to any of the office staff, either at their desks or during lunchtimes or perhaps later over a beer with Mr. Itoh, my neighbor at the dormitory, for example, I often moved onto the subject of work and how it ties in with their plans for the future, and was surprised every time that no one could countenance life without nine-to-five work, would not even consider it and hence as a corollary never wish for any such alternative existence. This attitude of thought really was the common currency. If I said something such as, wouldn't you like to make inventions or artefacts for a living, or do some acting, or produce anything else but *this* (referring to whatever paperwork task they were in the middle of doing), mostly my listener would look at me suspiciously or titter at my naivety, looking not certain whether I was even being serious. Most of these people agreed with me that they did not particularly enjoy going to work, but more on the grounds that they would rather stay in bed than enter the cold outside, or preferred to sleep all day or watch TV than get up and move. In fact, slumbering was the most frequently quoted preferred activity—inactivity, rather—to work that I heard from anyone, and seemed to be badly missed. I was dumbfounded that no one I probed wished they had time to read more, or explore more, or just feel the sun and freely amble about the city's parks and lonely forgotten points. No one had anything to build or color-in, examine with a magnifying glass or reach by telescope.

The state of their unquestioning conformity was also worryingly extreme—much deeper than just sportingly wanting to get ahead and not to incommode others by defaulting on doing their bit and chipping in to the smooth-running business machine. For a start, the people in the office were morbidly fearful of being late in the mornings, or spending too long at lunch and returning after the set time. Often as I made my way into Nimsan at eight-thirty, about to enter the gates just as the morning call-to-work siren started to wail, I saw people who had broken away from the weary herd moving along the sidewalks and who were running as fast as they could go—seemingly in a panic—blindly blundering through the throng to get into their office on time, gaze affixed on the building ahead. Heaven knows what would happen to any of these latecomers if a car came along just when they dashed across the road, because they surely did not look left and right! I wondered what consequence of being unpunctual could be so dreaded, in these adults.

Other customs and peculiarities I observed among the office workforce bore further testimony to the idea that something was very wrong within that population. One such bizarre piece of evidence corroborating my suspicions concerned the drip-coffee percolator kept in the small kitchenette area next to the office, which was supposed to be used by the office staff *ad libitum*, then replenished by the last person whoever finished the pot—that is, by replacing the filter with a fresh paper cone, heaping in some coffee powder and topping up the water. Every day when I went in to get a cup of coffee, however, I always found that it contained exactly enough left for one small mugful. Every day, the same. Evidently, after being filled first thing in the morning, the container was gradually emptied a cup's worth at a time as people came in, until only enough for one more cup remained. This must have been the case, because as I say, every day when I went to get a cup in mid-morning, there was always just this amount left. This extraordinary state of affairs could only mean that people were really so lazy, despite how they behaved in front of one another and their bosses inside the office, putting on a show of eagerness to be of great use to the company, that whenever no one was looking at them, that is in the kitchenette, they could not even make a pot of coffee; they would in fact rather have no coffee to drink than make it. But this was not all that the perpetually nearly empty coffee pot signified. It also showed that not only were office people too lazy to make coffee, they were also too scared to steal a cup and boldly walk off without refilling the pot. Each person who came in must have seen that only one cup remained, muttered a curse, and quietly stalked back out pretending never to have gone into the kitchenette. The pusillanimity of that! To what kind of state had capitalist civilization brought humanity!

Another peculiar piece of sophistry, which I could never quite work out, was the pretense evinced by everyone about to set off for lunch at noon, when I asked them, that they had no idea where they were going to go to get something to eat—either in the canteen or the food shops and stalls, there were several choices at Nimsan. Perhaps this charade was put on to ward me off in case I tried to invite myself to join them—but that does not seem very likely. If that were the case, they would use some other evasion, since not knowing where to go does not imply having to be left alone. Quite the opposite if anything. At any rate, it is not humanly possible to set off on a journey without having some destination in mind, even if it does turn out that it is not to be reached in the end. The pretense, so widely put on that it was a form of ritual, remains a mystery to me. It was probably associated with the general tendency I detected among the office people not to give anything away about themselves, to keep things close to their chest, further belying their true feelings toward each other, which were cutthroat.

The limit though, was what I observed in the men's restroom. The offices of the Communications Department had restrooms which were accessed via the outside corridor, opposite the aforementioned kitchenette. Whenever I went in to use the urinal, invariably someone was always locked in one of the two cubicles behind my back taking a crap. But the peculiar thing was, these persons never made a single noise. The atmosphere was electric with a static current of tension—the person within the cubicle had stopped like a creeping assassin and sat in wait for me to go out so that the coast was clear to continue. I could easily sense it—it was much like the feeling of being watched. Furthermore, sometimes on such occasions, the concealed person would flush the toilet two or three times in succession, probably to mask the plopping report of a bowel movement. How could they really be so timorous and afraid that someone might hear them and—they must have been so ashamed—know that they had defecated! Perhaps someone might even hear their feces dropping into the toilet? Were office people so squeamish and dandified that they turned away and withered from any such indelicate sensibility? Office people were so frustratingly tame and uninspiring, I just wanted to run out the building.

Only one person was different—at least in my mind I perceived her to be unlike the rest. Her name was Yumiko Baro—Yumi—and she sat at the far end of the office from where my desk was positioned. Oddly, I must have passed her up to fifty times before I really noticed her, which is unlike me; I can normally espy a natty chick all the way down the street, often sense one even before she comes round the corner and into view. But there was Yumi all along without me realizing. I had spoken to her every once in a while over minor work matters, but that was all and I had hardly thought about her each time after we parted company. The baggy identical work uniforms that we in the office all wore may have tended to obscure her, but if that were so I doubt by very much, since I certainly knew who were all the other fair maidens, and had a highly artistic mental picture of their bodies in wonderful anatomic detail beneath the unflattering overalls. No, the case with my not seeing Yumi from the first was an example of the phenomenon of active and passive attraction that seems only to crop up in offices and workplaces. That is, just as there were at Nimsan, both in my little office and to be seen round about at large, many ravishing beauties with whom, after initially instantly falling in desire, I had to learn to overlook the comeliness in favor of blandly collaborating in that cooperative business milieu—so that in the end I hardly noticed how beautiful they were at all—so there were also others whose charm I did not behold until passion was suddenly switched on by some event and expressed like a gene. With Yumi, the event in question was a dream I had, in which I found myself in a naked embrace with her. When I awoke, I was stricken with lovesickness, and that morning made my way to the office in a rush with thoughts of her batting wings in my mind.

I knew that Yumi was twenty-one, and like most people living in Tokyo, derived from some faraway province in Japan's mountainous countryside. She was slightly taller than the other girls, perhaps five-eight, and wore her shoulder-length hair, which had a lighter tone of ray-catching gold above the dark brown, in a loose ponytail and a forward fringe pushed aside to keep it out of her eyes. Her face was spotlessly pretty with a long nose, the face of my ideal imaginary junior librarian minus the horn-rimmed glasses—or after taking her glasses off. With her delicately pointed nose, pert lips and smallish chin that looked as though it might start quivering at any time, as in a petulant type of spoilt tantrum, she was quite similar to a Chardin-painted schoolmistress in profile. Her general manner was ostensibly demure and modest but palpably fun-filled, she was a beacon sending out a message of playfulness in a low radio-frequency undetectable to those without an attuned receiver. My radar dish was pointed at her all right!

That morning, the day after having my dream, when I went into the office and sought Yumi out, just as I saw her and she looked back at me, I started feeling a strange kind of painful embarrassment as though I were walking around with nothing on, almost an exhibitionist type of thrill. I felt like she knew that I had dreamed about her and what we were doing in the dream, as though we really had touched fingers overnight and become intimate. Could she have that knowledge? My heart thumped as I gazed at her, for long after she had made the first brief connection with my eyes and then looked away back down at her work-desk. She was just across the room about ten yards from me; I had to approach her and let her know that I was in love with her, but now that I wanted to get to her so badly, I was inhibited by paralysis, whereas always when I had spoken to her before, I had experienced nothing of the sort.

I sat down and decided to write her a message. Then I thought, I know, in Japanese. I took out my *kanji* dictionary and started writing a note: Hi Yumi, this is Tommy, would you like to have lunch with me today, what do you think, Tommy. This took me fifteen minutes to compose, looking up the Japanese characters and carefully copying them onto my bit of paper by hand. Throughout the fifteen minutes, I did not have a care in the world; however, as soon as I finished the short letter, I came out of my reverie of concentration and regarded it as extremely silly. Why could I not go up to her and ask her for a date? I looked over at her again, moved to stand up, then sank back on my seat in alarm. I was petrified by her looks! I thought about what would happen if I approached her at her desk. I would stroll over, say "Yumi," perhaps she would not hear my tremulous voice, so I would have to repeat her name; she would turn her face upwards looking expectant and probably also confused at my appearance, my pallor and shaking limbs, not understanding why I looked so wretched all of a sudden; I would start to speak then stutter to a halt as I saw that more and more people in the office were looking at us, looking at me especially, their listening ears bending the fleshy pinna my way, all watching, staring, and I would look back down at Yumi sitting there, and drop to my knees so as to hide beside her, and whisper to her, what? I could think of nothing winning to say. I was not the comic type who could use humor to cajole her, with the concomitant failsafe that if she refused it was all just a joke—I wished I could do that as well as some other gifted guys had a natural capability. On the other hand, I had never known any female to refuse an earnestly trying guy in bad grace, even if he was hopeless. The universal phobia of mortal man, that a woman might sneer or laugh at him or stick a knife into his heart for asking her to favor him, was as mythological as witchcraft. If I went up to Yumi and asked her to have lunch with me, and she did not want to, the most cutting reply that she might make would be to refuse with a consolatory smile, I was sure of that. The prospect was hardly unendurable, even if many people did laugh as I scuttled back to my place. Still, I could not find the courage to go over.

I began to sweat it out at my desk, thinking when might be a good time to talk to Yumi, over whom I was experiencing pangs moment by moment. At one point her desk-neighbor, Ms. Tanaka, stood up and walked out the office, leaving Yumi sitting all alone with no one else anywhere near within overhearing proximity. My heart bolted like a greyhound—I almost puked as it hit my gullet. As I studied the possibilities, I was so alert to Yumi's unguarded presence in the far corner of the room that if someone had walked up behind me and prodded me in the back ribs I might not have noticed. I shook from top to toe. Then just as quickly as Tanaka-san had left the room, she came back in and sat back down right next to Yumi again. Although I had not made a move when I had the chance, and no doubt was too chicken to take the plunge no matter how long Yumi was left sitting on her own, when I watched her colleague plant herself down and cut off the golden opportunity, I flopped into dejection.

The morning went by with myself trying to build up courage, then unstoppably and pitilessly the clock reached twelve noon and everyone including Yumi went off to lunch. What a total failure! I even attempted making excuses to myself in my head, trying to cover up the evidence of my inner cowardice with a barrage of perjurous mitigations from my ego's defense team. None of it succeeded. I was a chump and knew it. Ashamed, I left the deserted office too and went off toward the soccer pitch for my daily kick-around with the guys from the factory. As I bounded down the stairs and started to jog, however, to my astonishment I ran straight into the path of none other than Yumi herself, who came walking round a corner alone holding a takeaway lunchbox for eating back in the office. I did not even have time to think; I stopped or else I would have collided into and knocked her right over—and then there she was directly in front of my face. "Sorry!" I said. The heat-energy of running had produced the same symptoms as my nerves would have, had I met her at a walk, and so in not having to worry about my blushes showing, this soothed my mind. I asked her where she was going and she indicated back to the office since she had no one to lunch with. I may have been a chump, but even King Chump the First could not blow that offer. We went back up the stairs together and I sat at Ms. Tanaka's vacated desk while Yumi sat at hers, and we talked so fast that when the end-of-lunch siren sounded, I knew a complete précis of Yumi's family, upbringing, interests, tastes and travels, which were divinely matched to my own—as much by signifying a complicit sympathy of feeling as in their specific details—and furthermore had heard no mention of any competing boyfriend, which meant there wasn't one. As the staff filed back into the office and their voices interrupted us, I asked Yumi to meet me later that evening after office hours, and she responded with a yes and curtly turned to her work just when Ms. Tanaka came to reclaim her seat from under me.

5

That evening when the workday finished I waited for Yumi at the Nimsan gates, trying to avoid looking available for having a conversation with anyone I knew or appearing on the lookout for someone to invite me to go for a drink. On the other hand, I simultaneously tried to make it look like I was not hanging around waiting for anyone in particular either—I did not want everyone to know that I was dating a Nimsan girl. As the hundreds of employees drained from the buildings and passed me, just about everyone I did not want to see went by—they all had a good look at me in a knowing kind of manner or else said bye or started to talk to me. I eluded their inquiries and attempts to find out what I was doing. I was still very much a foreigner from distant lands and my movements attracted attention in a way that was part protective of me should I get lost and also a little bit because I was not without a modicum of celebrity-interest too. But one-by-one they moved on. At last Yumi arrived, practically the final person to leave, long after the flocks had dispersed. As she got near to me I saw why she was so late: she had made herself up and looked exquisite for our assignation. She was wearing tight jeans that showed off her long legs and a sky-blue rollneck sweater with matching scarf thrown on top. Her body was something else! As I took the vision of her in, I reminded myself of a Loony Toons animated cartoon depicting a saucer-eyed slavering wolf in a zoot suit. We walked along the river-path that led from Nimsan's grounds, following the concrete-enclosed waterway on its course eastward over to the docklands and Tokyo Bay. We talked away and eventually came to a brightly lit place with many restaurants and cafes. We ate a youngsters' meal of French fries and potato croquette burgers topped with brown sauce, all washed down with strawberry parfaits from Anna Miller's.

Yumi was absorbing. Her parents had been rich bohemians who moved out to Karuizawa in the western Japan countryside in the 1970s to breathe clean air and raise kids in view of mountains topped with snow, in order to instil in them a sense of nature's wondrous pledges and art. Yumi and her brother, Kimi, grew up in an environment of folk music, painting and filmmaking amid the many famous artists and musicians known to their parents. Kimi, a couple years' Yumi's junior, followed the typical course of similar children brought up in such circumstances, developing a fine aversion to earning a living and becoming a drummer in a local punk band, forever making recordings and playing in one of the bars in the village. Yumi, on the other hand, after finishing her schooling, moved to live with her Grandparents at their house in central Tokyo so as to attend a city university, and drifted into her job at Nimsan on graduating. She was keenly interested in cinema and music, played piano and wrote poems. Her sense of humor, which I had detected before I met her, was a delight. Her insights regarding people both known to us in the office and strangers who came and went in the street were brilliantly perspicacious and cunning; little escaped her notice and she was quite aware of human folly, which made her giggle a lot. We went and sat by the river in the cold night and I wrapped my arm around her as we talked, protective of my new beloved. At a certain dormant lull in the conversation, I thought, right, do it now and kissed her on the lips, to which she gave back as naturally as breathing, the subject of her talk abruptly sucked away. The kiss lasted several minutes while my hands moved all over her, each run of my fingers dextrously stopping just short of going so far as actually groping her breasts and squeezing her buttocks right in front of respectable locals out walking their dogs along the riverbank. I pushed my right hand up her jumper and stroked her back— her soft warm skin was so smooth and giving, my hand felt like it were on rollers. I looked at Yumi's thick shiny hair from close enough for it to touch my eyes. It was faintly scented and wafted, an olence of shampoo and clean oils. She was a luxury extravagance of stagecoach and ball-gown material. Her voice was a sonorous Oriental shehnai, her Japanese accent coloring-in the superb weirdness of her concepts and angles, her conclusions apparently all arrived at from somewhere round the back of from where my mind could probe. I loved to listen to her, so sweet she was. We looked up at the full, lover's Moon, the same orb that I have gazed at and wondered at all my life—how men have always wished to go there....

 Having a sudden impulse, I jumped up and urged Yumi to stand next to me. Ceremonially raising an outstretched hand adjoined, my left and her right, our other arms embracing each other round the waist, I said to Yumi let's touch the moon together with a pointer finger as elemental pledge of our destiny. The tips of our index fingers placed in contact, I looked up and landed them softly on the moon. "There, our avowal is made," I told her with an air of heartfelt earnestness.

"What avowal?" laughed Yumi. "I'm just pointing out into cold empty space."

I had forgotten the angle of parallax between our relative fields of vision. So I asked Yumi then to move our fingers over to touch the moon in her eyes. She moved them slightly over and stopped, saying "Now they are on the moon." To me, our fingers were pointing over the earth's horizon.

After our first tryst by the riverbank, I started to meet Yumi most nights of the week after work, usually smuggling her into my room in the dormitory. We talked all the time within the office, but never showed that we were dating and I doubt whether many of the office staff knew about us. This is how we sneaked into the dormitory. The second time that we went out together, we purchased a shopping-bagful of salty snacks, a bottle of Mumm's Cordon Rouge champagne, and several ready-mixed miniature cocktails in various bright electric blues, blood reds and orange, and made our way to the dormitory, Nimsan's male bastion. We arrived and stood outside surveying the four-story building from the street. Inside the gate, next to the drive and adjoining the main edifice, was the maisonette belonging to the dormitory's caretaker and his family. This man, Mr. Toji, was the epitome of menials who determinedly throw themselves into discharging their supervisory function to the letter of the law—especially, in Toji's case, regarding maintaining adherence to the dorm's no-women policy. Every evening he could be seen in his gray overalls policing the corridors, spot-checking the common areas, and generally tampering with the lives of the tenants over obeying regulations. Furthermore, like Loretta, from the outset he had correctly identified me as a troublemaker, and the fact of having me living in the dorm did not please him one bit. He was livid over my habit of bringing my mountain bike inside and keeping it in my room instead of leaving it out in the shed to corrode along with the other rusty boneshakers. However, there were no rules prohibiting the bringing of bicycles into the dormitory—no doubt only because none of the lawmakers imagined anyone would do it—and so, to a functionary of Mr. Toji's calibre, whose job was to enforce and not to make the rules, and whose legalistic mentality forbade him from taking the law unto himself, there was nothing he could do but to wait for me to drip rainwater all over the pristine polished hallways or mark the clean wallpaper with tyre tracks, so that he could bring the full weight of authority down onto having the bike banned. Alas, if only he could have me evicted as well, then he would have been perfectly happy.

Yumi and I looked over at the dormitory from the street. She was my girlfriend and I had invited her over to my place, and that was simply it: All I had to do was get her past the caretaker and inside. I crossed the gate and ducked past Toji's windows that faced onto the driveway. Toji had a habit of sitting at one of these windows in the early evenings, puffing a cigarette and letting the smoke out through the slightly ajar casement—as well as watching out for strangers approaching his dominions. Although he was not there at that particular time, he might appear at any minute. Myself arriving stealthily at the wall of the dormitory, as a black shadow of a sabotage commando, I waved Yumi over. She responded by walking out through the center of the gate right in the open under the street lights and, at a pace that was neither a quick run into cover nor slow and concealed, but more like a catwalk model's effeminate swing, made her way over in full view of Toji's windows, which thankfully were still not manned. When she reached me I reminded her that she was supposed to be incognito. Then I left Yumi waiting outside in the dark and darted into the dormitory through the main entrance. On the third floor, I nipped to the end of the corridor running along the wing where Yumi was located on the ground, opened the fire door, and fumbled my way down the emergency stairs in the pitch-darkness toward the outer exit. I unlatched it, opened it, and was once again standing right next to Yumi, having completed a Ferris wheel rotation of stairs and floors. We stepped inside where I had emerged, (I re-locked the fire exit door), then we were up the stairs, and with a dash along the corridor to my room, ducked safely inside with our stash of food and drinks.

The first night that Yumi stayed over in my room, after talking and listening to music for a while, we got down and kissed amorously under the covers of the bed and gradually lost our clothes. With my hands, body and tongue I enfolded her in long embraces until the time felt right—but then just as I motioned to enter her, she announced in a whisper that she was still a virgin. She lay back on the pillow and pulled me in toward her. Ever so carefully and slowly, I eased myself inside her. Her heart knocked against my chest as a rhythm subliminally generated and grew. And just before I came, considering Yumi's inexperience, I was tender and cautious to withdraw from her boiling fertile passage. We lay side by side in the bed and I exhaled long and hard. At length she winked into a gentle slumber and for some time I eyed at and learned her beautiful sleeping form as I caressed her shoulders, soft glossy long hair and the chaste untainted flesh of her torso.

Romping around and partying with Yumi in my room was wonderfully special. Over the weeks since arriving in Japan, I had been steadily replacing all my old vinyl records that I had left back at home by CDs, which I had till then always resisted buying since they started coming along in the mid-eighties some years before. CDs were badly inferior to records in terms of sound, and furthermore were not lovable like records at all. But records were dying out everywhere and in Japan were already extinct, so it was well nigh the moment for me to move with the times. With my extravagant new wealth at Nimsan, I had been buying CDs by the armful and already had over a hundred when I started going out with Yumi. Yumi was not knowledgeable about my kind of music but enthusiastically liked what I played to her, which was an essential plus from my point of view. She loved The Smiths best of all, followed by the Stone Roses. Some nights, sitting under my bedcovers huddled together, we listened to just The Beatles or Hendrix or The Supremes, the incredible musicianship and genius of the compositions and performances absorbing us in quiet concentration. Other times Yumi asked me to strum something on my guitar or read to her from my collection of books: poems and short stories which she rather intuited than understood, the words, feelings, images and emotions of western writers being as alien to her as Japanese life was to me.

One night lying in my bed, we got to talking about such things as telepathy, the future, clairvoyance and divination. I maintained that although I was pretty convinced of the existence of thought-transference, which I myself had done and witnessed many times over, as well as being as certain as I could be that chance and coincidence were guided by *some* power, which I thought probably came from within ourselves—again because of my countless observations of such events, and not due to gullibility, reading silly books and listening to charlatans, which I was more than capable of dismissing—I was, on the other hand apart from these, sceptical of divination and prophecy of all kinds. This was because, I argued, regarding the future there was nothing yet to see there; the future by definition had no shape to observe since any and every intervening event re-directed it in an infinity of alternatives. The future never exists. So I argued to Yumi. She however replied with a remark that challenged my assertions, and the words she used stuck tellingly in my mind in the months ahead, which were, strangely enough, destined to be rife with sudden changes: "I disagree with you," she said about the closed-off, occult nature of the future, "I think that we can influence how the future turns out, by our wishes and desires, if they are strong and keen." I believed her; for in this way she unified my outlook on psychic powers, chance and precognition, only the latter of which I had till then discounted, somewhat to the detriment of my belief in the other phenomena. Suddenly all three made sense.

On my birthday that late November, a strange thing happened to me, as I shall explain shortly. It was a Saturday, and Yumi had stayed over in my room the previous night. In the morning, she presented me with a sky-blue shirt that she had bought for me in the Ralph Lauren store on uptown Omote-sandō shopping street. I did not know what to think of it really, it was the first long-sleeve shirt I had possessed since wearing school uniform. It did not occur to me straight away that Yumi was smartening me up with some vaguely calculating notion about me being her long-term provider somewhere down the line, and that I was hardly going to get very far in Japan looking like a bum. Or perhaps at that point she was starting to feel embarrassed that she could not take me anywhere fancy, where I was not permitted to look like the council estate kid I was. At any rate, at the time, I hardly thought about there being any underlying significance attached to the gift, and loved the shirt. I put it on and we quietly slipped out the dorm in secret, I going ahead first and scouting for anyone around, and beckoning Yumi to follow when no one was.

Once outside we went hand in hand and ate a breakfast of sandwich rolls and coffee in a branch of the Subway chain. As I gave my money to the fellow serving behind the counter, who was big and quite considerably overweight, at least for a Japanese, something I saw in his large face, perhaps it was just such kindness, caught me by surprise and for no more than a second I started to weep. I had to turn away in case

Yumi thought I was a madman. A few minutes later, after we had gone over to our table, another incident happened, which is still not the strange event I have mentioned before, but another that struck me as memorable because demonstrative about the great differences between Japanese and western habits of thought, which when juxtaposed rarely failed to stimulate my own sense of shortcomings. We were eating our sandwiches when quietly somewhere overhead, on the café's speakers, emerged an Everly Brothers' tune, "Cathy's Clown." I immediately jumped up and tried to pull Yumi over to stand beneath the speaker; I wanted her to listen to the duet's harmony with me—I was going to make a point about it and how the art of singing in separate vocal parts had all but vanished from pop music since the 1960s. However, she resisted my invitation and stubbornly remained on her seat, so I ran off looking up, trying to locate the speaker embedded in the ceiling by its faint sound. Once tracked down and I was standing beneath it, I tried to wave Yumi over once again, with insistence since the song was only so long. For the second time she refused with an apologetic smile and shake of the head, probably embarrassed in combination with being uninterested, so I gave up my enthusiasm for the pop lesson. Just at that same moment, however, one of the local customers, a silver-haired senior citizen sitting near to Yumi, leaned over to her and intervened, uttering something or other in her ear. She smile-laughed back at him and raised the palm of her hand, a characteristic Japanese female gesture meaning that everything was fine. Meanwhile I was standing in the middle of the restaurant in the midst of diners going about their sandwiches. So I threw my hands in the air in surrender and walked back to our table, ignoring the old man as I sat. I was just a little bit annoyed at having had such a chivalrous knight spoil my fun. "Why didn't you come over?" I asked Yumi.

"Because I'm eating," she said, which was equally possibly evasive or true.

I digested her reply for a moment, then asked: "By the way, what did he want?" I pointed over my shoulder.

"Oh, he asked if we were looking for the toilet," said Yumi.

This is what I mean by misunderstanding Japanese motives and by usually taking a guess that lands on the misanthropic side of their true intentions once revealed.

After the meal, we made our way by train to the match ground for my soccer game with Nimsan F.C. After the game, which ended, with us winning, just as it was getting dark at about 4:30 p.m., the guys, who had figured out it was my birthday, seized me by my wrists and ankles and bounced me up and down into the sky a good twenty-four times—once for each year that I was celebrating. We then all adjourned to an *izakaya* bar near to the ground and ate and drank through till late. Sometime during the evening, Yumi went home to her Grandparents, and so by the time the party came to a close, I and a few stragglers made our way to the station and we found our way back home completely roaring drunk on *sake*, *shochu*, beer and whatever else we had been knocking back.

A few hours later, in bed in the dormitory, the strange thing that I have mentioned happened. Very early into the next morning, sometime before daybreak and still dark outside, maybe about 4 o'clock or so, I awoke lying on my back. I felt terrible, in the worst hangover state I could imagine after mixing and drinking binge amounts of wines and spirits. I just lay in my bed trying to decide whether I was going to throw up, and mentally asked myself the question, Shouldn't I get up and make myself a drink of water, try to sober up a bit, in case I fall asleep and vomit, choke on it, and die as did Jimi Hendrix? I used something like those words. I responded by concluding that I should lie still and stay put, and then I said to myself, again all in my head, "I bet that's what Jimi Hendrix said to himself just before he died." I lay still a little longer, feeling quite ill and almost being nauseous, when once again I thought to myself, I wonder whether I should turn over and lie on my side, since I had heard that that was the best way to save my life in case I passed out and was sick. And again, I just said to myself, No, I will be all right—and then I mused, Or, is that what Jimi thought before he died? …And in that same second, all of a sudden, in my room, in early morning darkness, a voluminous swell of music started playing—Jimi Hendrix's *Electric Ladyland*—all of its own accord on my stereo. I had to jump up and turn it off; it was on loud enough to wake everybody in the building. Then, since I was up I made my drink of water and washed my face, revived myself a bit, at least felt slightly better, and went back to bed to sleep it off till daylight came. Lying under the sheets, amazed at what had just happened and not at all spooked, simply incredulous, I remembered that Hendrix, my great hero when I was in my teens, a left-hander like myself—shared my birthday that day too.

6

I decided to leave my job at Nimsan. Yumi asked me what I was going to do instead, and the answer was that I did not know. However, I just was not interested in staying in the office any longer, whiling away the hours as the clock on the wall lorded it up counting off the days of my life. Anything was preferable to that, even poverty and discomfort. I wanted those hours and days to myself, to think and to feel the warm air and the atmospheric moods outside. I was fully aware of my time and how much it was worth to me, and the price was more than I was getting for it. Why work five days a week even for a good salary if I only had two free days left to spend it? Really, I was working mainly for the benefit of my tiny but warm and waterproof room. Even the amount of money I was getting paid did not seem all that much to me anymore. Now, it seemed that the income tax office, local ward office, utilities providers, telephone company, and just about everyone else in town had all received a tip-off about my novel wealth and came running to get their cut. What was left was handed out here and there in no time at all—Tokyo was expensive. I quickly adjusted from having bugger-all money before I arrived to having quite a bit to spend, then began to regard my nouveau loose capital as pretty small after all. I could buy the odd Paul Smith jumper or other frippery every month and eat out a lot, and usually had just about enough beer money to last till the next pay day, but I could not afford, say, to fly off to Hawaii for a week, or even travel round Japan by rail. Those kinds of excursions would require me to save up, or pay off in instalments later. I was not rich after all. And even if I were well off by all means versus a lot of folk, as well as compared with my previous student existence, I nonetheless innerly began to regard my monthly wage as something impertinent put upon me—a limitation and an imposition. It was my permission to lead a certain life just-so and no more. It was a confinement, decided by nameless outside judiciaries who considered my case. It was precisely and really my *allowance*—defining what I could do and where I could go. So was I not then a prisoner of it? Was my current lot all that I wanted in return for the boredom and frustration of carrying out repetitive and uneducating tasks? No, it certainly was not. On the other hand, I could not be a latter-day Thoreau on Walden Pond either, permitted to conduct a living experiment in self sufficiency while forgetting or overlooking that he was able to do so only because of the crucial benefaction of being granted free use of the land he cultivated and lived on by its owner, Ralph Waldo Emerson. In 1993, I could not see any analogous altruistic patron allowing me to build a log-house and grow a beanfield in his backyard. What was I to do to seek my fortune on my own?

I should also mention that nor was I at all against the idea of job-work *per se*. I was not very naïve or foolish enough to denounce work as an unnecessary detraction enslaving a narcotized humanity regulated by evil capitalists and warmongers who pervert the use of technological advances so as to keep themselves rich billionaires instead of letting progress liberate the workers toward lives of peaceful leisure, as certain utopians, anarchists, futurists, communists *et cetera* who stand up against the place of work in modern society have often espoused. On the contrary, what could be more obvious than that we depend absolutely for the advancement and survival of the species on work of every single kind, and that there is so much to be done that every able-bodied person must get involved to a degree. Every job that there is has some contributing effect: and it is those jobs that are usually called the most useless, underpaid and dissatisfying ones such as cleaning, serving food, standing guard, driving and the like that are instantly to be perceived as most essential. Office work, the tasks that probably occupy the majority of people—save perhaps service industries—is less obvious to prove in this respect. No doubt at least half the workforce sits around most of the time doing little that can be called highly productive or directly and demonstrably going to turn a profit for the company—but on the other hand, so long as things get done and the orders keep coming in, profits must exceed expenses or else the company is dissolved. What better proof could there be that all work serves a function?

As for the objection that one-by-one the trillions of things that we do not really need and that we could just as well do without, which arguably accounts for most of the items that we buy, accrue, store, consume, spectate, watch onscreen and otherwise amass, could be phased out and their creators, inventors and manufacturers relieved of their current positions and sent out to pasture *en masse*, so that eventually only the top professors, physicians, researchers, architects, programmers, designers and other dependables—whose level of expertise is simply too high for them to be replaced yet by computers and mechanization—remain employed at their tasks, (because without the minimum of their diligence and perseverance we would all die out), is equally as much nonsense as the idea that we would ever wish to do without our luxuries and novelty items in the first place. For, with most of the adult population hypothetically sitting around on their backsides on the beach, who on Earth is going to get up every morning and rush around a hospital in a white coat for eighteen hours, or stay in all day while the sun shines outside, devising a program that will allow computers to come up with tasty new cocktails that robots will serve to retired humans on their deckchairs? Work will not be eliminated for a long time to come while at least some people still have to do it. And besides this, there is the final *coup de grâce* on the matter, placed by the realness that on the whole people seem to enjoy and identify themselves with doing their work and would not wish to do without it anyway.

My objection to working at Nimsan or any other office, laboratory or teaching post, which would all be about the same to me, was that I was not at all interested in doing any of those jobs. I knew that I had to pay my own way, but I only wanted to do something that was artistic or inventive such as writing, playing music, painting or even acting to make ends meet. Many people make a fortune, or at any rate get by, doing those things, so why should I not be able at least to prosper in those ways as well? I wanted to give one of those types of occupation a try. Yumi of course pointed out that it takes time, perhaps a long time, many months or even years, to get going as an artist or performer, and then success can only be gained with the crucial combination of both ability and luck, without which no artist ever got anywhere—luck being the unknown factor, favoring some and ignoring others regardless of their potential or their brilliance. I myself knew many of my friends back in England were talented drummers and poets and spontaneous comedians, all who still had to keep their nine to fives. But, I insisted to Yumi that I wanted to have a go and to see how far I could get, and if nothing came of my ambitions and I got ready to give them up, I was quite sure that I could find another job quickly enough if it became necessary. Perhaps Nimsan would be prepared to take me back again. I might even be able to make arrangements for them to keep me a place in reserve if I took one year off, and in the meantime if I struck it rich with, hey, a blockbuster novel or choice movie part (or so I was crossing my fingers), then Nimsan would hardly require that I returned to the office on the morning of the anniversary of my departure, threatening me with decapitation by the Green Knight.

When I met Dr. Zen and told him that I was handing in my notice, quite a surprising look of sad disappointment suddenly ran over his face, a ripple, then was gone. Was that a moment of envy from a middle-aged man who had accepted spending his whole life in doing what I was trying to escape? No, it seemed more likely he was touched to see me go somehow, a loss of a kind of friend who was going away for good. My chair would be empty. When someone whom one sees and cooperates with every day for a while decides to quit, it chips a little hole in the illusion of permanence within the office, and subtracts from the feeling that the quiet hubbub and milling around of familiar people are the good times. At once after the brief reaction subsided, however, Zen shifted stance and accepted the thought of my resignation. Was I sure? he asked. Did I just want more money? No. What was I going to do next? I did not know, had nothing planned and no other job waiting. Nothing to go back to in U.K.? he responded. No, actually I was not going back to the U.K., I was planning to stay in Japan. I had a valid visa. Zen was mystified—he actually looked worried. What are you going to do? he repeated—for a job?

Christmas Eve, December 24th, 1993, a Friday, was my last day at Nimsan Co., Ltd. On that day and during the build-up to "The Festive Season," Tokyo including the office and everywhere else was entirely devoid of any Christmas decorations, changes in the routine TV programs, colored lights (except for on one long street, Omote-sandō, which had been illuminated with Santas, reindeers, and such like), or mulled wine, feasting, Christmas parties, or anything else that characterizes every mid-to-late December that I had known till then. Even the weather was warm. If I were in any other country in Asia, I might not have even hoped for Christmas celebrations—but in Japan, in Tokyo, everything looked so much like Europe, I was a little surprised that Christmas was not recognized. Being not a "Christian" country was not at issue—the West is hardly Christian, if one were to count the number of actual Christians walking around—but Christmas is nonetheless the West's most sacred tradition and its rites encompass every household. It just felt so unusual that a country like Japan that could adopt everything western had overlooked importing Christmas.

Not only was there no Christmas spirit at Nimsan, no one seemed even to realize it was Christmas Eve, a day that meant a great deal of excitement to me. Moreover, no one paid me too much attention on the occasion of my last day in the company of their employ either—which was also quite disconcerting. For the most part, everyone kept on working exactly the same as usual. Quite a few people popped by to say goodbye though, throughout the afternoon. I was also given several gifts from various members of staff with whom I had worked fairly closely, helping prepare their manuscripts and editing drafts. One person from the chemistry laboratories, Mr. Takadanobaba, even surprised me by coming in, putting a square piece of stiff mauve paper with Japanese decorative border down on my desk in front of me, and asking me to sign it for his memory.

The afternoon passed and I left after dwelling long on saying my farewells to everybody in the office. Then the day ended and I marched outside the gates with Yumi amid the throngs of people going home, none of whom I am sure remembered that it was Christmas Eve. Although Yuletide had little effect on the Tokyo population, however, New Year was a different matter; it is the most important holiday in the Japanese calendar, indeed the only set vacation of any length. In the Spring there is Golden Week, approximately a week off for the majority of the population, and in August most people again take a few days' to a week's holiday for *o-bon*, when they return to their hometowns to remember the spirits of their relatives—in theory at least. Neither Golden Week nor *o-bon* have any set dates from year to year however—like Easter they change. Golden Week is set by the authorities; *o-bon* is any time one feels like going home in August. Only New Year is naturally always the same date: January 1st. From about December 28th, every year a mass desertion takes place in Tokyo, and by New Year's Eve every office and shop is closed and few people are about on the streets. Tokyo—with few people about. It is unworldly. *Shōgatsu*, the New Year period, lasts through to about January 4th or a little later, depending on when the year's first weekend is, after which time the city refills and everyone goes back to work. Within a couple days, the holiday is all over and vanished.

When I left Nimsan, the offices were scheduled to be open as usual on the Monday to the Wednesday right after Christmas Day and Boxing Day—that is, December 27th to the 29th, then shut down thru till the end of the New Year break a week or so later. This was the regular pattern among businesses in Tokyo that year; shops also planned more-or-less to follow suit. On Boxing Day, Sunday, I was officially supposed to move out of my room, since I no longer worked at Nimsan, and I had accordingly sold my stereo (to a colleague in the office) and given my guitar to my old neighboring buddy Mr. Itoh, who told me he wanted to learn how to play, and I had packed my books and CDs into two boxes in readiness to vacate. But, because of the New Year closure, I was told at Nimsan that I need not move out till January when all the dormitory tenants returned. Up until that time I could practically have the entire dormitory to myself—even the caretaker, Mr. Toji, was going away.

In the meantime, however, I had to find myself somewhere else to live, such as, for example, a "*gaijin* house"—a dingy edifice consisting of cheap, dilapidated, weather-worn and cockroach-infested boarding rooms for back-packing, bar-working or English-teaching foreigners mostly on short stays in Japan, or shared accommodation in the YMCA or something like that. I had quite a lot of money saved—I could not spend all that I was making at Nimsan, and had just been in receipt of a "bonus" of quite a lot of money—and this was enough for me to be able to buy some sort of a roof over my head for a few months ahead at least, even if I did not make a penny more above what I had in the bank. I also could count on several ready-made students in the persons of Nimsan workers, all young women, who were eager to have private English lessons with me, which could be accomplished in a coffee shop for five thousand yen or so per hour. So I knew that I need not have starved no matter what else the immediate future held in store. However, despite my relatively secure prospects I could not help hearing my old friend in London Gary Gosling's words in my head: "You cannot protect yourself from the cold using paintings as a blanket, nor eat sheets of poetry for food." The mode of thinking behind that dispensation, which epitomized the point of view of Dr. Zen, my colleagues at Nimsan and just about everybody else in the world as far as I could tell, was exactly what I had just resigned my job to refute. Hence although I was on the cusp of being made to move out into the cold, I could not motivate myself to look for somewhere new to live just yet, to move in and immediately have to set about earning money doing all the same kind of chores all over again to pay for it. That would be precisely defeating the object.

Besides, I thought, as Yumi and I disappeared from view of the tops of Nimsan's high buildings, first and foremost there was Christmas to celebrate. We walked along the road going up to the local station in the clear cold early night with my noting that there was not a shred of evidence in view to suggest that the time was Christmas Eve. That was as may be, perhaps, but I was determined to make the night Christmassy. Hordes of people in suits and khaki overcoats filled the sidewalks and revolved around the entrance to the station just as on any other winter night. No one was merry; they were just commuters bumping into each other and rebounding off again as usual, not acknowledging anyone else around them. Back in London everyone would be highly aware that it was Christmas Eve, they would all be in a rush to get home or go out to the public house, a tangible holiday fever would obtain among the crowds that no soul could upset. Here, only the sight to one side of a ragged trio of heavily bearded homeless men with grimy hair all grown out into a wild hollybush sitting round a cup of *sake* provided anything like a Scroogesque note.

Yumi and I headed for the supermarket to stock up on food and drinks for the night and the next day. My design was to simulate Christmas inside my room at the dormitory—a week earlier I had bought a plastic Christmas tree that I managed to find in a department store, set it up in my window, and thrust Yumi's brightly wrapped presents underneath it. All that had not been organized as yet was Christmas dinner. I ran my eyes along the stocked aisles of the cavernous food store looking for Yuletide fayre: not a veggie sausage. No nut-roast, no salmon (except raw *sashimi*), no rich chocolates, mince pies or fruitcake; not even Brussels sprouts. For the first time in two months, I was dejected to see nothing but Japanese food. "No Christmas dinner, Yumi!" I cried out. I doubted whether Yumi was too dismayed; she had already told me that she had tried mince pies once and found them disgusting. At last I realized that dinner was off and consoled myself with Newcastle Brown Ale, champagne and a bottle of Amontillado from the import drinks counter. I also picked up a bottle of good bourbon whisky as an afterthought: Maker's Mark. I knew this brand because my Dad always kept a bottle back home and I sometimes used to sneak a sip. We next managed to find in the delicatessen some good Roquefort—fine cheese is a rarity in Japan, hardly eaten at all even though the Japanese generally are very knowledgeable and appreciative of just about every other type of European culinary provision. Green cheese is apparently too strong for them on the whole—but Yumi liked it. We paid and left the store and started on foot back toward the dormitory, but once outside, first quickly I had to stop Yumi with a press of my hand on her arm, separated away from her for a few paces, pulled the bottle of Maker's Mark whisky out of the carrier bag, and put it down among the three homeless fellows with a quick "Merry Christmas!" and darted back to Yumi.

Returned to the dormitory, I proposed to educate Yumi about the meaning of Christmas, which she had evidently been barred from being able to enjoy all her life. Lesson number one was a nice Christmas drink: Amontillado sherry which I poured into two small tumblers and we quaffed. Next was the unique, heavenly sounds of Yule: carols. Luckily I had purchased an excellent recording of a selection rendered by the choir of Salisbury Cathedral—the CD had first caught my eye because I love Wiltshire and the area around Salisbury, Avebury and Stonehenge. The main buying point, however, was the carols they chose to sing, starting with "Once in Royal David's City." As Yumi and I listened to it, I shuddered, and tingling points went all down my arms and spine, and tears like curious little silver fishes nibbled the bottom of the globes of my eyes; a curtain lifted and I was on a stage, a school Nativity play, memory of childhood primary school, so far away, wearing a tea towel on my head, my Grandparents both alive, were they sitting out there in the audience? The caroling brought my distant sensations back to me, a kind of constitutive loneliness, the black mass of winter stars, silence and bare trees, and I knew why I loved that hymn: it does not matter who sings it, which choir, only that Christmas carols must never be overdone and sung with too much gusto and power: children sing carols the best.

While the music played, I described the menu of a Christmas dinner and detailed the usual Christmas Day routine in a British household. By that I meant of course what happened in my household—I have never entered anyone else's home on Christmas Day. "Usually," I related, (drawing solely from my own experience living in Shropshire with two brothers), "children awake at around 5 a.m. and discover that: first, no adults have arisen yet and second, that their stockings (those, Yumi, are woolly socks) that had been hung out empty at the foot of their beds prior to going to sleep now contain tangerines, walnuts, Quality Street, and, for one year only, miniature bottles of cherry brandy and Warnink's Advocaat put there for a joke by my Dad, which went wrong because I drank them."

Yumi said she wanted to know more, so I poured us both another large Amontillado and we lay comfortably on the bed. "Round about mid-morning," I enlarged, "Grandma and Granddad drive over in their trusty beige Morris Marina. While Mom makes roast dinner, the old folks settle down into warm chairs in the living room and watch TV, which is showing all good stuff on every channel: films, cartoons and such like—instead of the boring programs that usually make up the schedule at that time of day during the rest of the year. In fact BBC Two, one of the only four TV channels, is normally not showing anything at all except for broadcasting a still picture of a little girl playing noughts and crosses during most hours of daylight, with the exception of at Christmas." I paused for a moment to remember what else usually happens on Christmas Day, then said: "With the admittance of Grandparents into the home, everyone is then assembled and it is time to open the presents—a long-awaited event. The parcels are doled out from under the tree and passed around to their recipients who open them while everyone watches their faces for their reaction to glimpsing the contents. This is particularly awful when it is your turn and you have to unwrap a book chosen by Grandma, or the newest Rolling Stones record from Dad, with the giver sitting there watching your face drop. The presents-unwrapping ceremony does not last very long, and ends abruptly with the carpet covered in multicolored litter when the final parcel is opened. But normally what you wanted is among the gifts, and a whole lot more too—Christmas is the best day of the year bar none for presents.

"After the presents have been played with for an hour or so, Christmas dinner is called and everyone gets up and goes to the kitchen, where the table is properly set out for once, with mats under the plates and a glass for everyone. Christmas dinner is an enormous stuffed roast sailing in gravy with a flotilla of swedes, potatoes and roast carrots bobbing about the prow. The roast is carved onto each plate, the vegetables spooned on, and then each platter is plastered in bread sauce. After this course come mince pies and double cream whisked stiff, or Christmas pudding. The entire dinner is without doubt the home feast *par excellence* with no equal during the rest of the year."

"And is that what happens in every home?" asked Yumi, playing at being absolutely naïve in her coquettish way.

"Well, most," I replied. And then an altogether different and Dickensian Christmas story came to my mind. "Of course, not everyone has a happy home to go to at Christmas," I said. "Once when I was a bit older, when I had moved to London for my first job, I was having Christmas dinner with my girlfriend, Nina, who was staying with me in my small flat, and I was dispatched out the house at some point in mid-morning by her to see whether any nearby shop was open, to buy some milk I think. So I put on my coat and strolled out into the cold. It was one of those days when there is not snow on the ground but only in the air, so fine that you cannot see the flakes in the wind, just feel their presence biting your chin as you walk. There were very few people about—I did not see anyone at all at first, making my way along the avenue toward Camden High Street. There were maybe three others I saw out and about, in an area that is normally filled with locals and shoppers, old people waiting for buses and static traffic jamming the whole length of the way. But on Christmas Day, the place was empty, and all the grocery shops that I had thought might possibly be open were closed up to boot. But then, just as I was starting to return home *sans* the milk, I heard someone speak to me: a young lady in her teens or early twenties. Homeless. She had run over from behind and caught me up, and started walking along beside me. She was so pretty, with wide-open hazel eyes and a Victorian china-doll's face, and also filthy, I imagined, with a highly prominent scab or cold sore on the corner of her mouth. But pretty—that is important. She attended me pertinaciously and struck up a conversation—where was I going and such like. Normally homeless people want money, but she did not ask for any such thing: she wanted to talk to someone on Christmas Day. That was so clear from her manner that I did not even think to offer her any coins—we just talked, I with half my mind thinking ahead about how to give her the slip some way short of reaching the vicinity of my destination—I could not take her there after all. Although I myself was not unwilling to taking her in, I decidedly doubted whether Nina would have been so welcoming. She had quite a jealous temper. I talked to the girl cheerfully enough but limited myself to answering her series of questions without letting the conversation catch flame; that is, every taper she held to my lips I blew out. I avoided inviting her to start talking about herself. And so we got to the last corner of the road, that Christmas Day, and I stopped and said that it was nice to make her acquaintance and goodbye.

"She responded: How about a Christmas kiss? Remember, she was a pretty girl, and there she was asking me to kiss her. If she were a bit more presentable, I might have complied straight away; but there again, if she were at her best, she wouldn't have asked. Pretty girls don't need to ask for kisses. We were in a curious reverse situation—or rather, she was; she was a reflection of herself and I was her mirror. What was I to do? I was not at all tempted to go ahead and kiss her, right on the cold sore. Only I had her feelings to consider. Where were her home and family, and why was she walking around a freezing Camden alone on Christmas Day? Why shouldn't I just go ahead and kiss her? What kind of a person would I be if I said no? I had just a few seconds to react to her request, because no sooner had she asked than she began to show signs of backing off. The reluctant reality was sinking in: Was she at such a low point in her life, that this most basic attribute of her femininity, till then unquestionable, was also now to be denied and defeated? So, I…."

Yumi moved forward toward me on the bed, placed her hand on my mouth, and said: "Don't tell me what you did."

"You don't want to know?" I asked. "Why not?"

"Because either you kissed her, which would be in an odd way gentlemanly, or you left her standing there, which would have been cruel, or perhaps you gave her just a hug which probably would have saved you both from heartache—but whatever you both did, why tell it? The story benefits better by leaving it at that."

"No it doesn't!" I said. "I hate stories with no ending."

"That depends on what you mean by an ending. To me, it's where the story stops."

"I mean a conclusion." I said. "A place where the story leads to, and one's expectations are either met or there is a surprise. At any rate, a point where no more narration is necessary, because we feel that the tale is complete. The ending—the conclusion—is the main point of having a story."

"It was complete, just where it ended, to my mind," was Yumi's reply. "That's why I stopped you."

I could see that Yumi meant what she said. I had encountered another puzzling piece of the large difference between my and her Japanese thinking: climax, the required constituent of stories, music, film, plays—anything that moved and could be developed, in fact—fireworks shows even—all these I would expect to evolve toward a certain direction of build up, then end with a coming together or flourish. In the Far East—not necessary. This was why Japanese pop music was such a cacophonous racket, that went on all over the place with no discernible repetitive motif or hook to lock onto, to detain my ears' attention, and inexorable collaring toward a release sounded by a relieving chord change or pause. Also the few Japanese films that I had seen made no sense at all, with no apparent connection between the various scenes and actions, apart from the same actors' faces, no story development to speak of. Japanese day-to-day logic meant almost as little to me as well—much of it was unfathomable. I had read Yukio Mishima's stories just before I left for Japan, thinking that I might learn something useful from the doing, and remembered a passage where one of the books' central character, a young student priest, was assigned a problem to solve by his master: "After a testing day of troubles and setbacks, a man returned home and placed his shoes on his head—Why?" Now, I cannot even remember what the answer was, but it was just as meaningless as the problem, which no one who is not conversant with Japanese Zen, I presume, could go about breaking down. The point was, it did not give any indication of a direction, by following which one could approach some sort of an answer, a destination, a *conclusion*. The Japanese might occasionally take pains to try, but do not actually need, to get to the bottom of things and work them out to obtain their satisfaction.

Half an hour later, we were lying in the bed feeling a deep and pleasant warm mellow, thanks to the effects of the Amontillado and brown ale, when Yumi, who was no doubt still concentrating on my reminiscence about the homeless girl, bridged a connection with earlier events of the evening and turned to me. Why, she asked, did I give that bottle of whisky to the homeless people outside the supermarket? I said because it was Christmas Eve and not very cheerful to be out in the cold with no home to go to, so I thought that I would improve their lot slightly with a warming gift.

"But you should never give anything to the homeless," she insisted. "They don't want to work—that's why they drop out of society. If you help them, they will never learn to assist themselves, and will just become dependent on others."

I was amused to hear such a harsh opinion especially from someone who lived comfortably at the expense of her Grandparents and more recently at mine most of the time. On the other hand it occurred to me that, like just about everything that she or any Japanese person said, she was voicing the unanimous sentiment and unequivocal position of the entire people, since I never heard any disagreement among the Japanese on matters of the heart, so I assumed that her words reflected the general consensus rather than represented just her personal fringe minority outlook, and therefore that there was nothing I could say to talk her out of it or convince her to the contrary by suggesting that homeless people mostly lose their jobs, are evicted, thrown out, left to fend for themselves, had bad luck or something like that. I also concluded, looking back over my period of stay in Tokyo, that it was true that the homeless in Japan kept themselves to themselves, never begged or asked for anything or even were seen very much. I thought that they themselves probably concurred with Yumi's idea and felt that they had to shoulder their destiny without asking for aid from anyone else. Even though they were destitute, they remained Japanese—insular and private.

The next day, Christmas Day, passed with Yumi and I having a lot of merriment. In the end, we decided to eat out in a restaurant, and after looking around for any establishment that made anything approximately like festive food with no success, eventually we settled for spaghetti. Before that, we exchanged our presents including a shirt (very smart) for me, and a leather jacket for Yumi, when we got up in the morning, then went out in the frigid, clear mid-day in search of our Christmas dinner. The southern sun that cannot get much off the ground in winter stays low in the sky over Japan, but fills one side of heaven with an intense brilliance of beams that are so blinding that no one can face the entire half of the day it is in and see a thing. Cycling is practically impossible without shielding the glare with one hand held at a constant salute. In this gilded dazzle we went out and greeted the beautiful air outside, clad in our newly opened presents: two young romantic lovers. After spaghetti we walked in the big central park, Yoyogi Koen, kicked a ball around with some people we met and latched onto, a couple of Britons and some Germans enjoying a Japanese un-Christmas outside. After the game, we all went in search of somewhere to have a drink and found an Irish pub nearby, where we sat till late night laughing and talking away over pints. At around midnight, we said our goodbyes and dispersed; Yumi went back to the dormitory with me for our last night spent under its roof in which I was an official resident.

On Boxing Day, we stayed in the dormitory all morning doing nothing except feeding on packets of potato chips which I went out and bought in the local convenience store. Later, Yumi went back to her Grandparents and I spent the day alone reading in a small play park opposite the dormitory. My book was a new copy of Edgar Allan Poe's *Collected Works*, and I started reading *The Narrative of Arthur Gordon Pym of Nantucket*, the writer's one and only novel he finished. Engrossed and captivated by the story, I soon could not bear to stop reading it. Chapter after chapter after chapter, I kept going, past one then two hundred pages and more, finally finishing the entire *Narrative*'s journeys and sailing voyages and mutinies and adventures in the South Pole, looking up and slightly puzzled to be sitting in the same place I was when I had started reading many hours earlier. It was getting late at night, past ten o'clock I thought, and cold. Never before had I read such a book that overcame me so much. It seemed to me highly telling that a mind such as Poe's could not resist taking an adventure story that begins at home and transfiguring it into a saga of secrets. The problem I had always had with novels in general was their very fictiveness, which the less didactic they were the more I found them of no use to me. However, Poe in his *Narrative* had seemed to take an autobiographical character, Pym, written in the first person, and placed him in all sorts of fabulous situations, commanding unreal actions and feats of survival, and still managed to retain his, the writer's, personality with aplomb.

I looked up from my seat and over toward the sleepy dormitory building across the road. Stars languished naked above it. Most of the lights were on, the various occupants would be getting ready for bed. I was the only one of them who did not have to go to the office or lab the next day. The idea pounced on me—No more work. I was free. I was free! It felt good—no matter that I did not have any means to make money, or anywhere to live, those could take care of themselves. Something would work out, I was sure. I was unafraid, just full of excitement. I was free.

Gōman: Hubris

7

The next day I met Yumi in a coffee shop at eleven in the morning and we sat there for an hour exchanging ideas about what we were intending to do in the near future: an action plan. However, nearly everything we suggested was more-or-less associated with making money, as though our psyche was obsessed with acting like that. The talk of writing a book I had been thinking about evolved into how we were going to get it published and marketed; we also discussed my starting giving English lessons and doing some editing as a freelancer. Without being aware of it, we could not get away from the habitual idea that days were to be occupied with earning coins, which could then be used further down the line for unspecified purposes in the future. Putting off and postponement, or aiming and planning at some target inducement, were liable to take up more life than could be spent on savoring the goal itself. After roughly an hour of this, I realized what we were doing and stopped us. "I am not going to do any of those things for the time being," I said. "For now, all we are going to do is enjoy every minute of our freedom." We agreed. We downed our coffees and walked outside into the busy sidewalk, and I mentioned that we should go into a branch of my bank to see how much was in my account and take out some money.

"Which bank are you with?" asked Yumi.

"You know, the green one with the monkey character," I said. "Saruda." All the banks in Japan, along with most of the big companies and professional sports clubs, had a cute "*a-ni-me*" (animation) animal character as a mascot in their logo and ad campaigns.

"I know it, that's a new bank," said Yumi. "A small minor one. Not so good I heard. Their ATMs didn't work on the first day they opened, and as a result half their customers left in fright. It was in the news a few months ago. In Japan, when a bank goes bust, everyone loses their money."

"Oh well," I said. "It was the only bank that would have me, because of the stamp. To open the account, I didn't need a stamp, or something." I indicated what kind of stamp I meant by pretending to impress ink on an imaginary document.

"*Hanko*," said Yumi.

"That's the one. Come on, let's find a Saruda Bank." We walked along the street and passed several banks that were not a branch of Saruda—in fact we virtually went by every other bank I knew—until at last we saw a Saruda and went in. It was very small, perhaps the smallest bank I had ever been in—no more than a counter and back office consisting of three or four desks rammed together in a cluster so that their occupants had to face each other across them. Sitting at the counter was a solitary, young, very thin, hollow-looking chap with his hair brushed from one side over the top in order to cover the bald dome of his crown. He looked kind of gray; if anyone could be perfectly applied the epithet cadaverous it was he. He was occupied with doing something behind the counter and did not look up when we came in, so that for a short period I found myself studying the effects of his woeful way of coping with hair loss. Next to him was just enough space at the counter where another cashier could sit alongside, if there were another cashier. Perhaps he or she had gone to lunch. Behind the scenes a couple of "O.L." (Office Ladies) in blue bank-tellers' uniforms—white blouses, green Saruda-theme-color waistcoats and matching ribbons gathered in bows at their necks—sat at the desks. Although really only set back a few feet, they appeared miles away. Apart from these three people, there were two customers present, a man and a woman, not together it seemed, loitering around as though they were set on waiting patiently in the bank all morning. No one looked at anyone else.

After up to half a minute of staring at The Cadaver's skull, and seeing that he was purposely ignoring us, I made a beckoning sound and he looked up uttering a tuneless "*Hai*"—Yes—which was ambiguously either obsequious or contemptuous. Since my Japanese was still unquestionably Level One Beginner, Yumi took over in translation. I wanted to know the current balance on my account, and wrote down my name and number filled out in big block letters on a Saruda bank-slip. Although all Japanese people can read the Roman alphabet, most appeared to have difficulty in deciphering free-form *gaijin* handwriting, so I carefully rounded out each letter in capitals: T. P A R K E R. The slip was handed over the counter along with my foreigner's ID. I had applied, but still did not have an ATM withdrawal card. In 1993, ATMs were a new entity in Japan, eschewed by a lot of people who preferred to manage their accounts in a more watchful way—prudentially sticking to good-old account books and material cash. In any case, Japanese ATMs were only activated approximately during the same hours as the banks were open: it was impossible to withdraw money anywhere in Tokyo after six o'clock at night. In addition to all this, since my account was created on my behalf by Mr. Ōmori of Nimsan Personnel Department and the process was conducted more-or-less in secrecy, all in inscrutable Japanese, I did not have much of a clue about it except that each month I knew that my salary went in, various automatic debits went out, and I withdrew a standard amount of a hundred thousand yen to last me for the forthcoming four weeks and carried it around in my pocket till it ran out. Two weeks previously, however, in the middle of December, I had been paid what in Japan is called a "bonus," which is not an unexpected or earned or favored extra as it sounds at all, but part of my as well as every other person at Nimsan's salaries: one bonus in July, and one in December, in my case of about five hundred thousand yen (five thousand dollars) each time. This was what I was expecting to live on for a while, my December bonus plus whatever else was lingering in my account, perhaps half that amount again I was estimating.

After a few minutes, The Corpse, who had walked off, came back with a small rectangular print-out, gave it to me without any form of expression—(watching his utterly dispassionate manner was really quite intriguing)—and appeared to doze off on his chair with his eyes still open, dropping their gaze back onto what he had been writing before we had awakened him, two lusterless stones.

A number jumped up at me—No—my neck had reflexly craned my head down toward the slip in my hand, magnifying it. My brain sparked and threw ideas around. What on Earth? According to the chit I was holding, my account contained forty-five million, one hundred eighty thousand, nine hundred nine yen—nearly half a million dollars. I composed myself sharply, looked up at the teller, smiled although I was sure he was not even looking at me, and stepped away from the counter pulling Yumi by the arm. Over to one side of the room, I showed Yumi the balance. We looked at it for a few seconds, trying to see what was wrong, for there had to be something. I spotted what it was: the account number was different to mine. The name, Mr. T. Parker. Was there another T. Parker banking with the same company as I was? It was a bank that accepted foreigner clients after all. I looked at Yumi. What should

109

we do? I was breathless. Half a million dollars. Before I could even think, I was back standing in front of The Cadaver. In Japanese, I asked if I could withdraw forty-five million yen, which I wrote on another white paper slip from the tray on the counter, signed, and put down on the surface between us. The Cadaver picked it up without a sound and got up, then looked back at me for the first time: I saw his darkly ringed eyes. "*Gaijin torokoshō*," he said. My *gaijin* ID card. I took it out of my wallet and put it on the tray on top of the slip of paper.

Now was the time to sweat. I stood with Yumi over by the window and tried to look like a normal customer somewhat in a hurry and experiencing tedium at being kept waiting, certain that my instructions would be obeyed. In a hushed but insistent voice Yumi was asking me about the balance I had just showed her. Had I received that money from somewhere? I had not told her what I was doing! What was I doing! Acting in a blizzard. Not for a moment did I let myself consider my impulse—I just went along with it. Yumi wanted to know about this colossal amount of money that all of a sudden had materialized, not previously mentioned by myself. I winked at her, keeping calm. Then I heard my name called—by The Cadaver over at the counter. He did not look sinister any more: beside him on a wheeled trolley was the most cash I had ever seen, stacked in bails the size of house bricks. I went over, and he gave me a receipt and my ID card. From the top of this factory of money, he picked one bound deck of notes, tore off its paper seal, and dealt out ten hands of ten notes apiece, to indicate to me that each little deck contained one hundred brand-new ten thousand yen notes. Then so slowly—but he was doing it, to my supreme relief, he started to count the decks. On and on he went counting aloud. Each time he got to ten he packed the decks into a neat oblong and placed the pile in front of him on a lower shelf behind the counter, right under my nose. Finally he finished counting: forty-five decks of bills packed into four dictionary-thick blocks each containing a ten decks of one hundred banknotes, and a smaller clump consisting of five hundred notes. Throughout the transaction, apart from to count the notes slowly, his face had not moved one iota; there was no sign of prevarication, suspicion, uncertainty, amazement at the sum I had just withdrawn, as though what he was doing was not being processed by any overseeing brain at all. Perhaps he always counted that much money during the course of the day. Yes, he probably did.

I picked up the cash clump by clump from the pile, placing it carefully in my bag, but as I picked up the deck that he had opened, which was at the bottom of the pile, in my nervous state with my hand shaking I dropped it onto the floor scattering the hundred sheets across the carpet. I stooped to retrieve the brown paper leaves, and as I did so I found to my surprise that I was joined on the floor by the bank's two other customers, who quickly darted over from their waiting positions beside the counter to help me. Yumi helped too. Thus I found myself being handed cash from all sides as the money was picked up bit by bit by my smiling courteous assistants. When they had finished and all of the money had been redeemed, I bowed to the man and the woman who had helped me and walked out the door with Yumi.

Back outside in the street, the heavy load of money in my shoulder bag, I was in a state of nerve-wracking exhilaration combined with intense stress. What had I just done? Stolen money, a lot of money, from someone. No matter that the person would probably get it back, I thought, from the bank and its insurers, someone must lose out while I still had it. The question was, how long could I keep it? From the minute I took it and walked out, I was bound to be—*wanted*. This thought rushed into my head as a barbarian horde clashing spears and tridents. Fear and paranoia were starting to become overwhelming and I almost dashed along the sidewalk, Yumi keeping up behind me in a trot. Surely I would soon be hunted by the police? I needed to sit down and explain to Yumi. But I could not stop—where could I go? Could I be seen in public? I was not in a capable state to think properly. A flight of stairs going up a building came into view and I ran up it, Yumi following. At the third floor level, I sat down on a step and exhaled a long, long breath. I looked at Yumi perched next to me; I was very ashamed and expected retribution to start from her. It must have shown on my face, a kind of boyish uncertain smile perhaps. It was the first time I had looked directly at her since we went into the bank. But to my surprise, instead of viewing me with nameless horror, as I was preparing to observe, she looked decidedly excited, as gleeful as anyone might be if given or having just won a huge amount of money legitimately. She was excited about the money. She had seen me take it, and was not really perturbed to find out what had actually happened in order for me to be in receipt of it, even as a secondary consideration, almost a bore beside the fact of the money itself. That is what her facial expression told me.

"What happened back there?" she wanted to know. She seemed bursting to be in on the game. I told her that the clerk in the bank had confused my account with somebody else's with the same name, Parker, and that I had withdrawn the entire balance on the spot, give or take some small change. "You took all that money from the bank!" exclaimed Yumi. Her mouth was wide open in surprise, but not dismay by any means. She looked more like she thought it was very funny and daring—there was no sign of moral opprobrium or condemnation mixed in the expressed arrangement of her features. Nonetheless I still could not face myself what I had done. I tried to start saying something such as the teller had made a mistake, and I was confused by it, and before I knew it I seized the opportunity, and that I did not know whose money it was, the bank's or some filing error, or....

Then Yumi's face really did look concerned, and sympathetic to see me in distress. She was surprised that I was not jubilant at the coup I had carried off. I took some of the money out my bag and we looked at it. I was an outlaw, Yumi was an outlaw, we were Bonnie and Clyde! The paper money in a thick stump on my lap exuded a powerful vibe. What was done was done. My face bended into a smile—why not have an adventure. Why not! It was only money we had taken, it were not as though we had mischievously harmed anyone in doing so, or tricked anyone or broken into their property or snatched a handbag, or any of those vicious crimes. And how did the real owner of the money acquire it anyway? Most likely by swindling other people in some way or other, either in business or by employing functionaries to slave away and work hard for him in return for not very much. How else could he have saved up all that cash? Thus I tried to excuse my actions to myself, not wholly succeeding but making the attempt.

"This money is not ours," I said to Yumi. "Very soon if not already, there is no doubt whatsoever that somebody will notice it has gone, and then people will try to find it. They will start to look for us."

"So what do you think we should do?" asked Yumi, in her highly teasing non-serious manner which was most arousing.

"What else can we do?" I said. "Try to avoid getting caught, using logic."

"How do you mean?"

"I mean, by putting our minds to a consideration of what tactics our pursuers might use to trace us, and then by taking extra care not to oblige them by falling into their traps."

By means of illustration, I related the following story to Yumi: "For instance, sometimes when I'm out riding on my mountain bike, I forget to take my bicycle lock with me, and only find out that I've left it when I've gone all the way to my destination and go to lock up—which of course always seems to happen when I've ridden too far to warrant going back. So, in those situations, I am left standing by my new precious mountain bike, with which I do not want to part because I am loath to leave it unlocked and unguarded in case someone will steal it. I want to secure it for a while without being able to lock it up. Hence I apply logic to this predicament to see if there are any ways around it. What kind of people steal mountain bikes, and how can one outdo them? Okay, there are those who go out looking to steal; those who, while out, suddenly impulsively desire a bike to go home on; and those who were thinking of nothing like stealing a bike but by chance observe a tempting unlocked specimen and therefore pinch it. I think that covers everybody. So, the next step is to devise a way to defeat all those people. The methodical thief would have to go to the places where people leave bikes in order to stake one out—hence to evade this thief's scrutiny, logically I should leave mine somewhere where no one normally leaves a bike. That's the first thing. However, there is usually nowhere to secrete it completely out of eyesight, and so I am still left running the risk of it being observed by one of the impromptu band of bike-pilferers, wherever I should leave it. But, I ask—what makes someone who wasn't planning to do so, suddenly steal a bike? Its unguarded availability. So, the best place to leave a bike unlocked, to prevent it from being stolen, is both well away from the usual bike garages, and also where it appears under such close watch by its owner that a lock is superfluous. Hence the ideal place is right under the nose of someone who is not going anywhere, such as a shopkeeper; I usually leave mine propped inside the doors of a supermarket adjacent to one of the registers. For all anyone knows, it must then belong to one of the cashiers, who is keeping a beady eye on it. Without tempting fate by being too sure of myself, I can be reasonably certain of its safety there, even if I left it there all day."

By likening the expedience of taking such kind of a reasoned approach to handling the precarious position we were in, I managed to persuade Yumi that we could prevail if we kept our trust in logic. If we were going to be hunted, I argued, we should estimate by whom, as well as to what methods they might employ. First, it seemed quite unlikely that the owner of our money would come after us. He (the other T. Parker) would not be told about us and besides would sue to be paid back by the bank. Once he was reimbursed, he would be completely out of the picture. On the other hand, the bank would naturally be very interested in getting the money back, and so must definitely in that case go to the police. It did not seem a possibility that they would recruit the use of a private investigator or bounty hunter to find us: big companies such as high street banks do not involve themselves with unseemly types on the shadowy edges of the law. Yumi and I could not actually be certain that such detectives even existed, at least not for doing criminal police-work. So, the police would be involved.

But did the police in Japan or anywhere actually hunt people? No, they either caught them in the process of committing crimes, or suspected that they had committed crimes and went round to their address to try and haul them in, or else sometimes their customers turned up in their attention for other reasons, and only afterwards did they discover that those people were responsible for felonies long out of mind. But apart from in the case of dangerous individuals, they never really tracked down and went out in search for people, did they? They could afford to wait for their everyday quarry, thieves and the pettier lawbreakers, to make mistakes, to commit more crimes and get caught. But we were not going to do anything of the sort. Besides, what had we done at bottom except take money out of my account? It was not my mistake, it was the bank's. I only compounded it and acted on the chance. Of course, if we were caught I could never maintain that I genuinely thought it were my own money that had got into my account somehow, been given to me by so and so—and cover up my subsequent disappearance, which was the very next move Yumi and I were going to make, by pointing out that I was due to move out the dormitory at any minute anyway, which was in fact true. No, I could not pretend that I was innocent. We were going to have to keep out of the way of the police, not even get stopped for the slightest reason such as looking out of place, not knowing where we were headed, anything to attract attention and suspicion. We were going to need to become invisible. I would have to dispense with my beloved mountain bike—foreigners riding bicycles were a magnetic field for officers of the law. I would have to wear a suit and tie and look like I were on business with a job, never seeming at leisure except for during weekends. And also importantly, we should keep moving and not frequent any places often enough to get known by our faces. So we agreed, on these rules, at the start of our novel adventure—to stay on the move and to avoid the police. As it turned out, the police never did come looking for us, because they never heard a word told about us. What did happen was completely different to how we had judged our status, and our cautious avoiding tactics were not to do us any good at all.

8

Our first task that we had to accomplish was to vacate my room in the dormitory. So as not to raise any undue suspicion as well as to provide us with some sort of alibi should we need one later on down the line, that is if there were any chance that we could plead that we simply moved out because we were going to go traveling, I gave the place a thorough tidying up, wiped all the top surfaces and swept up. I put my better clothes in a big shoulder bag and the rest in a white plastic bin-liner along with everything else that I did not need—letters, souvenirs I had picked up here and there, a big blown-up photocopy of Walt Whitman's picture from the inside cover of *Leaves of Grass* that I had made in the office. Throwing away letters is a reluctant maneuver; I found it only accomplishable by closing my mind to the clean-out and putting everything into the bag in a frenzy. I was also sad to leave my books, but at least they were only massed-produced copies of works that I could buy again any time. Anyway, I was still sad to throw them out. The bin bag and box of books I took outside and left in the recycle point. Returning to my room, where Yumi was sitting cross-legged on the bed surrounded by empty space all except for a box of my CDs and mountain bike leaned against a bare wall, I beckoned her over to the door and we kissed on the threshold like olden-day movie stars. Then I wheeled the bike out into the corridor and locked the door behind us, leaving the CDs in the room in case anyone found and wanted to keep them.

Downstairs, I posted the keys into my letterbox, and then quite quickly Yumi and I were outside in the cold late afternoon. I pushed the mountain bike with one hand as we walked along toward the station. When we arrived, I wheeled the bike into the middle of the row of parked bikes and left it with the lock, key in the hole, sitting on top of the saddle. Then we entered the station and bought tickets to Ginza, the most upmarket part of town, twenty minutes down the line.

From the exit of Ginza station it was a short walk to the Imperial Hotel overlooking the green traditional gardens of Hibiya Park. We checked into a double room under Yumi's name. It seemed to me a little strange that no one paid us any more attention than usual—I felt conspicuously as though I emanated suspicion and unease. Even the braided blue uniform with its gaudy gilded buttons and badge worn by the security guard standing across the lobby set me on edge. I imagined the fellow marching the police over to arrest me. Every time I tried to put the image out of my head, as I stood beside Yumi at the registrar's desk, it turned straight back round and popped in again, getting sillier and sillier with each return. By the time Yumi finished filling out the guest registration form and was picking up the card key, I was imagining being apprehended by a man resembling Bismarck with white whiskers and flamingo-feathered spiked helmet, accompanied by goose-stepping military police. We crossed the lobby past a huge decorated Christmas tree and Winterland display with a model railway and train going round and round, and stepped into the elevator, which smelled faintly of carpet.

No sooner had we dumped our few things down in our room, which was a large double on the seventh floor, nothing extravagant, than I was stepping back out into the heavily carpeted corridor and closing the door behind me, leaving Yumi to soak in the bathtub. In my pocket were five ten thousand yen notes folded in a paper envelope. I went down to the first floor, crossed the lobby, and strolled into the darkly luminescent bar, which was nearly empty except for a few waiters and bar staff whose crisp white shirts glowed purple-orange under the lamps. I sat down on one of the tall stools at the bar and picked up the cocktail menu. This was fun! I looked around at the sparse customers, all foreigners with baggage crammed under their tables. The waiter approached and I ordered a Long Island Ice Tea, for want of any better reason than it seemed to justify the price more than the other cocktails on the menu by dint of having more shots than the rest. It amused me to think that I should take this line of reasoning with all the money I had just acquired; I had not drastically changed as yet, then, by the sound of it. My drink arrived and was quite good after all. I opened my book, pressed it down on the bar, and started to read under the faint glow of the lamps overhead, sipping occasionally.

After a few minutes, I noticed a super-fit–looking old man of about seventy years of age come into the bar and sit down a seat away from me, ordering a beer. Lean, craggy and suntanned, he had on a cowboy's pale-blue shirt and suede hat, down from the brim of which an Apache Indian's long white hair hung at the sides. Looking like that, he could not be anything other than a crazy Vietnam vet I imagined, as American as anything in his mishmash of traditional costumes. Once settled, he politely nodded good evening to me then started on his beer looking dead ahead, a curious supplicant of both welcomes to approach combined with admonishments to be left alone. I went back to my reading, but when the smoke from a cigar the vet lit reached me, I looked up again. The vet noticed and asked if I wanted one, and when I said yes he almost went to take one out then shrugged and gave me the whole pack, introducing himself as Skip Atwater at the same time. I thanked him, told him that my name was Tommy Parker, lit one of the cigars, and placed the pack on top of my book on the bar.

"Where are you from?" I asked.

"I live right here in this hotel," said Skip.

"Really? But I mean, where are you from originally?"

"The States."

"Which one?"

"California."

"Oh yeah?" I said. "Same as my Dad."

"Is that so. Ever been there?" he asked.

"Nope."

"It's a nice place."

I was quite surprised at how down-to-Earth the vet was in spite of his crazy appearance. I asked him what did he do.

"Now, I'm retired," was the reply. "Before that I had my own company, construction business, and before that I was in the army thirty years. Company grade officer, a captain, in a small Sixth Army unit, working on the atom bomb tests at Camp Desert Rock, Nevada."

"Oh yeah? Did you ever see any of those bombs go off?" I asked.

"Saw lots. They would detonate them all the time. Way up in the sky from a balloon, mostly."

"That must have been pretty amazing, to see something like that. May I ask you a question? Now, you kind of look like the last person I would have guessed to serve in the army. Is that because you didn't like it there so you repudiate the whole shaven-and-shorn look?"

"No, no. It was okay, it was my job. I had some good times there, back in the '50s and '60s. I was young then, just goofing around a lot. Here, look at this." Skip held up his right hand and showed me a big reddish-pink mass of scar tissue covering the palm.

"What's that?" I asked.

"Occupational health hazard. In the base down in Nevada, there was a room where they put a metal ball embedded in concrete, just the dome of the upper half sticking up. We used to go in there and put our hand on it for good luck. It was hot—radioactive plutonium. The first man-made element, which had never existed before, except possibly during the first few moments of the creation of the universe, apparently. In the '50s no one cared about contacting those materials. We used to lug the bombs around in trucks: A-bombs, and H-bombs too. A few years after they closed down the plutonium room, my hand went bad like this. But that's nothing to worry about now. I figure that the fallout from the tests affected my brain in those days. We used to see all kinds of crazy things such as UFOs up in the sky every night."

"I saw a UFO once," I told Skip. "When I was a kid playing outside under the stars one night. Went right over my head, a real *Close Encounters* UFO, with four little red lights spinning round."

"Well there you go," said Skip. "Maybe I wasn't so crazy after all."

"Do you believe in all that kind of paranormal stuff, psychic powers and such things?" I asked Skip, finishing my drink and looking round for a waiter. One came over and we both asked for more drinks.

"Well, I don't know about that so much," was the reply.

"I do," I said. "Watch this." I looked around for a likely person, someone sitting alone and not too far away from Skip and myself. On one of the tables nearby, a man of about forty-five years wearing a pale-yellow polo shirt and beige pants sat legs-crossed facing sideways on from us, a half-empty glass of beer in front of him. He appeared to be passing the time, arms folded on the tabletop, not in any especial hurry to get anywhere. Perfect. "See that guy over there?" I said to Skip. "I'm going to concentrate on making him get up and leave the room."

"Well, maybe he doesn't want to leave the room," said Skip. "He looks like he's just having a rest over there."

"That's the whole point. If I concentrate on making him get up, and if he does get up now, that would prove that I was the one who made him do it, right?" I said.

Skip shrugged his shoulders as though resigned to observing the experiment, not too comfortable about making the poor man get up when all he probably wanted to do was relax for a while. I closed my eyes and concentrated on the man in the yellow T-shirt. Go away! I thought. Go away, go away, go away. I kept it up over and over again. Not sending any hostile thoughts or enemy messages, just simply charging up a laser beam with that one instruction, for the man to get up and exit the room. With my eyes closed tight, I excluded every other notion but that one thought, nodding my head slowly so as to insulate it from incoming sounds, colors and scents, as well as to radiate the waveforms from my mind over to the target. For about twenty seconds I concentrated, then thirty. I looked over, and the man was still sitting there. I shut my eyes and started again, Skip observing as his cigar burned down between his fingers. Go away, go away! ...I concentrated so hard on polo-shirt-man that I was able to open an eye occasionally to observe what he was doing, without breaking my train of meditation on my message. Go away, go away!

He got up and walked out, leaving his unfinished drink on the table.

"Hey hey!" said Skip, chuckling. "That was pretty far out. How did you do it?"

"Just by thinking about him leaving and saying it over and over again," I replied. "I discovered that I could do it by accident one day, and since then it has always worked. I bet you can do it too. See, we are all psychically linked, all of us, and the channels that run between and among us are like sounds to the ears, we can respond to them from the direction they come. I'll show you: Keep an eye on that waiter over there..." (I pointed at a waiter standing at the far wall, who himself was abstractedly surveying the groups of customers in his area at the other end of the bar, unaware of us.) Skip and I both watched him for about a count of ten, when suddenly he turned and looked over at us, making us both break our glance away from him and get back to our conversation.

"Okay, I'm convinced," said Skip. "Now try that again, make him walk out too!" He tilted his head toward the waiter enthusiastically.

"I don't think it would work on him," I replied.

"Why not?"

"Because, he's doing something. He has a will too, and he is intent on staying right over there since he has a job to do. He can't just walk out. The trick only works on people who are more-or-less indifferent to being impelled to move on, without a hint that they are, and who are therefore receptive to suggestion."

We both sat in silence for a moment. I was still almost surprised at myself at what I had just done with polo man, and Skip was apparently chuckling about it too.

"Must be quite expensive," I said, after a minute, "living here all the time."

"In the hotel? Well, I can afford it. I've got more than enough put away to last me for the rest of my days. Made a lot when I sold my company. And I like it here in my suite of rooms, where I'm looked after pretty well."

I finished my drink again and looked around for a waiter, but noticing me doing this, Skip got up to leave. "It's been a fun night," he said, "but I've got to dash. See you around." With that, he picked up the check from the counter in front of us, got up, and went the same way as the man in the yellow polo shirt, out through the door, stopping at the register and handing over the white chit on the way. Then in a puff of smoke from his cigar that left only his jeans and boots fleetingly visible, Skip Atwater vanished.

Skip's departure prompted me to take a change of scenery too, lest I sat in the bar all night doing nothing. I strolled over to the register to pay for my drinks, ready to produce my wad of ten thousand yen bills from my pocket, but was waved on and told that Captain Atwater had already taken care of the check. So I nodded and went to the lobby and phoned up to our room to catch Yumi—no answer. I waited for another ten ringtones then put the phone down. Yumi must have gone to sleep after her bath as she often did. I looked across from the lobby counter at the glass doors and rows of windows: Outside the hotel, the Ginza shimmered and rolled alive.

I walked out the doors into the freezing-cold night. The weather was still and the sky black and clear, no wind but cold. My denim jean jacket hardly provided any warmth, so I looked around the narrow little brightly lit and busy streets on the first block for what I was vaguely seeking—a sushi bar to duck into. I found one that looked not bad through the window, walked in, and sat down shaking. This was a *"kaiten-zushi,"* wherein the solitary chef stood in the center of the counter, surrounded by an annulus of customers, he preparing sushi on little plates and popping them onto a conveyor belt that revolved round the top of the counter looking like a rickety mountain railway line at the level of the customers' noses. I always liked these places because I did not have to ask for any of the dishes, whose names I did not know, I could just take my pick from the continuously rotating fare till I had had enough. The waitress came up behind me, and I indicated that I would like to have a beer please! Then I took a little clean saucer from the stack in front of me and poured in a drop of soy sauce as a dip for the sushi. However, as soon as I picked up one of the plates from the conveyor belt and went to eat the tasty snack plumped thereon, a hand reached over from my right—it belonged to the elderly man sitting next to me—and indicated with a point toward a stack of cups and teabags in front of me that I should drink some green tea with my sushi. A helpful instruction! I thanked the man, who wore a suit and with his elegant white hair worn mid-length like that of a retired professor looked way too old to be still peddling his services in the business world, and gave him an emphatic nod that was the equivalent to a bow from my sitting position. Seemingly taking my response to his gesture to be my invitation for him to talk to me, the professor then asked me where I was from in English and we soon got talking in the manner of travelers "met a-night." The waitress was beckoned several times over the next hour or two, at first to bring beers and then *sake*, the potent rice wine beloved of Japanese working men.

At some point, with my head swirling and the professor also presumably drunk as a lord, our respective piles of spent plates were counted by the waitress and a bill was presented to us, totaling nearly ten thousand yen. I indicated to the professor that I wanted to go to the toilet to relieve some of the alcohol from my system prior to stepping out into the cold, and when I returned a minute later, I found that the professor had paid and, by vigorous hand waving, made it clear that he would not think of asking me to pay my half of the bill. Therefore when we stepped onto the street, I offered to buy the professor, whose name was actually plain old Mr. Yamazaki, a drink in an adjoining pub-type bar I observed in front of us. He agreed, and we went in. It was a small Cuban-style beach bar, with tropical pot plants and postcards pinned on the walls. A few people occupied each of the five or six tables, so we sat at the vacant counter and ordered cocktails. Time flew by and our conversation, which hardly amounted to covering any more important topics than making comparisons between life in Japan and in Great Britain, steadily wandered from one point to the next without getting anywhere really, a drunken discussion stealing time from my life. After a few cocktails, which went down like creamy soft drinks, once again I went off to the toilet and returned to find that Mr. Yamazaki had likewise paid the bill, which must have been dear, and was standing by the exit. Without making an excessive fuss, since presumably it was a point of honor for Mr. Yamazaki to heft the expenses that night, I offered to pay for the drinks, but when I saw that that was out of the question I thanked him once again and on the street outside we parted company with a bow apiece. It was almost midnight so I returned to the hotel. On my first evening as a homeless person in Japan, with five hundred dollars of stolen money in my pocket, I had consumed countless drinks, a good dinner, and cigars, and had not disbursed a penny all night.

Back upstairs in the hotel room, Yumi was lying on the bed idly watching television when I sat myself down next to her. "How much money do we have?" I asked.

"Forty-five million yen," she replied, with impressive precision.

"What can we buy with that?" I thought out loud. "I mean, what does the money mean to us?"

"A big house with a garden, maybe. In the suburbs," said Yumi. "All in one go, with no life-long mortgage to worry about."

"We can't buy a house, or a car for that matter," I replied. "We would have to register ourselves as the owners and do all kinds of paperwork. We don't want to draw any attention—we're on the run, remember."

"Well," replied Yumi, "in that case we could hire a car, in my name, and travel around for a while. There's nothing to connect me to you, Mr. Outlaw, or that money you're carrying around."

"That's too dangerous. What if we were stopped by the police for any reason? I would have to show my driver's license. I think that it's probably safe for us to travel around a bit, but only by train."

Then I paused and remembered my original emergent thought for a minute, and said: "Well how about this idea instead. As an experiment, let's work out what a million really looks like. That is, the number, one million. It might make us realize what we have. We always talk about city populations of millions, or millions of millions of atoms in a cup of water, or of millionaires as having millions of cash, but how does a million really look?"

"Like those stacks of paper in your bag," said Yumi drolly.

"No, not like that. Each of those notes abstractly represents ten thousand yen. A million yen is only a hundred of those sheets of paper, not a million of them. I want to know what a million objects looks like."

"Okay, let's try to picture it," said Yumi, getting in on the idea.

I paused. "How big is an ant?" I asked. "Say, half a centimeter long, and two millimeters wide?"

"I suppose about that," said Yumi.

"So if we put five ants side by side, they would cover a surface area of one centimeter long by half a centimeter wide?"

"Yes."

"And so five *hundred* ants marching side by side would cover a strip a meter across by half a centimeter wide, and two such rows of ants in formation one in front of the other, head to rump, would occupy an area of one meter by one centimeter and would contain a thousand ants?"

"I think so."

"So therefore a million ants is a thousand of those two-row lines of ants, which when put together so that all the ants are packed as closely together as possible, would cover an area one thousand centimeters long, which is ten meters, by a meter wide, entirely filled by ants. That's equivalent to an ant-carpet along this hotel corridor."

"So that's what a million looks like!" said Yumi, switching off the light by the bed.

The next morning, December 28th, I was in an elated mood. We were planning to go shopping in Ginza, but first were going to have breakfast in the dining room down in the lower floors of the hotel. The prospect of this breakfast was somehow almost unbearably exciting for me. I could not think why that was so; it was just a thrill to go down to breakfast that had already been made and to help myself from the buffet. I supposed it was simply a treat to be pampered in luxurious surroundings. Down in the dining room, I looked briefly round for Skip Atwater, but could see no sign of the old soldier. I ate several slices of toast with some bland elastic cheese and drank tea, while Yumi delicately polished off a croissant while reading through a newspaper. The domestic news in Japan, as I had perused in *The Japan Times*, one of the English-language dailies, over most mornings during the months of my stay thus far, was, like much else in this strange land, a curious mix of the deceptively innocuous and the downright crazy—and highly revealing about Japan's society. Most days the important national news reports would hardly displace the kind of trivial stories that make the local village couriers in the U.K.—petty industrial scandals, company takeovers, boring stuff like that of no interest at all. However, some of the criminal misdemeanors disclosed in the Japanese headlines, usually at an appearance rate of once per week, were horrifying: knife-murders and poisonings of moms, dads, grandparents, to rob them of cash or for insurance money; arson of shops by their owners to cover up the theft of money and a few trinkets, killing staff and occupants of adjoining apartments alike; murder, dismemberment and disposal of love rivals; child cruelty and infanticide; suicide pacts between failed corporate bosses and their spouses....—the striking points about these tragedies and crimes, apart from their callousness, were first that they invariably involved killing family members and friends or colleagues, that is close intimates, at home or in the perpetrators' normally frequented locale, and second that the crimes were committed in the face of almost certain detection, as though criminal forensics and analytic pathology were not available to the police, or the police were not capable of putting the facts of each case together to solve it: the crimes reminded me of the annals of late-Victorian detective-work, pea-soupers, Scotland Yard and Baker Street. Most of the killers, according to the news reports, apparently turned themselves in, or rather went to the local police box and told what they had done before anyone knew about it. What resentments and cruelties boiled underway among a few of these mostly so peaceful people, the Japanese, who never disobeyed the rules unless to go crazy?

Another odd point, I thought, was that during courtroom trials, as reported in the papers, the contriteness (or not) of the person in the dock stood for a lot: genuine heart-felt apologies and much guilt afterthought as reckoned by the jurors often led to light sentences, whereas lack of regret was always listed next to the crime itself as cause for sending the prisoner to the gallows. Even in court, whereas in other countries showmanship, lies, perjury, settlements and conviction deals are continuously played out, in Japan the actors applied only straightforward logic and followed open, fact-based deliberations. Discourse with the accused normally assumed the pattern of a reasonable discussion and the trials invariably concluded with the sought conviction and expected sentence: In Japan, a verdict of not guilty and acquittal are virtually unknown—for, why else might anyone be sitting in the dock unless he were a criminal?

After breakfast, Yumi and I went out and traversed the few streets that ran between our hotel and the center of the Ginza. It was a frigid day and Yumi suggested that I procure a wool coat. I had previously never stopped to think that there was much difference between cotton and wool coats or polyester coats for that matter, but Yumi insisted that to stay warm in Japan's freezing winter months, only a thick coat made of wool would do. I went along with her and we checked out the department stores on the main street, which was nearly as bustling as ever in Tokyo but not overflowing with uncountable numbers, because of the time of year. We eventually found a blue Crombie knitted wool coat with a silk lapel, which seemed to please Yumi no end (with me infolded inside it and not in my usual slacker's get-ups), so I paid for the garment from a pile of notes that we had abstracted from our fortune that morning and walked off toward the escalators with yours truly still wearing the coat above my jean jacket. Next, Yumi insisted that I purchase a leather wallet in which to keep my money. In Japan, the sound of loose coins jangling around and the sight of wrinkled notes pulled from a trouser pocket are considered very rude and gauche. So we picked a nice wallet from among the wares on display on the accessories floor and after paying for it I transferred the various contents of my pockets into its folds and compartments.

What next, I asked? Suits—two suits, so that I could always be wearing one even if I scuffed the other. Yumi seemed to know where we were to go for men's suits: the Ralph Lauren store nearby. We went there and walked inside its Raffles Club-styled interior, and I looked around at the funny outfits hanging on dummies among the casual wear: chinos, jodhpurs, tweeds, flat caps, elaborate jumpers stitched with teddy bears on the front. My initial assessment was that there was not a hope of Yumi getting me into any of this stuff, which although amusing and perhaps fun to wear as a dressing game, was the uniform of my opposite numbers: privileged twerps, young conservatives and rugby-playing students who were practising to become stockbrokers. I was a punk rocker and against all such people—after a decade of Thatcher and Tebbitt I was not going to go around looking like one of those villains. However, we passed through to the suits and I found the wares there to be classy and refined:

navy, charcoal and brown versions in robust materials and well cut. With the assistant's help I tried on a dark-gray pinstripe and a standard blue suit, the traditional costumes of the restless businessman, and liked them well enough. These were to be my disguises on the streets of Tokyo.

Next Yumi picked me a couple ties that I would probably not have considered buying forever, but which when I focused on them were in excellent taste after all: a cream flowery embroidered one and one in baby-blue silk patchwork. These were hoisted onto the sales counter by the immaculate male shop assistant, who ran back and attended us pertinaciously while chattering to Yumi about what I might wear as though I were putting on my first school uniform. They selected me an assortment of tidy shirts (I stood up straight while Yumi held each one up under my chin, still talking to the assistant), as well as two pairs of smart trousers made from fine virgin wool, then it was time to find me some shoes. Yumi did not like black shoes, so I chose a pair of chocolate brown slip-ons, which were good for going around in Japan, where people are required to take off their shoes all the time. I was amazed at the price of the pair—nearly five hundred dollars—but like everything else on display in the premises, the shoes were beautifully constructed and the tag conceivably made sense. At the last I observed an eye-catching piece dangling from its hanger over to one corner at the back of the store: a silky purple velvet smoking jacket with two columns of glittering gold buttons that, for all I could tell, were hewn from real nuggets exhumed out of a goldmine. The buttons were minutely detailed with some kind of heraldic crest including lion, unicorn and all, very mystical such as the sigils of a secret society. The price of this fabulous coat was... nine hundred ninety-nine thousand nine hundred ninety-nine yen—ten thousand dollars! I took it over to my pile of new clothes draped on the sales counter and threw it on top. Then I retrieved my new wallet from the breast pocket of my Crombie coat and paid for all the things. I was thus all complete and the assistant explained that the whole lot was due to be delivered, after tailoring adjustments, to our hotel that day.

I had had a lot of frivolity during the morning and did not mind at all paying large amounts of money for expensive items, since I had so much cash. (And this was not because of the ease with which I had come across the money; I would have just as eagerly disbursed great chunks of it had I earned it legitimately in exchange for labor.) What I felt, was along the lines that although some folks might consider it wrong to pay more money on a single pair of shoes than half the world's people can earn in a year, and that shoes from fancy stores should not cost ten times more than ones on sale in low-budget supermarkets—I did not share those concerns. I believed that the rich should be duty-bound to spend their money on finery, since without their patronage there would not be any fine things—in the past no historical palaces to marvel at, no paintings by Raphael, Van Eyck or Tintoretto, no Chrysler Building or Portmeirion and other monuments. There was nothing great in existence and were few noble achievements that had not been bankrolled by rich men and women or by wealthy foundations and institutions. And I too was determined to be a model rich person and spend my stolen money.

After we made our egress back onto the street, which was filling out with a denser crowd of people dashing about as the morning grew on toward lunchtime, Yumi announced that she wanted to buy new outfits as well, so we went off going round more ritzy shops for the next couple hours, picking up whatever Yumi fancied. In one place she bought a pair of jeans with fancy military braiding going down the side of the leg, and in another a new coat and in another an expensive tan handbag decorated with straps and buckles. At two o'clock we stopped for a sumptuous luncheon of Japanese seafood curry with pickles followed by chocolate cake, washed down with a couple glasses of champers, then we agreed that we had bought enough stuff for the day and decided to spend the afternoon in Ueno Park to the north east of the city, wandering around the wide open spaces and zoo. The park was extensively laid out with open promenades and a collection of museums and galleries. Behind these, we discovered one further area of constructions that was quite shocking to behold. Occupying an area the size of a wheat field, a substantial tent city of what must have been hundreds of small self-made shelters for the homeless all fabricated from the same blue plastic sheets, which presumably were supplied municipally. We circled the park looking around and finally spent an easy hour rowing on the boating lake. By early evening, as we returned to the hotel on the train, the city was noticeably emptying out of people. New Year was coming. Hardly anyone rode on our train and the station platforms were almost deserted, as were the streets outside our destination. Very few shops remained open; the majority were dark and had their iron shutters pulled down. It was the first time that I had not observed dense congregations occupying every possible space since I had landed in Japan some months earlier, and felt strangely unreal since I had become accustomed to the massive overcrowding. All the citizens were leaving Tokyo to spend New Year in their hometowns far away across Japan and beyond. In the cold midwinter night, the city although still brightly lit, looked deserted.

We spent eight nights altogether at the Imperial Hotel, including New Year's Eve, which we celebrated in the hotel ballroom slow-dancing to a 1940s-reproduction big band along with the other guests. I wore my exorbitant velvet jacket and to complement the part smoked a big cigar that I had picked up in one of the hotel's shops, puffing it while standing in the lobby gazing at the toy train going round and round the little one-inch-gauge alpine track of the festive Christmas display. I thought I was having a wonderful time, drinking champagne in the hotel bar every night and spending the days wandering around the emptied city with Yumi. We ate well in the hotel and, since all the shops everywhere outside were closed, took our lunches from the morning buffet and brought them with us wrapped in paper napkins. Each day we looked at somewhere new around the city: Chinzanso in the northwest, where we saw working trams and the remnants of a little hermitage that once was home of Bashō the *haiku* poet; the National Park for Nature Study, westward in Meguro, a wild, extensive, walled-off forest within the city; we strolled an hour along the elevated, wind-blown suspension Rainbow Bridge that had just been built across the bay from Tokyo's wharfs and waterfront to the man-made isle of Odaiba; visited the wild bird sanctuary snuggled at the end of the desolate docks down at the farthest southern reach of the city, where the jutting land stops a giddy mile into ocean bloom.

In the evenings, we sat in a local play park, setting off fireworks under the clear stellar skies and looking up at the winter zodiac: Taurus, Gemini, the Crab, the Lion, on black a decorated chapel of heroic icons: the twin Bears, Sirius, Lepus (the Hare), Orion with his sword of emerald stardust. As we sat back, settled down, and looked up, we were assured that that night's star-studded performance—the chandelier above—was hosted by the silver-lamé Moon. With Yumi's head on my left shoulder I pointed out the twinkling pinpoint that is the left shoulder of Orion, a red-giant star named Betelgeuse by the early Arabic astronomers who first charted the zenith. That star, I said to Yumi, is one hundred times bigger in diameter than the sun; that is, if the earth were one centimeter across, a shirt button, then our sun would be one meter across, and Betelgeuse a hundred meters, the length of a sprint-track. It is so big, that if it were positioned so that its center coincided with that of our sun, engulfing him, our world would be somewhere inside Betelgeuse's infernal flames as well.

On nights when it felt too cold to go out, we idled around indolently in our hotel room reading or drinking cocktails. I was still high on the thrill of not having to go to work, and congratulating myself for my cleverness at ducking out of my job at Nimsan, but nonetheless I was in need of something to do. Reading, looking around at interesting corners and niches, and buying nick-nacks and souvenirs were merely pleasant activities and sensations that were inadequate for keeping me amused all the time. Within a little over a week of being a man of leisure, I was desperate for a creative project to fulfill. My hands fidgeted and fingers tapped on every surface within my reach as some undecided need became more and more urgent. I had been making sketches of Yumi and of various outdoor scenes occasionally over the preceding weeks, and for a time I wondered whether to paint Yumi's picture on a more ambitious scale. I envisaged a house-sized mural or something even grander, an inverted Leonardoesque fresco on the rooftops visible only by helicopter or a flying machine. Alternatively I considered starting a rock 'n' roll band and being a singer with a group of musicians. These notions came and went-in then out my mind, and at first I did not realize why they were not pursued and translated into action—then it struck me: I was powerless because, after all, I was still a prisoner, and the hotel was just my new prison. I had acquired a lot of cash, which meant that I had free time, but that was gained at the cost of space to move around in, for I could not live anywhere except in hotel rooms so as to keep moving and to conceal my identity. I could not freely socialize and meet new people nor advertise who I was, in case I were caught. I was wealthy but had to live kept in a tower, at least while I remained in Tokyo. I could not even leave Japan, certainly not by conventional travel where I would have to show my passport.

But I knew that I had to do something.

9

By January 4th, in all appearances, the city had returned to its pre-holiday state. Congestion filled the tarmac, people were everywhere, so compactly compressed onto the streets and narrow sidewalks that they just seemed quite casually to resume their life of colliding into each other, rebounding a step, and continuing ever onwards into the crowds. Men in beige, women in dark wools, and children in gray tweed coats for school criss-crossed the wet paths in all directions. Noise of cars, motorbikes and construction work, which was ever in commotion behind temporarily erected enclosures round the block on almost any corner, deafened relentlessly. Yumi and I checked out of the hotel at about 11 a.m., and made our way to the grand old Tokyo Station. We procured two one-way tickets for Shimoda, a beach resort town on the Izu peninsula jutting out into the Pacific south of Tokyo a few hours away on the slow train. It was at Shimoda, so said my book on Japan, where in 1853 a flotilla of "Black Ships" (that is, iron ships) of the American navy forced a landing on Japanese soil—an invasion of sorts—and once encamped thereon coerced the Tokugawa shogun to open up trade with the rest of the world, thus ending Japan's centuries of preferred isolation. It was the beginning of a bullying relationship of the U.S. over Japan, the two industrial–military giants at the far ends of the Pacific Ocean, that has persisted, apart from on one day in 1941, ever since.

Yumi and I had decided to travel all round Japan by train, going clockwise first down to Izu, round that peninsula, and southwestward-ho! through Shizuoka and Aichi prefectures to Nagoya and beyond: thereafter lay Kyoto and Osaka, Hiroshima and then hundreds of miles of mountains, lakes, national parks and islands infused with Japanese spirit, mist and greenery, temple and rock. The first day of our travels unraveled mostly as we watched the scenes of the country going past the panel of the large square train window with its rounded metal corners. The lie of the land beyond the city was much flat, as we followed the coast, with long vistas of fields showing the thick leaves of root crops dominating off away toward the horizon farther inland where steep mountains hulked. There were no grass fields and arable land of golden grain, or any horses, cows or livestock to be seen: on mile after mile of flatland grew vegetable crops alone. On the contralateral side of the train, however, from the station of Hiratsuka onwards past Odawara and progressing along the east side of the lobe of Izu peninsula, blue buckets of the sea down below were more-or-less constantly visible to us in a series of peeps and glimpses. All in all it was a beautiful train journey.

Getting off at Shimoda, a small, fairly bleak seaside town, we made our way to the Kurofune Hotel (the "Black Ship Hotel") and checked in. The hotel was venerable and traditional with *tatami*-mat flooring and futon bedding in all the rooms. When we entered our room, we were welcomed by a hair-tied maid in traditional green silk kimono covered in embroidery depicting regal wading birds and mountain scenes, who was kneeling before a low black table preparing green tea and *okashi*, palm-sized soft sweets. No sooner had we walked in when she was gone without a word, leaving just the orange enamel tea-set and a pair of small rectangular plates bearing the little cakes to testify that she had been there at all. It was late afternoon and we changed into the two *yukata*, Japanese dressing gowns, that had been left folded on the bedding for us, and sat around entwined together having a long rest. This hotel had, outside on a balcony on its rooftop, a series of steaming hot spring baths exposed to the cold winter air. As the disassembling afternoon light gradually rolled up and was folded away, the sun retired, Yumi and I went up to the hotel's uppermost floor and parted company for the respective men's and women's al fresco baths. I stopped at the drinks machine and purchased two tins of beer, then pushed aside the curtain suspended over the entrance, got undressed in the small changing room within, and hefted open the glass door to the outside, a freezing current of air pressure resisting my effort. Stepping naked out onto the roof, however, the chilly night, not yet dark enough for stars to see, was calm and windless. I plunged quickly into the hot bath and opened one of the beers sitting submerged in a soft heated mineral pool.

After some lost minutes of sinking in the bath, and feeling slightly overwhelmed by the hot water and steam, as well as dizzy from the two beers I had finished off, I stood up, stepped out the bath, and quickly went back inside to escape the cold winter air which attacked me instantly. As I stepped through the door back into the changing room, I caught sight of another guest, a Japanese gentleman, as he turned and went back out the main sortie leading through to the hotel corridor, at the far end of the changing room. Since it was a common daily event for

Japanese to display signs of timorousness and all kinds of misunderstanding toward foreigners, I shrugged and concluded that my presence had scared him off, and cared nothing for that. However, when I went to retrieve my *yukata* gown, which I had left in one of the green plastic baskets provided for guests, I noticed that the garment was, if not exactly folded, far more carefully placed in the basket than I remembered having left it—I had flung it in unceremoniously, but when I returned it was neatly rolled up. Suddenly I became alarmed. Had the person I had just seen been trying to rob me? Had he been looking for my room key? If so, with all the cash that was in my duffle bag, he would have had quite a find if he did. Fortunately Yumi always kept our room keys, and earlier we had arranged to meet back in the room after a short bathe. This was perhaps a lucky escape: I realized that Yumi and I should have to be more careful about securing our money. When I went back to our room, I told Yumi about what happened and asked her whether she had seen anyone prying around, which she had not. I opened the fridge and got myself another beer, and sat on the bed sipping it quietly.

After a while, Yumi said to me: "Tommy, why don't you not drink tonight. You have been drinking a lot recently, just about every night for weeks."

I was taken by surprise by her remark, and replied: "I'll drink if I want to drink. I'm paying for it, so I'll do what I like." Then I glared at the TV. I finished my beer, then, feeling put upon by a perceived intrusion by Yumi on my state of relaxation, I got up and went out the room without a word to her, closing the door with a slam. Once out in the hallway, I made my way to the beer machine and bought another can, and sat drinking it in an armchair in the corridor. As I raised the can to my face, swirls of aromatic wheaty-sweet whiffs hung in a drowsy barnyard. When the can was finished, I threw it in the bin and went up to our room door, knocked once with a knuckle and said through the wood panel in a raised voice "I'm going out, see you later," then walked off without waiting for any reply.

I cannot remember where I went. Afterwards, I could only recall glimpses of speaking to people, drinking cans of beer, walking along the windy beach and looking at crashing surf and foam in the night, wandering around the small town center looking at the closed and fastened shops. At some point, I wandered into a bar and got talking to the middle-aged barmaid while the only other customer, an old guy, sang *enka*, Japanese warbling folk songs, standing in front of the karaoke machine. Apart from those fragments of memory, I cannot recollect anything else that happened, including how and why I found my way back to the hotel. The next morning, I woke up in bed with Yumi. On the floor next to the bed was a carrier bag containing unopened bags of potato chips and wrapped sandwiches, along with more cans of beer, from a convenience store. My head bulged. Yumi hardly said a word to me, but all morning I was prepared for her to make a complaint about my leaving her alone in the room and going off without her somewhere mysteriously, and I was getting ready to explode back about how she had pushed me out by telling me that I could not drink when all I wanted to do was to relax quietly. How could I relax quietly in an atmosphere like that?

That morning I sat at the window watching the rain come down, blearing the soggy green hills behind the hotel. The hills were fascinating beehive humps, volcanically formed mud-olive bubblegum blown up from the ground. The feeling of bliss at not having anything to do, no deadlines to meet, no one to tell me to get going and perform a boring task, just freedom to go wherever I pleased, to look at whatever took my curiosity, was the next nearest thing to being an infant again, before school, before education, before having to slave at making a living. It was a flight of fantasy made real—and I had enough money for it to last forever.

Since Yumi did not wish to go out from the hotel in the cold and rain, I went out for a walk alone, arranging to meet her for lunch later in the hotel. Without an umbrella, I wandered around Shimoda town getting wet through, but did not really mind the discomfort. I strolled into a few shops that sold items for the beach: flip-flops, plastic balls and trinkets. Since I had sobered up, most of the layout of the town came back to me as I ambled about, including the location of the bar where I had been, which was closed during the day. I remembered having walked down several of the streets, and of meeting and interacting with various people, and it seemed that I had covered the entire town nucleus the night before. After having filled my lungs with cold wet outside air, I turned about and returned to the hotel, where I met Yumi in the lobby. We went through to the dining room and were seated at one of the tables next to the window-front looking away across the beach and ocean. My clothes were still damp through. We ordered lunch and coffees and talked while we waited, when all of a sudden Yumi noticed one of the customers sitting across the room to our side. In a low whisper, she told me what she had seen: "See that man over there? Don't make it obvious, just look." I looked over at a man, who glimpsed up as I did so, our eyes catching, who then looked back down at the newspaper on his table. He was a slender Japanese man with a slightly unhealthy appearance, it seemed, wearing an open red Hawaiian shirt. He looked like a holidaymaker staying at the hotel.

"I think that's the man from Saruda bank," said Yumi.

"What man from Saruda bank?" I replied.

"The one who gave us the money."

I froze for an instant then involuntarily and automatically looked right over at the man, staring unabashedly. Quickly I got hold of myself and looked back toward Yumi. "How do you know it's him?" I gasped.

"I remember him, from the bank. See, he has the same balding hair and thin appearance. 'The Zombie,' you called him, or something like that."

"It can't be him." I protested. "How did he get here?" I couldn't help but glance over again for another look at him. I could not remember what he had looked like.

"It's definitely him," insisted Yumi. "You know that it's hard for westerners to recognize Japanese features. But I can recognize him easily. It's him all right."

"Shit," I said. "Is he looking at us?"

"I don't know, I don't really want to keep watching him."

I tried to make sense of the surprise. It suddenly occurred to me that the man might have been the one I had seen loitering around the hot spring changing room the previous night, maybe trying to get our room keys. Was it really him, had he been following us? I was starting to become very worried. What would he do to get our money? The answers I estimated seemed dangerous. So I had an idea. "Listen," I said to Yumi in a low voice. "I am going to try something. If that is really the same person, and he is watching us or following us, he will be quite determined to sit there spying on our whereabouts, won't he? But if it is someone else, and he is just a traveler taking coffee and minding his own business, then I can probably make him stand up and walk out, using this little psychic trick I have."

"What little psychic trick?"

"I can make people go away just by thinking about the idea strongly. It nearly always works if I send them the signal—so long as they are not set upon staying put or doing something, in which case they are never receptive. Only people who are absent-mindedly sitting about take the hint."

"I've got to see this!" giggled Yumi in her kittenish way, having fun although I was starting to feel highly nervous about the man in the red shirt sitting across the room.

I closed my eyes and concentrated hard on the man. I filled my mind with nothing but his image, and of the spectacle of him standing up and walking out. Over and over again, I imagined that one thing occurring. "Go away," I repeated. I thought of nothing else but the sole possibility, making it an inevitable outcome. "Go away"—the concentration wracked my brain. "Go away." Still poring over nothing but this, I opened my eyes and looked over briefly, noting that he had not moved, so I re-shut my eyes and continued at it, mesmerized in meditation. After a while, again I looked up and flashed him a glance, but he remained in his seat looking at his newspaper. Another minute went by with my concentration redoubled. I looked up again, saw that he was still there, then at last gave up and focused my eyes on Yumi. In utter seriousness, I said to her: "I can't do it. I think that he's watching us." I looked over at him again, and this time met his cold stare—beams of light transmitted from the black dots of his eyes knocked into mine, making me cold. I shivered in my still-damp shirt, and said to Yumi that we should get up and go.

We walked out the dining room and stood in the elevator. I explained to Yumi that we had to pack and leave. I would pay our bill for the hotel while she got us a taxi. We could take the taxi as far as we liked, to another town somewhere, and hide. Since we had found out that The Cadaver—I remembered my nickname for him—was following us, we could take precautions to escape from him. Everything began to unravel itself in my head. Of course his presence chasing after us made sense. He must have realized once he had given us the money, what he had done in dreadful error. He had made a big mistake and given a huge amount of money away to the wrong person, because he had not made thorough-enough checks. He had unwittingly robbed his own bank and would be made responsible and punished by his employers. He would be out of a job for good—so then it must have occurred to him that his best option was to get the money for himself, by following us and relieving us of it. He could see the real address of where I lived from my bank account record, knowing that my name was Parker. Right from the first day, he must have been snooping us all along, waiting for a chance to confront us. And we had performed wonderfully in accordance with making his design all the more easy, by leaving Tokyo and going to the countryside, where, as soon as he could find us alone, he would step in. Suddenly some words jumped into my head as I considered this situation: "When following someone, it is better to stay in front, not behind." What if he was armed and tried to kill us, I asked Yumi? She shrugged, looking scared as a little bird. From that moment, we should consider ourselves running for our lives, I said.

The elevator stopped on our floor and we ran out along the corridor toward our room, got inside, and slammed the door shut. We thrust everything we had into our two bags and were ready to leave in just a few minutes. Then I went toward the door again to re-open it. What if The Cadaver was waiting outside, holding a gun? As soon as I unlocked the door, he could kick it open and force his way inside.... I turned the latch and slightly opened the door ajar, just a few inches, and stood back waiting. At a count of ten, nothing happened. I opened the door and looked out along the corridor, left and right. No one was there. I beckoned Yumi and we rushed out, past the elevator entrance, and ran down the stairs to the ground floor lobby area. Yumi took our bags and went outside and hailed a taxi from the waiting cars, while I checked us out at the desk. Audaciously slowly and meticulously, the receptionist made out a bill. Eventually, he took my cash payment and went off with it, disappearing through a door into an anteroom behind the desk. I did not wait for any change, and rushed outside to Yumi who was sitting in a black taxicab. There was no sign of our stalker. I jumped in and Yumi asked the driver to take us out of town and to head south. The mechanized door swung closed, and with a stomp on the accelerator we were moving. I looked out the back windscreen, imagining that I would see another taxi containing The Cadaver closely tailing us, but no car followed as we left the driveway, and none emerged as we rounded the first several corners and turns going away from the hotel.

Eventually, after about ten minutes, I thought that we could not be at all being followed. However, this too was perplexing. If that was The Cadaver back at the hotel, and he had followed us all the way so far, why should he let us go now? I started to question whether it was the same person we had seen after all. Was having all this cash continuously about our person making us feel paranoid? Was it just because I had seen someone, whom I had thought was suspicious, when I left the changing room in the hotel on our first night, that we had begun to imagine we were being chased for our money, and this culminated in our conjuring up a fanciful scenario of being tracked by a sinister huntsman? Once we were sitting in the safety of the moving taxicab, and our feelings of extreme vulnerability began to settle back to normal, our behavior of that morning quickly started to seem very irrational—our imagining guns being pointed at us and promptly running out of the hotel in fright. Counting from the time that we had seen "The Cadaver" in the dining area, we had checked out in less than fifteen minutes! We both started to laugh as the embarrassment tickled us. Soon we were holding each other in an embrace of hysterical chuckles on the back seat. I looked out the back windscreen one more time, and saw dozens of cars, vans and trucks behind us, going away in the opposite direction, and moving around on all sides in a chaos of town traffic. Could any of those vehicles have been following us? It seemed ridiculously impossible.

We left the town and traveled along the coastal road going southeast around the base of the local peninsular past a place called Ino Point. There the sand was white and inviting, the sea blue and clear, and among the isolated coves caves and rock formations formed a grotto piled high with chests of pebbles and shells. Arches of ruddy bedrock, here and there broken, looped a ruined abbey casting shadows over the flood.

Quite suddenly the car stopped hard. We had pulled over by the side of the road, the cab was parked on a layer of fine sand. The driver turned round and motioned for us to get out, urgently. He repeated the command in basso Japanese. I questioned Yumi with a look? Car trouble? She concurred with a pressure of her hand: I should obligingly slide out of the open door of the taxi. I got out, thinking that Yumi was coming too—when to my amazement the door slammed closed and the taxi drove off, Yumi still inside with all our luggage in the trunk! I flipped and ran after the cab for a few paces, watching it disappear along the beachy road. Did Yumi even look out the back windscreen? I do not think she did. I was astonished, to say the very least, and slowed down to a halt. Then it hit me right in the eye: That was the Cadaver once again, driving the car. I became sure of it—and he had driven off with Yumi. It was the same man. What was going on? Where was I then? What had just happened? I stood by between the road and the sea in a whirlwind of sensations and conundrums, not knowing where or how even to begin to start sifting through them to a resolution, lost for where to commence reconciling order with the day's events. At low tide, the primordial sea swept over massed ranks of entrenched shells awaiting a signal to invade.

In a short while, I realized that I was not feeling well. There seemed no use in dreaming that Yumi and the taxi were ever going to return; the car had hurtled away at speed and was far gone. So I turned and walked toward the sea's waves and clambered down through links of gorse and rocks to the level of the gray-sand beach, then sauntered toward a pile of high abstract rock formations. The sea was strangely un-voluminous, muted, although the waves rolled in vehemently and were brimmed with white. Only, there was no roar, just a muffled quiet. It seemed to be a sonic property of the architecture of this particular cove, its acoustics. Reaching the rocks, I sat down on sand and held my head, trying to clear my thoughts. I was exhausted. I had been out till late the night before, but that did not explain why I felt so sick. Examining my feeling and extrapolating backwards over how I had felt earlier during the course of the day, it seemed to me that I had picked up a chill when I ventured out in the rain for my stroll that morning. I still had on the same clothes that had been soaked during my walkabout: dark gray suit and a dress shirt—indeed, my only clothes that I had left now that my belongings had all driven off. At the same moment that I was considering the cause of this gaining malaise, I began to feel feverish, as though my detective work was gratified by physical reckoning as the price of proof. Acquiescing, I lay down and closed my eyes, incanting sleep. It was not a time to disturb myself with worrying about how I came to be in this hole. That would wait till later.

When I awoke sometime afterwards, it was nearly getting dark—and I was as cold as I had ever felt myself to have been. Not merely freezing due to the elements, exposed as I was on the shoreline; I was shaking in extensive spasms. I curled up and tried to warm my trunk and limbs by insulating body warmth on huddled self-contact, but continued to shudder and shake with an icy chilliness all over. All I could assume was that it was a freezing cold evening and that I could keep warm by nestling under. As I lay on my side, however, I felt myself disgorging and before I could try to prevent myself, vomited down the side of my face onto the sand. Worn out, I tried to return to sleep, or else passed into unconsciousness again, only to emerge back into some groggily alert sensorium a moment or perhaps hours later. I was in a fit of confusion, it seemed to me as though I were reasoning from the outside as a spectator. I tried to get up but could not, so began to crawl inland going toward the empty roadside away from the sea. As I motioned along the soft sand on hands and knees, imperceptibly slowly, I felt myself—once again, as though I were watching someone else and not me, with a detached observation sense—I saw myself push my head back and ululate an animal howl. Up and away it went. I was frost-cold and shaking in the throe of a tremor, a high fever affecting both brain and body. Eventually I desisted in trying to move myself and just lay shivering on the sand, and soon passed out again.

When I awoke it was daylight, I had slept overnight where I lay, and my severe fever persisted. If I had been more conscious, for I was delirious, I would have felt lucky to have survived through the night. I lay inertly exposed on the sand all day long, passing in and out of a sleep snapped by visions and dreams. Powerless and insensible, I could not think to attempt to move or to seek help from anyone who might be on the beach or should be passing by on the road, which was a stone's throw from where I lay prone on the sand. I shuddered endlessly, feeling frozen to the bone, but had not realized that, had I tested the temperature of the surrounding air and that of the sand beneath me, I might have found that the weather was not treacherously cold that day, as I might also have assumed from the mild ambience of the previous days when Yumi and I had been traveling and residing in the hotel. Fortunately, it did not begin to rain as I lay helplessly on the beach.

The day stretched and passed into late afternoon and still I could not move. Apart from the pain of my fever, my back and flanks burned and ached as though I had taken a walloping body-blow in the region of the kidneys. Because of this smoldering pain, I shifted position onto my side and curled up into a ring, unconsciously drowsing and falling into deep bouts of dreamless black sleep. Once, I awoke feeling sick and tried to vomit again, but my stomach was empty caused by retching the day before and subsequent deprivation of food intake, and I merely pulsed and hacked out watery phlegm. But still I was too paralyzed to lift my reason and see that I had to find help, because my situation was assuredly perilous approaching a second night of abandonment on the rocks.

Not seemingly very long after I was sick, or had tried to bring up whatever was left in my stomach, my attention was brought to life as I detected something touching me. A hand was pressing on my shoulder. I stirred myself and brought my head up to look: the hand belonged to a man of about forty years old with round specs and short hair dyed coral-orange. His inquiring frown demanded, was I all right? He spoke something quietly but I could not gather what it was he said, in Japanese. I murmured some sounds and expressed facially my sick condition, and pointed to my lower back to indicate where I felt pain. The man helped me up off the sand, first onto all fours then slowly and uncertainly onto my feet, where I stood leaning against him. Once I was standing, he indicated that we should walk and, slowly and stumblingly, we made our way up to the road, I pausing for a rest every moment or so. By the roadside at last, the man left me sitting propped against some low boulders and sprinted off up a country lane going into the verdant tree-covered hill rising opposite the sea. Drifting, I fell into a dozy slumber while time passed. Not a car went by. What day was it? I did not know. Eventually, a compact white pick-up truck emerged from the small lane up which the man had made his way, and I noticed from his orange hair that it was he driving. The truck pulled over next to where I was sitting and the man helped me inside. He explained that his name was Rokuro, which meant "Son Number Six" in Japanese, and that he was going to take me to hospital. This I could understand and remember, but I was still relentlessly shaking all over, frozen cold, and almost insensate. All I could do was nod my assent as we set off.

10

Soon we arrived at the "hospital," which was nothing more than a small clinic situated amid a clutch of shops off the main ocean road. Rokuro helped me inside the glass doors fronting the building, and I sat slumped on a row of metal seats while he spoke to the nursing staff at the reception window. Presently I was admitted and led via the elevator to a tiny three– or four-bed ward on an upper floor, stripped off and gowned, put in one of the beds, and connected intravenously to a saline drip. I was not especially moved very much to hear from the white-uniformed nurse that I was dehydrated and running a high fever, but was struck to learn that my body temperature was forty-one degrees—dangerously high—when I felt like I was freezing cold. Drained of energy, I slept all through the night, forgetting even to thank Rokuro for helping me.

In the morning, feeling much better but still shaky, I was examined by a doctor. A sample of my blood that had been routinely drawn and passed to the clinic's biochemistry lab showed abnormally high levels of a substance called CRP, C-reactive protein, which spelled an acute inflammatory reaction: something morbid. The doc remarked that although she did not think that I had had a heart attack, just the mention of which was a jolt to me, she had to rule it out by tests. I possibly had pneumonia, she added. I was taken away and connected up to an ECG device and monitored, but did not display any signs of a heart attack. Next I was positioned supine on a droningly bombinating CT imaging apparatus, in a white room that housed that bulky machine alone, was left lying on the coffin-narrow gantry looking at the ceiling lights while the nurse and technician ducked behind a screen, and was borne head-first through a ring containing an X-ray tube that painstakingly took three-dimensional images of my chest and lungs.

The outcome of all this, I was told by the doctor later on as I lay on my bed back in the ward, and with heart attack and pneumonia established as unlikely, was that the pain I could still experience in my lower back suggested a kidney infection. "Pyelonephritis," she said. This did not necessarily require inpatient treatment, only much rest and to keep warm and dry, and so there was no reason for me to stay at the hospital for any prolonged period, occupying a bed at considerable cost.

Sick and cloudy-minded as I was, I had recovered enough sense overnight to be aware that there was going to be a bill to pay. I had lost the great bulk of my fortune but knew that in my wallet I had some remaining cash, which until of late I had been prone to carrying about in thick decks and disbursing frivolously. As my healthcare options were being explained to me by the good doctor, my savior Rokuro had returned and was present listening, acting as my lone hospital visitor. He had arrived in the ward at lunchtime to check how I was doing, and when I mentioned that I was not pledged to go anywhere in particular next, he straightaway offered to let me recover at his home by the ocean, where he ran a bar overlooking the sea from the cliffs as a business. Apart from my not having any other choice of where to go anyway, this seemed an excellent offer in its own right, and I was at a loss as to how I should express my acceptance of this lifesaving invitation without sounding like I was accepting merely due to lack of alternative options. Instead, I just said yes and thanked Rokuro unreservedly. At length, I would have to tell him my story as to how I came to be near to death swept up on the sands when he came to my rescue, but for the time being I had to rest and be thankful of salvation.

After the somewhat protracted process of getting out of the hospital was completed, I limped from the glazed doorway to Rokuro's white truck and we drove along the coast to his house and shot-bar, which went by the name of "Da Da." Rokuro, with his granny glasses, orange-colored hair and all-round out-of-date punk appearance—on this day he was wearing a pair of multi-striped flaxen pantaloons held up by twine—seemed a likeable borderline dropout and, like all Japanese, appeared harmless. He spoke good English and told me about Da Da, which was a Hawaiian-style cocktails-and-shots beachcomber hangout where regulars played music and drank all hours. "It's a quiet place, nice and relaxing, and you are welcome to stay for a while," he told me. "All you have to do is make space for yourself, blend in, and take a good rest till you are better."

Once again, all I could do was thank him. Feeling embarrassed to be a burden, I changed subject and asked Rokuro why he had named the bar so.

"Because I 'Love to Say Da Da'" was the reply. "That's the name of a song by The Beach Boys, you know. It's far out and trippy, suits the atmosphere of the place, and I want all the people who go there to remember to love it too."

As this conversation was ongoing, we steered into and started negotiating the steep country lane that led from the main road up the hill toward Rokuro's place. Behind us over my shoulder I could see the sands and desolate rocks where I had lain under the spiraling seagulls a matter of days earlier. Soon we pulled up in the small car park, among the dunes, of a two-story chalet building that looked like it was made of chocolate logs. Over the door was a neon sign announcing our destination: "Da Da." We climbed out the truck and I crept inside as quick as I could, wherein Rokuro instantly assumed proprietor mantle and disappeared off behind the scenes. The bar itself, which was open and serving a few customers diffused around the tables, took up the downstairs floor-space while Rokuro presumably lived in the area above. True to Rokuro's word, Da Da was quiet and inviting and effused home comfort. Windows on three sides provided vistas of sky and sea, and there were low sofas and cushions to sit on dispersed round the perimeters of the room. Behind the bar was a faithfully wrought reproduction of George Grosz' desolate painting "Going to Work," juxtaposed with photographs of the bar's smiling and laughing customers holding their drinks pasted all over Da Da's interior.

Since I had no luggage, all I had to do was ensconce myself and I had moved in. I motioned over to and got down on a set of mustard-yellow cushions placed between two potted bamboo trees whose nicotine skeleton-finger–like trunks formed an arch, leaves intertwining overhead, reminding me of the Big W in the movie *It's a Mad, Mad, Mad, Mad World*. I was not restored to health by a long shot and was sleepy from the exertion just of getting out of hospital—I had to rest my head.

Examining Da Da a little more closely from my throne of cushions in the wings, I noted that apart from low, ebony Japanese-style bar furniture designed for kneeling or sitting cross-legged on the floor, the place was adorned and decorated with one or two musical instruments and a few books scattered round, and there were pictures of sixties-era Swinging London and American pop stars on view at the bar and hanging unobtrusively on the walls. There were The Beach Boys, right next to a portrait of a young Dionne Warwick. From this evidence, I deduced that Rokuro was nutty about music and saw in me a kindred spirit, someone to get to know and talk to, a bona fide natural born gleeman schooled and reared on the sounds he loved. I had met a few people like this in my time in Japan, always eager to gabble about their favorite monomania, classic pops, and if our tastes happened to overlap we were henceforth friends for life.

I spent a total of four days at Da Da, hardly moving much from my cushions except on my final night, when at last I got up and did something there. But about that later. For the most part, I rested well and ate of the wonderful cooking that went on invisibly and aromatically round the backroom of the bar. I was basically a customer who never went home and paid for each meal as it arrived. As for money, I had just over thirty thousand yen left from paying my hospital bill— approximately three hundred dollars. And after that:- nothing. I was killing time till impecuniosity.

As I spent the mornings, afternoons and nights in Da Da, my mind kept turning back to what happened on the last day I saw Yumi. How could I comprehend it? Had she known it was The Cadaver driving the cab all along? Had she made a plan with him to take the money? If so then they must have met and colluded in the hotel; it did not make sense that they could have had any contact prior to our elopement from Tokyo on the train. Yumi had been with me the whole time. Did she encounter him on the night when I went out of the hotel alone, or during the day when I took my ill-fated walk in the rain? None of it seemed probable. But what of her? In the cab, when I had started to get out, the car drove off with her still inside. What would have happened next? Was Yumi in terrible danger? It was impossible to know or to find out. I could not think that there was any necessity for The Cadaver to harm her once I was out the way. Either they were in it together from the first and divided the money between them, or more likely he jettisoned her just as he did with me. It could not have been too difficult. Maybe he reasoned with her as they went along and then paid her off with some of the money, enough to get her home. After all, the adventure was over as far as we lovers were concerned.

The niggling part of this outcome, as I had formulated and construed it in my mind, was along with the banality of how easily the money had changed hands once again, the contributing factor of Yumi's deserting me. That is, if she had connived with The Cadaver to take the money, possibly because he had threatened her even, and persuaded her that it was better for the three of us if she complied with his instructions and had me ejected from the scene *sans* a struggle—or else on the other hand, even if she was unaware of The Cadaver right until he revealed himself to us at the last minute, and had driven off with her in the cab, in either case she had gone on quietly with her captor. As the cab drove off, I could not see Yumi fighting to scramble out or halt The Cadaver in his tracks. She had gone along with him wordlessly and left me, and did not come back afterwards. So, she must have realized that going with The Cadaver was a better way out for her. As I faced this conclusion, I came to see what I had been like to Yumi in the weeks that we had been together. A drinker. And selfish. I had drunk every night since leaving Nimsan as well as frequently before that. Not drunk so much as to the point of being slurred or soused, but tight all the same. That took quite a lot.

What did this drug alcohol, ethanol, do to me? To my perception inside myself, when drunk it felt like I was liberated by it from a state of my normal reticence to one of verbosity, with my mind racing to pour forth such enthusiasm as I momentarily felt for whatever topic to whomever was listening, Yumi *et cetera*. Or often I read a book while drinking alone, my concentration constantly breaking off from the page to go down new avenues suggested by the text, my hand scribbling notes on a bookmark. And then after I had put the book aside, or the talking was finished and my companions had gone off home or retired to bed, I would be moved to play music on my headphone set. Hours I spent in this activity, it was a continuous pattern of my drinking habit. First the fanatical talker, then the lone listener. Both these personae were narrow and introvert, the scope of their attention converged on themselves: one's talk was stuck on monopolizing the themes and bolstered by much bluster, the other was a closed-off penitent begging some harmonic musical angel for solace. That was the outcome of alcohol on me, to reduce all perception inwardly till I could not sense anything beyond my own skin and nerves. In the mornings-after, as well, I was usually quick-tempered and ratty, a further extension of that hubristic form of assurance caused by the drug ethanol. And the effects noticeably lasted longer than the twenty-four hours between each binge (for I never drank during the day): always I felt vaguely depressed and glum about unseen and make-believe perils during periods of drinking a lot. It was inescapable not to turn introspective while on alcohol. It elicited the opposite of the psychoactive, so-called "mind-expanding" drugs such as marijuana and LSD; alcohol's effects were mind narrowing. I decided that from then on I should try to stop drinking it.

Seeing how I had been to Yumi, I could not be surprised that she had run off eventually. Maybe she had eloped with The Cadaver after all. There was enough money for both of them. As for me, what was I to do next? I had at first expected that I could be welcome to stay at Da Da for a night or two at best, but as it happened no one interrupted me from sitting in my little coop in the corner during the whole time I was there. Rokuro sometimes came over to ask how I was and often stopped to talk for a while, but apart from him, no one else bothered me and I was not asked to leave by any of the other staff. In truth, I was a paying customer and since the bar-café was open round the clock there was no pressing reason to expect me to move on. On the other hand, I was fulfilling an invitation from Rokuro to sojourn at Da Da and was therefore a bit more than one of the joint's normal patrons, and for my part I had accepted in my head that once I was recovered, my tenure must expire as part of the deal. So even though I was not urged to leave, by the third or fourth night I was feeling restored to my former strength and decided that I had stayed for long enough.

Quite a few of the customers had talked to me and been introduced by Rokuro, and I noticed that the same faces tended to come and go day and night. It was all very familiar. On the first evening that I stayed in the bar, a duo of musicians who announced themselves as "The Tug" squatted down cross-legged on a rug and played an assortment of acoustic guitars, mandolin, pipes, conga, maracas and several other instruments which, I found out when I talked to them after their set, included kazoos and pixiephones. Their music was a surprise. As they started playing, the various customers assembled round about the darkened bar-area one-by-one seemed to become mesmerized, rhythmically swaying back and forth while the elfish guitarist–singer, who was wrapped in a home-made cape and whose long black curly gypsy hair cascaded over his hippy garb, sang incomprehensible slur vibrato in strange and unfamiliar language and his sidekick percussionist moaned and shrieked along in harmony to the poetic verses of his leader. It was highly affecting and immediate music, drawing me in and quelling all my alertness to other extrinsic matters. It seemed not in any way forced by the two musicians, and not loud by any means, and the beat variously was plunked or else willed along by lacunae—so that the listener compensated for what was actually not there. Later on, after the gig was finished, "The Tug" hung around drinking at the counter and I went over and spoke to the duo. They informed me that the letters of their name, T U G, stood for "Token Underground Group." It was a nice hobby, they said, playing the local bars.

On the day that I had concluded it prudent to end my stay at Da Da, I had to make two further decisions consequent with taking this action. One was of course what I should do next, starting from the minute I left the door, and the other concerned how I had to express thanks to Rokuro for his kindness in rescuing me and for looking after me for nearly a week. The first decision seemed inevitably that I had to return to Tokyo: there I could find populations and livelihood, business and commerce, thriving inexhaustible multitudes and all their activities. Just to survive, I needed to immerse myself in life's nutrients. The far-off citadel was a surrealist hand holding up superabundance. Exactly what I would do when I got there was another matter; but it was clear that I could not stay at large where I was, out on the coast or on rural land, among a rarefied society dotted around who owned and patroled every acre. Without a cent, I was and had about as much chance to prevail as a runaway slave. An earlier impression returned to prompt me again: I was still a slave, a prisoner. I was born into slavery—unless I could find some way to break out.

As for the second of my problems, how to go about parting company with Rokuro, I had an idea given me by The Tug: I should stand up and bow out to all my new friends at Da Da by playing a few songs on the guitar. I would call myself "The TUF"—the Token Underground Foreigner. After all, I reckoned that I must have been the only foreigner ever to set foot in Da Da, and all the locals dug me for being a refreshing change to the usual clientele. With all the pictures of The Beach Boys and so-on on view, and what with home-grown boys The Tug as staple mainstay of entertainment, I thought what could be more appropriate than if I played some rock 'n' roll with a dash of Englishness. When Rokuro came down the stairs that lunchtime, I went over to him with my idea and asked whether I could perform that night. He instantly uttered that I certainly could, and sprung into animated action pulling out a small p.a. amplifier with mass of wires and cables plus a basket of microphones from under the bar. These were quickly assembled into a working sound system connected to a pair of big speakers situated at either end of one wall facing the counter. Rokuro adjusted the volume level while muttering into the microphone in his hand, and before I knew it, I was given the mic for a test vocalization. This took me a little bit by surprise: I belatedly realized that there was no turning back and that I had to entertain whomever showed up that night with songs. I mouthed some sounds into the mic and assented that it worked fine.

There was also one further problem, in that the only guitar available, an acoustic sitting in the corner, was a right-handed instrument while I am a southpaw, a left-hander. I would have to strum the guitar and finger the chords upside down. Luckily, I was well used to playing guitar like that, from years of toying with whatever instrument I picked up round friends' houses and the like, and could play the chords inverted while plucking the strings with an upward glissando instead of the usual down stroke. We lefties were seemingly rare in the guitar world, judging from the minuscule availability in guitar shops of custom-built reverse-strung axes—despite that rock's greatest guitarist and most wondrous bass player were both left-handers. That night I would manage to play bottom up, but it did not help having the additional awkwardness on top of simply playing in front of people in the first place. I was not exactly a seasoned performer—as a matter of fact, the evening's scheduled event was the first time I was prepared to play in front of anyone except Yumi since I had been in a band at school.

I spent the afternoon sitting on my bed of cushions with the upside-down guitar trying to work out a set-list for the evening's performance. I slung together a few old folkie songs, a couple of rockabilly numbers by the King of Rock 'n' Roll and some sixties Hit Parade favorites, all familiar classics that everyone was bound to know. In no time I had a fine roster of repertory—if only I could remember the words! Then I told myself that so long as I mumbled something and got the choruses more-or-less right, it was doubtful whether my audience of late-night Japanese drinkers would notice any travesties or nit-pick. I was all set to make my debut. As I waited around, watching punters start to arrive, I became quite anxious about having a decent-sized audience in the house. The time to get up and play was approaching, and it would certainly be a disaster if there were hardly anyone there: I would be made to sing to each individual intimately. Better to have a big company, even if no one listened. At least then I would not have to face any person in particular. As time wore on, whenever customers cheerfully left in ones and twos, I grew disheartened, and when a few more serious people arrived, I trembled afresh because they would soon be watching me. There was nothing I could do about my nerves except try to put the audience out of mind. I considered knocking back a couple of draft beers, then remembered my vow to stay away from the stuff.

At eight o'clock, Rokuro approached me and asked if I were ready. I assented—but was taken off guard by how suddenly he waved for the bar's background music to be shut off, emulated responsively by the quieting of voices, and Rokuro was standing at the mic announcing that I was going to perform. He stepped aside and I trundled up to the vacated spot amid cheers of encouragement, jollity, indiscernible witticisms and whistles. On the guitar, I thumped out the opening ringing chord to The Beatles' "A Hard Day's Night," and before even I myself was really aware what was going on, I was caught along by it and lo! was singing. I managed to pull the song off with aplomb, and when I came to the end, everyone in the bar burst into enthusiastic applause, far more than I deserved, affording me a secret hoot and a chuckle. I smiled all round and pledged myself to them with a musician's formal bow. From then, I was on a roll, and confidently advanced through the set without overmuch chord-fumbling (despite playing paranormally) or excessively warbling off-cadence. Next I thought I should do something a bit more up to date so I played the Lemonheads' "It's a Shame about Ray" and "Higher than the Sun" by Primal Scream. With each song, the assembled men and women sitting on bar stools at the counter and kneeling behind various drink-laden tables clapped in time and joined in the singing. The night was quite a resounding success considering its spontaneity and minimal amount of preparations.

In what way did I feel about all this? I was startled at how commanding one can be just for holding a guitar and standing up in front of a bunch of people. That is, the *ad hoc* utterances I spoke between songs, desultory asides and pronouncements mostly about the next number, were greeted with solemn expressions of heeding and abidance, whereas I might have normally expected everyone to turn away and start chatting or that elements among their number would mock me with derision and try to debunk me. I even wondered whether the audience actually understood my words, but when I said something humorous, smiles appeared on the bank of faces to show that they had got it. Also during the singing, when I mixed the words up and got them wrong altogether, people were very forgiving. I was intrigued that their receptivity to music was so overt and palpable.

When the music was over, I put the guitar down and mingled in with the usual faces I knew, and talked late into the night. One by one, people left Da Da, and when just a few stragglers sat around hunched over their drinks at the bar, I took the chance to thank Rokuro for helping me and for looking after me so well. He was tending the bar, mixing cocktails for a group of customers seated at one of the tables. Without wishing to dwell for long, I bade him cheerio and made out that I was going to sleep, then instead slipped out the door into the short corridor housing the men's and ladies' bathrooms on one side, with the outer door looming at the far end. The corridor was cold; it was mid-January and bitter outside, situated where we were, up on the hill facing the raw sea. It was perhaps four in the morning and still night. In the glass door I saw myself clearly reflected on black sheen: a young, vital man, a bit scrawny because I usually ate so little. I had long hazel-brown hair that had not been cut in months. I was still wearing my only garments I had left after The Cadaver drove off with all my other possessions: gray pinstripe suit, cotton dress shirt, old green jumper that I had kept with me from England over the years.

I went out through the glass door and braced against the cold. Because it was so late into the night, constellations normally viewed on summer evenings had come round the back of the earth and assumed their places in the clear sky above—the effect was to be transformed in time and period, not to be in winter any more. Distantly, the rhythmic music of the sea faintly could be heard, also from another time. In response to the cold air, I took two steps away from the building, then leapt forward into a run. I quickstepped across the car park and onto the road, starting down the hill at a jog. I was exhilarated. At the pace I went, I felt as though I could run for weeks without stopping. My heart beat at its normal sedate rhythm, not increased by exertion. No tiredness visited my legs, no strain pulled across my chest. Breathing was as slow as if I slept. In hardly any time, I was at the foot of the hill at the junction with the main coastal road. I could hear the sea coming in across the darkness, white wavetops rounded into their pen by shepherd's whistle. I turned to the left and took the direction going toward Shimoda town some few miles away. The road was unlit except by starshine but was manifest enough to see where I was going. The sea on my right, I marched ahead. A voice within told me: "With the Stars on my side, and Truth as my guide…." It sounded like a good slogan so I repeated it to remember.

What else came into my head as the road passed away under my feet? Alone unconnected to associations and senses unfed in dark, quiet, and cold, "the palimpsest of the brain"—where did that inscription come from?—split the deck and turned up what may. Chance memories from my past in England fanned up: being so in love with Sonya, a girl at school, with such romantic impulses, never put to the test, just a dream—of sitting in a field idly noting a tractor go round far away, its driver at work, intent and set on something—of being cornered in the schoolyard and punched to the ground, blood raining from my nose, then bully and spectators strode off—of being picked out at school in another, more pleasing way, of being singled out by the headmaster, Mr. Ingham, during Assembly on my last day at primary school and being touted to make it as a writer, referring to those most likely to succeed in some way as "the Tommy Parkers of this world"—next I remembered an early inchoate nightmare I once dreamed, of a volcano eruption in the distance beyond the garden of our family farmhouse in the Shropshire country, and Mom determined to walk toward the fires, I unable to stop her by tugging at her wrist. I remembered that dream clearly, and found it wondrous to think that in its scenes my Mother was twice my height—I was just a little boy when I imagined it.

When I got to Shimoda, the day was starting to light up. At first, white streaks and lacerations appeared in the black sky, which seemed covered in soot without any stars to be seen. Within moments, the land all round was illuminated, and when I looked up again at the sky it glowed white—the soot was all gone. I saw no reason to stop in Shimoda except to go to any convenience store that was open to buy *onigiri* (balls of starchy rice wrapped in a crisp olive-colored wrapper of paper-like seaweed) and a pet-bottle of oolong tea. I soon saw one such place by the road ahead and accomplished this errand. I ate the meal outside the shop and threw all refuse bags and wrappers in the bins provided, then kept going at a walk to let the food go down properly before I started running again. I had timed this stop to allow myself to walk through the center of town once more so as to re-exercise my curiosity at its features, and also partially (I detected buried amid my motivations), to give myself another chance to see the "Black Ship Hotel" and thereby know from its aura whether Yumi and The Cadaver were in there together. I had no suspicion whatsoever that they were there, or that they were even with each other anywhere, but I knew that if they were, then that I must see them. Thus do the laws of chance always see fit.

Soon I was standing on the beach promenade across the road from the hotel. The wind fluttered and animated the hotel's bunting and hangings. As I looked at the grand old building of stone and heavy brick with slate roofing and fittings of bronze and copper, for the first time since the day I had lost everything, I felt as though I missed Yumi, the money we had and all the opportunities it had offered to us. We could have been inside the hotel right then, I thought, in our room, loosely making plans about where we would go next, what to see, what to try and explore.

There was no trace of her. I turned away and ran along the compacted flat sands of the beach, continuing in the direction of Tokyo.

Jyōka: Catharsis

11

Using a map of Japan inside my crumpled guidebook as route planner, it took me six days of continuous running to reach the outskirts of Tokyo. On the first day after passing through Shimoda I continued going along the unbroken beach toward the hot springs town of Atagawa almost nonstop except to buy a small snack to eat and to drink a soda (I had thought that anything more substantial might give me stomach cramps in running motion) or else to take brief resting periods in which I did not stop but walked easily for a while before inching back into a jog. I found those walking episodes frustrating—each time, even objects fairly close by in the middle distance ahead seemingly remained fixedly remote and could not be perceived to draw any closer as I perambulated pace-by-pace toward them. I made no progress unless I ran—only then could I observe that I was steadily passing milestones. In the six days of my remote odyssey, jogging came to be known to me as the perfect velocity for a person: neither so fast, like a car journey, that nothing can be taken in on the way, nor too slow, as is walking, to make notable progress in a short time. Running should be advocated as the only way to get from A to B.

The white-shards-of-shell–strewn sandy coast followed a scalloped line of one curved bay after the next with grassy dune-capped promontories and isthmuses poking out to sea in-between. To shorten the journey to my destination as much as possible, these land projections over water I avoided by making my way up the strand onto the coastal road for a few hundred yards or so, each time one came up, passing it, then hopping back down the sandbank to run the length of the next stretch of beach as it came into view. By this means I saw that I made significant headway in next to no time: each bay must have been an arc two-to-three miles across, lined with beach houses, flags, hotels and diners in the distance, but always I found that very rapidly, my mind on other matters, I was neck and neck with what had looked so far away not many minutes before, and soon afterwards I would find myself coming to the far end of that bay and wishing it all goodbye as it vanished behind me. I was quite astonished to see what it actually looked like to cover a long distance in a matter of minutes—because normally by running on a circular racetrack or round city park we do not get to view that farness opened out in front of us.

The sand underfoot was gray and looked dirty as though an oil slick had washed in and drenched the shore. This was gravelly volcanic basalt: Japan is a mountain range sticking up above sea level, its towns and cities built on what appear plains but are actually foothills above the deep. To my right, as I pressed on, brim of the sea overwhelming underwater vegetation and shoals of fish; over to my left, the ridge of land rising giving way to trees, farms and rocks swarming with life, birds and people. I imagined myself microscopically on my opened map migrating toward my goal: from Atagawa thru Ito to Atami on the second night; next stop Odawara with its white castle fortress; next Enoshima, then by road to Yokohama and Tokyo. For the first time in my life, I was all alone. I remembered my Mom and Dad back in England—how long was it since I had telephoned and spoken to them? Several weeks—they did not even know that I had left Nimsan, let alone that I had run away with stolen money. What had I been doing? I was still running…. From what? To what?

More spontaneous words entered my psyche: "What road will take me home?"

I tried to plan what I was going to do when I reached Tokyo. I was already without anywhere to live, but where I had been so far that had not mattered—most people at the seaside are visitors alike stopped in temporary accommodations. Once I reached the city, however, I was going to have to adapt to being homeless in that context, a stray, on streets and alongside other homeless people not to mention among seething human crowds who may or may not be hospitable to an outcast. I had no apprehension of what I was to expect. Nonetheless I could appreciate that, unless I might somehow acquire more money, I was soon going to be without that as well, and then must sustain myself by other means than reliance on being able to buy food. As I ran along, images of my former life in Tokyo came before my mind: the streets and the multitudes of shoppers at weekends; my days spent in the office at Nimsan with Dr. Zen and Loretta and Toady; my dormitory and its built-up urban surroundings. Next time my stay in Tokyo would be quite unlike those experiences—I would have to spend each day absorbed in myself and end it by being filtered out from the crowds rushing to their homes, leaving me extracted somewhere.

On my long journey on foot, at nights I stopped and slept away from the pressures of the sea winds coming in from the beachhead in whatever shelter I could find. Going to sleep, anywhere, after running all day was not a great difficulty: I was exhausted each night. I took care to wash every day and night, at the washbasin of public toilets dowsing my limbs in cold water and drying off with paper towels. I was not one to sweat much, even while running for several hours, and considered that my clothes hardly smelt at all. Whether anyone else might have agreed with that I did not know—but since I had no company to keep and spent all my time by myself there was no way to test that theory. As insulation against the night-time cold air, I wrapped myself in my suit jacket and slept in sitting position with my back against some vertical support such as propped inside a doorway. I found that there was nothing in the way of litter or loosely secured items to borrow for use as cover, nor was there any access to secreted areas to burrow inside. The whole country apparently was secured, accounted for, partitioned and neatly put away. Every square inch of flat surface in urbanized areas was taken up by road, sidewalk, or buildings whose orifices were shut off by closed doors. Greenery areas were dense impenetrable and inaccessible hedgerow and shrubbery; parks at night enclosed by high fences and locked gates. Parks themselves were paved or asphalt walks and running tracks bordered on all sides by bushy flora with no lawns or sometimes some patchy grass designated "Keep off!" There was not a public bench to be found anywhere, nor any restful bus stops with seating. I looked around and could find nowhere to sit down except by the roadside or in an occasional doorway. There were no low walls except those that were topped with prickly shrubs, and nothing else served as a convenient perch either. This must have been why so often I had seen young Japanese squatting on their haunches when hanging out and talking together; it had not occurred to me till I had begun earnestly to look for places to repose that there simply was nothing on which to stop and sit, anywhere.

What oversight had led the town planners of Japan to neglect providing the people with any place to rest when they were outside? It seemed very deliberate, to deter anyone from stopping still for a moment. Perhaps it was somehow seen as not proper for people to be observed sitting around doing nothing in a nation where the population prides itself on working round the clock all the time. Or perhaps it was felt that if there were park benches some individuals would sleep on them or take them over for their permanent residences so that they would not belong to everybody as intended but only to a minority of antisocial elements. That might make sense in Japan, where people's social responsibility seemed to be taken care of not so much by teachers and elders encouraging personal morality in each individual from earliest youth and leaving him or her to get along with all the others, but by keeping all-comers in line with having a code of rules and set ways for just about everything all through life. Japan really was quite a bossy place, I thought, with regulation precepts everywhere backed up by endless officers and sentries hired to police the people's obeisance and browbeat them what to do. I never encountered disorder of any sort. In Tokyo there was a police box outside every Metro station and on every other corner, uniformed guards at every construction site, road repair, or even toilet clean. Stewards issued orders to motorists on where to park and marshals directed shoppers in line at queues. On the trains, porters gave interminable directions and announcements and helped herd passengers onto the packed carriages as the doors closed like clockwork on the appointed minute of departure.

This was the real machination of Japan's *"wa,"* its cherished social order and harmony—gently enforced by grinding everyone down into coexistence rather than letting them truly feel congenial or by experimenting in free love for all, which had been tried and failed once in the occident. Japan's solution to governing amid immense popular overcrowding was to ensure quiet and peaceful community by overlordship, albeit perfectly jolly and benign at first appearance. The samurai never went away. Among neighbors, in business, at every level of Japanese society, this order was implemented. Companies paid their employees' railway commuting expenses, and insured them against accidents in the workplace or while traveling to and from work on the trains; in this way the railway and insurance companies mutually benefited with all the city businesses to which they delivered their people. Symbiosis was everywhere. Nimsan, my erstwhile company, did not compete with the other Japanese pharmaceutical manufacturers. Instead, each of these "pharma companies" restricted itself to specializing in developing drugs for certain therapeutic areas—cancer, cardiovascular disease, ophthalmology and the like. Each was aware of the other companies' operations and kept out of their respective ways. Shops that stocked the same brands of goods all charged the same prices for those. At sale times, each charged the same reduced prices! There was no such thing as a bargain in Japan—only consistency characterized by high quality at an equal price. Wherever you looked, you could not escape the uniformity.

Thoughts such as these occupied me as I kept running toward my destination. In all the days when I was on my toes, I made contact with no one and spoke to no one. I saw people only as I passed them. Occasionally the still negative of a striking face was developed and mounted in my mind, but afterwards the image faded as I passed from the scene. It did not occur to me to consider what impression I might have made on all the people whom I overtook: a white man in a gray suit running non-stop past them. Apart from people's faces, more memorable sights and sounds on the way there were: a close-by attendance of vivid white-topped Mt. Fuji huffing alongside me as constant companion on my left, for two or three days till finally the big hulk fell back and stayed behind; a bamboo forest—swaying olive-hued poles rising the height of a temple in a density of clattering, an enchanted place that made me feel reduced to the size of a flea riding on the back of a ladybug deep in someone's nicely mown lawn. While I contemplated this green curtain, I heard something, an unforgettable, lush, dulcet warble, sung from the throat of an unseen songbird, and I knew it to be the melody of the nightingale, bearing witness to truly the loveliest sonorous jazz notes in nature.

Later, on another occasion, I stopped on the beach and sat down to tuck into a soft sandwich roll I had just bought in a local store. It was a lovely warm winter's day, and I looked out across the flat waves of sea absentmindedly holding the bread out in my left hand, my elbow rested on one knee. I hardly paid attention to the harsh squawking and croaking of the numerous big black birds that filled the air at all times, but did seem to notice a shadow going about in figure-eights on the nearby sand, for a moment, before suddenly an enormous bird of prey with beaten doormats for wings swooped and slammed into my hand sending my sandwich bonking onto the sand, thus agitating a mass descent of crows and more of these great birds, which looked like eagles, or some kind of big kites, onto the ground scrambling to devour it. They were frightful birds in size and voraciousness. They eyed me from behind their beaks for more titbits on my person, and walked around like Roman thugs in gold and bronze going about the marketplace.

Later that day, as evening encroached, I was running along the sands far beyond where I had had my encounter with the eagles, when I saw a vast fissure of electric giga-watts split the sky, then nothing, then heard a thunderous report impacting my ears. No rain fell, but more explosions followed: a dry tropical thunderstorm befitting the wild scenery of botanic palms and beach. Each stroke of lightning transubstantiated the silver sky into copper. The scale of it exceeded the thunder and lightning I had hitherto seen in England, which had always seemed to leap from low black clouds bubbling just above the rain-hit rooftops. The blazes of lightning in this Japanese electrical storm, no less, were laser beams fired from fixed satellites orbiting at heaven's upper capacity, each pulse posing in the sky for a period of seconds. I stopped and decreed to rest for the night beyond a bank of sand dunes amid thick green rushes, watching the lights of the storm—a hit-and-miss bombardment by distantly emplaced artillery that continued late into the evening.

On about the fourth or fifth day, much farther along my journey, I was running through mountainous country going inland from the coast of the Hanto peninsula northwards, with the Kanagawa region ahead and the port city of Yokohama beyond. It was around midday, when I rounded a bend on the gray tarmac lane deep in thought and saw across a deep gorge spreading out below me a sizable lake flanked by barren peaks topped with flossy clouds. The intervening valley was green with woods of pine and cedar. I stopped and contemplated the wild scenery. I was not sure whether Nature here made me feel at home—the forest could just as easily be English heart-wood or the jungle, the pasture either clover-heather or creeper and vine. To decide which, I conducted an experiment by projecting onto the view in my eyes first a country gentleman in tweeds trudging through the grass, a small herd of deer nearby, squirrels and hares pelting about, then after imagining this, second, a menagerie of long-tailed monkeys, parrots and caramel yellow snakes hanging from the branches, so as to picture which would accord with the verdant frondescence more suitably. It was decidedly the latter. I was still in Asia.

From those mountainous areas I seemed to be running thereafter constantly downwards at a gently declining plane on the long and warping road as the scenery changed imperceptibly into suburbs. First mountains drew back and were replaced by long vistas of flat fields and bright white homesteads, increasing in numbers as houses filled level valleys on either side, then by degrees more and more buildings, mostly truck-stops, family restaurants and motels at first, followed by offices and shops, came parking right up to the roadside I jogged along and eventually lined it every foot of the way. During the course of a day I made it from what had been appreciably mountain country in the early morning to city outskirts by the afternoon. I was nearly there.

That night I spent sitting upright on the cold concrete floor of a telephone box. I slept at length, and dreamed that I was walking with my two brothers back in time, in the Shropshire fields where we grew up, making toward our old "camp." This camp was a large tree in the corner of one of the fields near our home, which had a broad spread of low branches that we used to balance-walk along and depend from by the arms. When we were kids we kept precious possessions such as a bag of coins and penknives hidden in the bowery limbs of the camp. As we tried to find the camp, which would not have been difficult were this reality and not a dream, but, as usually happens in dreams, something was wrong, the set and stage props were not the grassy cow-fields as I remembered them. We found ourselves walking in dense forest amid green, huge thick trees the size of California coastal redwoods. We remarked among ourselves that these woods were not there before, and carried on looking for that corner, our camp, but the territory was all changed. Then, next we were walking through a nouveau housing estate of well-to-do mock Tudor houses that appeared between the trees in these woods that themselves had suddenly mushroomed up like magic beanstalks inside our familiar old farmland. New construction development had encroached in the area, I thought, as we passed through the cul-de-sac of elegant houses. In dreams, we do not have our waking pattern of reasoning and never question the strangeness we encounter. We are illogical. My brothers and I carried on walking, but by the time I awoke, we had not found the camp.

Still half in sleep, lying prostrate on the floor inside the telephone box, I again asked myself: "What road will take me home?"

Opening my eyes fully and looking around, I noticed that my little Perspex bed-chamber was embroiled in thick gray fog. I could not see more than about six feet through it in any direction. I got up and stepped out of the telephone box, and found myself standing the central axis of a cylinder of vision caused by the fog's presence, I the light bulb inside a translucent lampshade: nearby objects such as a roadside post box and parked bicycles in whose company I had spent the night infused into this microcosm of space and materialized inwards as I stepped cautiously around. I tried to recall correctly which way along the road I was supposed to run. It was a phenomenal pea-souper! Reasoning that I had been moving along the left sidewalk when I stopped for the night at the telephone box, I made ready to continue on the same course. I looked up toward the bright white sky. Fog rolled downwards from above, curling sideways in plasmic tendrils overhead. I angled myself in my intended direction of advance, which was along the sidewalk with the road to my right, and started to jog, very cautiously at first then increasing in confidence going through the nebulous gray ether. I could see nothing ahead except the paving slabs immediately underfoot, curb and gutter at the lip of the road. I wondered whether I might be able to stop in time if an obstacle suddenly came into view. I did not fancy the prospect of blindly dashing into the clammy solidity of a brick wall for example. Or running into someone. Worries aside, I kept going like that all morning, slowing only for uncertain changes of the path's mosaic that were indicative of upcoming hindrances and detours. On the whole though, I ran unknowingly and unseeingly onwards getting always closer to whatever would emerge ahead.

12

I finally stopped running on February 1st, 1994, a cold clear day of dazzling sunshine. I wound up my journey into Tokyo legging it along Daiichi Keihin Dori, Route Number One, or Number Two, depending on which set of road signs you believed (nothing is straightforward in Japan) akin to a triumphant marathon runner reaching the finishing line. Even the roadsides were lined with a crowd of cheery welcomers, it seemed, there were such multitudes out and about on the pleasant airy afternoon. To check the day's date I entered a convenience store and picked up a newspaper. It seemed that nothing much had happened while I had been away. Except that, one news item I read caught my eye. It was reported that two men had broken into the headquarters of a religious cult based in mountainous Yamanashi prefecture in order to try to rescue a cult member who was being kept there against her will. The men had been captured during their attempt and as a nasty punishment were ordered to kill each other, in a fight to the death, by the cult's leader, whose picture adorned the page. I looked at the photograph and recognized the leader as the obese, sari'd guru I had observed chanting (what was it? *shōko-shōko-shōko-shōko*) outside Ebisu railway station on my first weekend outing, after landing in Japan, being laughed at and made fun of by schoolgirls.

From the magazine rack by the window (convenience stores in Japan always put newspapers and magazines next to the window to act as bait to catch browsers, who stand there reading and when viewed from the outside make the shop appear full of customers and thereby ward off shoplifters) I picked up a copy of the U.K. style-magazine *The Face*. Flicking through it casually, I took note of a minor article tucked into one footnote, a tip-off about a new band of Mancunians to look out for in the coming year, who called themselves Oasis. Since the bandleader interviewed in the magazine quoted Neil Young and John Lennon as his main musical influences, I decided that this was a band that I might like. I looked forward to hearing their songs. I placed the magazine back on the rack, took a newspaper over to the cash register, and bought it along with a can of milky ice coffee then sat on the step outside the store sipping my drink and reading the paper.

After finishing reading the news, something occurred to me and I decided to conduct an experiment. In my mind I took a bearing, and calculated that I was not far away from what I wanted to investigate, so I got up and started walking down the street in the direction of my inquiry. Men and women in suits and work-wear shuffled along on either side of the road mixing in with pensioners and a few children out and about. I had for long completely forgotten about my former need to go to work, hitherto conditioned in me as an unavoidable necessity. I glanced at all the people I passed: every one of them seemed to have the imprint on them, that the children were being schooled in preparation for joining the workforce, the younger adults were all currently in work, and the elderly people had worked till their retirement and still looked businesslike in old age, going about their shopping and bowing to one another in the street.

After about twenty minutes I was on the last stretch of my experiment, walking up toward my old local station near to Nimsan Co. and my former dormitory. The area was all freshly familiar. Crowds of people strolled in and out of the entrance to the station buying tickets and going through the gates. Was what I sought going to be there? I looked at the bicycles as I walked along. Yes! I could barely believe it—my mountain bike was still there, lock lying on the saddle and all. I was very happy to be reunited with it again, my old friend I had abandoned, loyally waiting for my return. I extricated it from the clutter of shopping bikes that were parked in the row as in a junkyard and got on.

I had nowhere to go.

I had almost no money.

I pedaled off down the road and rode past Nimsan then my dormitory heading toward the docks and ports on the east side of the city. The dormitory sent a yearning grasp out toward me as I cycled past it—is this what keeps the spirits of the dead lashed to their former living residences? It was an emotive connection. As I passed beneath the window of my ex-room, and was about to ride on, I had to brake suddenly to check that what I next noticed on the other side of the road was really what I thought I had seen: Dr. Zen was over there, in his Nimsan uniform, standing at the curb waiting for traffic to halt, evidently passing on foot from one of the many subsidiary Nimsan buildings back to his office in the main complex. He had over his nose and mouth the surgical mask that he often wore, but I could clearly see from his eyes, hair, lean build and overall bearing that it was Dr. Zen, my old comrade. Cars continuously passed by between us, keeping me from crossing over to say hello. I tried to catch his attention by looking over at him, my hand poised ready to wave when he noticed me. After a short spell of waiting for him to see me, though, I could detect that Dr. Zen was purposely keeping his eyes fixed away from me. It was taking him a bit too long to notice me staring at him, I thought, perched directly opposite—he seemed very determined to look away. Then still under my gaze, he started to walk off. Had he seen me and just not recognized me? No, he surely would have known it was I across the road. Was it because I was no longer a member of his work and social group that he had since then felt disinclined even to acknowledge me? I did not wait to find out and rode on.

I traversed several blocks lined with small commercial buildings then burrowed down narrow streets not much wider than a delivery truck, kept in on all sides and above by buildings, power lines, bunting and decorations. In many streets of Tokyo, it is easy to assume that you are not outside at all but imprisoned under frosted glass through which pale sunlight diffuses. Soon I was crossing a series of road bridges over increasingly wider canals as land, at first the age-old natural bedrock then reclaimed isles, was taken over by the gray sea. At the docks I observed scores of giant cranes of iron girders, built to unload the rolling cargoes of the ships that fed the city. At no point as I cycled along the seaboard could I more than glimpse seawater past all the industrial fortresses. Even the air's smell was of iron, not brine and chloride. There was no access to the sea anywhere. Eventually I stopped at an extensive green park with baseball grounds and soccer pitches. Pedestrians milled about walking dogs and taking exercise. I jumped off my bike and wheeled it around the periphery of the park till I found a spot with lush overgrowth of vegetation out of view of the open field. Getting down on my knees I crawled inside a gap in the hedge. Beneath the low canopy of green was a natural hollow chamber with carpet of moss. It seemed like a good place to set up camp. I was thirty minutes by bike away from the busiest streets of central Tokyo but here was all the quiet I needed. No sooner had I decided that this would be my base camp than my next immediate thought was how to secure it from intruders. It occurred to me to adorn it somehow with apotropaic totems to ward off rivals. Then I thought again: who would move into here anyway, I had nothing to steal, and in any case if someone did take over the place I would just find somewhere else to sleep. There was no need to demarcate the place as mine. I sat down on the soft green floor and looked around the inside of the bush—a good home indeed.

   I spent the subsequent days pottering around the area near to the park and cycling to remote parts of the city. I awoke at sunrise always and spent the first few hours of each morning walking around the park in solitary except for the occasional company of the stray cats and early foxes who were my neighbors. The park was so clean, like the city as a whole, that I never found anything of interest scattered by the edges of the playing field, in the wastebaskets or chucked in the hedges. The city's bin-men came round regularly and cleaned up what little was thrown away by the park's visitors. After my walk, I usually ate a breakfast of rice cakes with a can of sweet coffee that I bought in one of the 24-hour stores near to the warehouses erected along the shore of the bay. I rarely ate bread, which was relatively expensive: rice cakes, on the other hand, hardly cost a thing. In mid-morning I got on my bike and cycled to one of the local centers. I then wandered around amid the crowds all day, watching people mostly, or stood reading in the bookshops. In Tokyo, patrons seemed to stand around in bookshops browsing the books for as long as they liked—the staff never disturbed them. I read entire books in those places; I read Shakespeare's plays one by one—each can be accomplished in an hour or so. Despite sleeping rough every night I did not consider that I looked like a vagabond. My erstwhile long run from out of town had gutted all my body fat so that I was stick-thin and could feel all my bones sticking out. In particular my rib cage felt like just that, a rib cage with no skin to cover it. I had not shaved for a week or two and had a visor of gold bristles round my jaw. My cheeks itched.

   Back out on the streets I was content to follow my nose and wander round. On some days I conducted experiments such as calculating the slowness by which city dwellers walk the streets compared with the speed attained by those unencumbered by urban obstacles, or estimating the number of times Tokyo drivers continued through traffic lights after they had changed to red every day—trivial investigations that nonetheless kept me amused for the doing. Sometimes I decided that I would allow myself to go anywhere I felt like so long as I did not have to break in or trespass. I spent whole days walking into offices, police stations, hospitals, unobtrusively observing what went on in those places from day to day.

No one paid me any heed. I elevated to the top floors of high buildings then clambered out onto the rooftops and jumped or climbed over from one edifice to the next, making my way around a block from above. I searched in vain for the full-sized galleon I had seen one time on top of an office building, going backwards and forwards over and over again in the area where I had seen it, and could never find it.

I was inwardly surprised that not once did I feel that I was missing out on something or that I should be occupying myself with some useful work. Anyway, what actually was more useful than walking around? I had to define useful: it meant of use, to someone. Alternative activities that I could be undertaking were more likely useful to someone else and not me. I was happy just to walk. Tokyoites were an endlessly interesting spectacle. Despite all the hundreds and thousands in view out and about every minute, there were several constant patterns of types, at least judging by appearance, which seemed to exemplify just about everyone as a stock example of a certain compartmentalized group. There were school kids in uniforms not unlike those to be seen in any other country: gray and navy tops and bottoms with a white shirt or blouse. The girls dissented from conformity by bleaching their hair a sallow ocher; the boys un-knotted their ties and let their shirts hang out. They did not carry themselves with any sort of hoodlum or aggressive demeanor though; their rebelliousness was conveyed by giving off a lackadaisical impassivity amid all the bustle of the grown-ups. Young women above school age dressed much more smartly and looked as though they were out boutique-shopping or about to meet chic friends at a café. All appeared to follow similar fashions: many girls wore pleated skirts down to the knee with calf-length shapely boots—one after another sashayed past me in that same get-up. It was the current fashion. I never saw girls dressed in loose sportswear or who were carelessly turned out. They all looked perfect: their beauty radiated. Then there were the endless office crowds—and among those the males truly did all look the same. Their gait was an unhurried although respectable shuffle, indubitably in a determined direction although tortoise-like. No one stopped to dawdle as he walked past me, just pressed on. Their suits were uniformly gray, shirts cream white. No one wore anything flashy—there was no pinstripe, no silk kerchief bedizening a breast pocket—ties were plain, un-patterned in un-dazzling tones, gray or brown mostly or burgundy. Nearly all of this flock held a lit cigarette wedged in one paw and puffed it between stops at the curbside. This applied to office men across all age groups, of which there appeared to be no upper limit. There were legions of old men who must have been going to, from or between the workplace as well. All wore similar suits and carried a brief case and followed the same smoke-clouded tracks as the rest of the herd. Some of these old fossils seemed past eighty. But they were still sprightly and looked ostensibly as though they felt just as much part of the business world as their inferiors. Clearly they had no intention of retirement.

White-collar workers in groups of three or more always walked side by side ranged neck and neck across the sidewalk, further increasing the press of obstruction and preventing anyone with a faster step—that is, me—from ever getting past the picket-line. This was consistently the case with such groups—they did not split into lesser nuclei of colonnades in file, for example, which surely would have made a more streamlined process. It seemed very determined and natural of them to walk in an even line spread across the sidewalk like that, talking in turns, part of the Japanese love of leveling all-comers to sameness, I supposed—no one wanting to march ahead and none being left to lag behind. Individuals out alone or within their groups never gave anyone else a second thought. No one lifted a finger to help anyone else except those within their group, and that was no one else at all if they were on their own. No one altered their actions or movements in any way out of consideration that they might hinder or incommode another person, they just went about their business regardless. If they walked through a shop or office door, they let it swing back in the following person's face. If there were anything up for grabs such as a place to sit, all converged on it and the first to arrive sat down without even looking up: the runners-up adjusted their step and walked off. Not a glance, let alone a word, was ever exchanged between strangers. If someone bumped into them they made no reaction whatsoever, no apology, no excuse me, no look of annoyance. It were as though nothing happened; they mutually got in each other's way and made each other walk round them, but without any complaint raised. They ignored each other to perfection.

The more I watched I began to notice other types amid the crowds as well. Not everyone was apparently affluent and respectable. Some bore the marks of poverty and failure, the way they walked head down and searched the ground. It was not what people wore that gave them away—this was probably why I had not seen those who were on the lowest rungs before. They still attempted to put up a decent appearance. But the clothes they wore were backdated and their look was surrender. Then there were some with a more malignant air. Men whose face bore a scowl. These men moved with more boldness than the rest, maybe it was more speed, and reminded me of gangsters with their style of Dayglo patterned rayon shirts, black pants and loafers, hair greased with lotion. Like in some film centering on a gang who hang out in a bowling rink, they even wore fat rings and chunky necklaces. All were thickset or getting obese. After I first noticed them I began to see them all over the place, standing around regarding the others go by. Did they see me? Their mannerisms were bullish and ugly and this showed on their bloated faces.

I kept walking around the city. A cavalcade of black propaganda vans belonging to a right-wing group, with great big white loudspeakers stuck on the rooftops like grafted human ears, and a similar black battle-bus lined a roadside near to a railway station. A man stood on top of the bus ranting into a microphone as flocks of people walked past and ignored him. He held no audience and no one stopped to listen to his speech, with the exception of myself. From a safe distance, because I had heard that this group was nationalistic and anti-American, as well as above all anti-Soviet, Chinese and Korean, in other words anti–non-Japanese, I held back and observed with curiosity the man's hopelessly outmoded method of addressing a crowd: hysterically he implored those who were not paying any attention to him to pay him attention. Around him, his corporals stood up sharply in militaristic uniforms of olive twill and black leather, a vague menace.

After I had watched the ranting orator, I next made another weird discovery, that every car on Tokyo's streets was alike in identikit achromatic tones: by far the most were silver-gray, nearly all the rest black or white. I had not previously noticed this colorlessness probably because of the infusion of yellow and orange cabs in all the passing traffic. But after it first occurred to me, when I was standing at rest waiting to cross a road, watching cars go by, it became plain to see—private automobiles in Japan were gray. Why did everyone choose the same shade for their car, and why was that shade gray?

Afternoon moved into evening. Two blue-uniformed policemen

strolled ahead of me in foot-patrol away along the sidewalk: then a salaryman in a suit, visibly drunk, for fun pretended to kick one of the officers up the backside, stopping his foot just short, and brayed back at his group of friends, who all laughed as well. The officers kept walking in front without taking any notice of them. No sooner did I witness this when I saw something quite similar: amid the throng on the sidewalk not far from me a man dressed in black shirt and black pants screamed something—which first caught my attention and made me look over toward him—and then I observed him high-kick martial arts-style another man in the throat, scream something again, at the man he had kicked, then disappear into the midst of the crowd, leaving his adversary standing clutching his neck in shock. Squabbles and strife were more frequent than I had previously thought, but just did not escalate beyond a margin of self-control. All incidents were resolved quickly in seemly fashion then blew over. Those who temporarily lost their cool vented their annoyance in a flash without further going on the rampage. Two young men caught in the pressure of all the multitudes in the street and swept right into an oncoming other turned to him with the aside "*Dokei*!"—rude slang for "Get out of our way"—which induced him to turn back on them and growl some unheard words close-up in their faces, causing them to look apologetic if nothing else. Smiles followed as the lone man walked off on his way and the two friends rejoined theirs. Genuinely, it looked as though they considered the encounter a harmless incident and was quickly replaced by some other more important topic for their conversation. After this, I saw another, bespectacled, man in a suit and raincoat wandering around, wailing in grief. He was sobbing as he circled among the hordes of people, blindly bouncing from one to the next, howling tears of pain and sadness. What could have happened to him to make him so inconsolable? Maybe he had just lost his job or only suffered a minor setback like that, it was impossible to tell.

 Each night I was gripped by an encroaching excitement at not having anywhere particular to go. My feeling was such as entering a secret, a dark secret. Night-time represented possibility and assignation. Those who were out at night were concentrated on feeding their desires. They entered into and emerged from underground nightspots connected to the street down stairwells. I did not try to enter any of these secretive dens; I did not have the money to go in, and besides, did not want to meet people and talk to anyone. Once while I was working at Nimsan, sometime before, I had been taken to a hostess bar, wherein gray-haired men in suits shared at their tables with glamorous young women in silky colored gowns with their hair done up in curls like bridesmaids. At the time I was taken there, one night after I had been drinking beer with one of the older doctors whose research reports I regularly edited, apparently on a spur-of-the-moment whim of his and no doubt to educate me about Japan's after-hours nightlife, I remembered that we had to negotiate with the bar madam at the door in order to be admitted—at first it looked like she was not going to let us in, then she relented. These inns were selective and only those who were known to the purveyors could enter sometimes. Once inside, nothing improper seemed to be going on however. Hostesses sat at the tables with the middle-aged men who were the sole customers, conversing with them and pouring their drinks: beer from the bottle or whiskey mixed with water and ice. The hostess bar, like every established custom I observed in Japan, was genteel and distinguished.

So I did not go into any of the myriad hostelries, bars and diners that were open all night while I walked the streets. I observed the night owls coming and going between various stopovers but did not indulge myself in trying out any inveiglements or sipping magic potions. I had not drunk any alcoholic drink since the last time I was with Yumi in the Black Ship Hotel looking out over the coast of Shimoda many weeks before. I just wandered from spot to spot, stopping here and there and always observing what went on around me under the artificial streetlights that poured faintly orange illuminations onto the herds of nocturnal mavericks. At the end of each long night-time ramble, just before sunrise I wound up by climbing on my bike and cycling back to my base camp in the corner of the playing field, arriving there at around the beginning of dawn. To sleep, I did not want to be seen either passed out clothed in the street or to wake and see people walking busily around me. Also, there was an element I suspected within me of not wanting to sleep in a field in the blackness of night. I would not be able at all to drift off and pass out in such a vulnerable position; I would be alert to every sound I could hear out there, approaching?—wild predator, spectral wraith, fugitive killer? So I chose to lie down and sleep in the early hours of morning as it was getting light, trusting my preservation in the sun, just for a couple hours till I stirred myself for breakfast and began the day again.

After some unknown period of this pattern of activity, when I was having one of my night-time rambles, as I was passing through the midst of one mixed group of people, who apart from taking up the entire width of sidewalk were all drunk and making a merry loud noise, one of them, a big oaf of a man in a dark gray suit whom I could see backing toward me as he looked with a besotted expression at his companions, who were surveying the menu displayed outside a late-night diner, so that I had to skip out of his way to avoid being squashed, abruptly swung in my realigned path and blundered into me—then as if nothing had happened the oaf righted his posture and continued engaging himself exclusively with his fellows.

A crimson mist floated between us. All the endless raucous cacophony and stridor, compression and claustrophobia of the city, people's inconsiderateness, blind unawareness and being looked past that I had witnessed and felt during the preceding days and nights seemed to flow from this one boorish individual, and I strode up to him, grabbed his suit lapels with both fists, and thrust my face into his screaming in his eyes to feel sorry that he had stumbled into me. Much against my expectation, for I had considered that he was large, he contracted and shrank in my grip and went so limp as I clutched at his neck that to a spectator it might have looked like he had swooned from my kiss, were it not that I was assaulting him. Still I continued spitting insults in his face for good measure before finally letting him go and backing off from his group, looking at no one in the face. They parted as I barged my way out.

Then insidiously, an unnameable indefinite kind of dread crawled all over me as I left the scene, following me around. I could not identify its cause—but what it felt like I must describe only as:- horror. I could not rid myself of it, I was gripped by fear of I knew not what. I started to run along the pavement. When I reached my bike I got on and pedaled quickly in the direction of my camp in the playing field. I felt nothing but deep fear and—horror, of nothing in particular, except a vulnerability and exposure to an imminent worrisome presence advancing on me. But, I did not know what it was going to be. When I eventually reached my camp in the bushes I lay down on the cold hard earth surrounded in darkness. In the quietude, my fear redoubled. What was it? I had attacked someone more-or-less at random; I had not struck him but almost as bad had threatened him with a promise of manic violence. Then I myself had become scared. Why? I tried to get over it. I told myself that it was just my imagination, therefore I should just imagine it away. Think positive. As I analyzed the night's events I considered that my fear might have existed prior to my assaulting that man in the street, at a low level, then increased till I became conscious of it conjured by the act of transgression. It had probably been with me since I lost Yumi. I missed Yumi. I missed my Mom and Dad, my brothers and the people back home. In the weeks that had passed since Yumi had been gone, I had seen no one but myriad strangers, had been alone and fending for myself all the time. I had heard no voice except my own in my head, with no others to counterbalance and outweigh it and oppose it from rambling where it may. There had been no one to reassure me, to compliment me and nod and listen or else to doubt me with a wrinkle of the nose. In other words, no one to put me right. I had not interacted with anyone in any meaningful way except to swap a word at a store counter or to throw a look toward a passer-by for the last several weeks. Loneliness was making me confused. What I had thought was pursuing me was unknowable because it was madness. All the other madmen and madwomen I had seen skulking around the wrong side of the city's streets were not disheveled and destitute because they were crazy, it was the other way round—their aloneness had made them mad. I lay back on the cold ground in my woody nest and stared upwards.

Over the canopy of leaves above my face shooting stars criss-crossed space. Someone was potting pool balls up there. The black spotted silk of the firmament was not still and infinite and frozen set at all, but moved in every quarter with bits of floating clouds and man-made lights, the stars blinked and flickered. I recalled that I had once seen what I believed to be a UFO some years previously. I thought that then if I looked at the sky intently, another flying saucer would be bound to appear. I studied the heavens as I ruminated about what I should do next to relieve me of my forlorn predicament. Could I go back to Nimsan and ask for help, a job, or some kind of assistance, a roof over my head? I remembered seeing Dr. Zen outside my old dormitory on the day that I had come back to Tokyo. He had not even acknowledged me. I was no longer a member of his old group. In any case, really I did not want to go back to Nimsan; I preferred to make it a rule never to go back and try to re-live and recapture some role or occupation that I had earlier undertaken. The place and people would have changed in my absence—a return would be bound to lead to disappointment, and sour the good memories of how it was before as well. Better to move on I thought. As I scanned the sky for something out there, I recalled leaving Nimsan and the events of the day that Yumi and I had fled with our stolen money, and our stay at the plush Imperial Hotel. Who was that old-timer I had met downstairs in the bar on the first night? Skip—that was his name. Didn't he say that he used to see aliens and flying saucers passing over his military base somewhere out in the midst of the Mojave Desert? I went over my memory of meeting Skip in the Imperial Hotel. He was living there as a permanent resident, in retirement. In the early hours of the morning, I thought about the past and wondered about what I should do next.

I was tired having been awake all night and soon fell asleep, when I had the following terrible nightmare. I was walking about in town, perhaps London, crossing a road in broad daylight when I happened to look up into the sky. I glanced up, and what I saw was astonishing. A spectral, gigantic hand poking in through the clouds. The hand of God? What else could that have been? The hand was side-on pointing an outstretched finger vaster than an airship down at the earth. The hand's palm was adorned by a razzmatazz of pale pink scars and lacerations. At the wrist, the point where the huge hand mingled into the clouds, were two yellow lights. I looked around me incredulously and observed others were stopped in the street looking up at the hand with its two yellow lights. People were gasping aloud and quizzing each other. Some had flocked round a policeman. Radio fizzing, he had no idea what it was either. Crowds started to gather, all looking up. The hand started to move round gradually, the pointing finger moving toward us. Eventually the hand was pointing down right in our direction. I looked again at all the surrounding people filling the street one last time, then looked up again—quickly—the hand had changed into a white missile, a nuclear Cruise missile raining down on us, the two yellow lights were the afterburners on its rocket engines. As it seared toward me in fright I jumped, jumped out of the dream, landing safely awake in the bushes of my camp.

13

That morning, instead of consuming my usual breakfast of two rice cakes and a can of café au lait purchased from the convenience store, I hit upon a change of routine and instead went to a Denny's family restaurant and ordered scrambled eggs, toast and jam and American coffee to wash it all down. I was still feeling somewhat nervous, that sensation would not leave me alone, so the change of scene and what was for me a lavish breakfast were attempts at putting myself at ease with some treats. As I waited for my order to arrive I opened my wallet, spilled out the contents on the table, and calculated what money I had left. After paying for breakfast, there would be my last one thousand yen—the equivalent of a ten dollar bill.

When I had finished eating I mounted my bike and headed out in search of one of the city's public bathhouses. These are common in Tokyo and throughout Japan, a throwback to a time, not yet over, when many living-quarters did not have enough space inside to build a bathroom. Lately the public baths were mostly used by university students who lived in crumbling digs without wash facilities, as well as by some other impoverished individuals in similar situations and elderly widowers with no one to run them a bath at home. Apart from and distinct to a shower for scrubbing themselves under with soap, the Japanese relish a pure clear bath to bask in and relax, one of their rituals. Hence in each city ward public baths were still in demand. Only, I had never been to one and did not even know how to find one. According to my battered old guidebook to Japan, which was kept perpetually in my suit jacket pocket, there was a public baths at Tokyo Station, the gigantic complex of ticket halls, platforms, shops and department stores that was the terminus for Shinkansen bullet trains coming in from the north and south of Japan and a connecting hub for various Japan Railway lines and the city's underground network. So I cycled to the mammoth station, and once there walked around inside looking for any sign of the baths.

Finding the way in, I purchased a ticket and entered, for my first bath in weeks. Then with the remaining few coins I had left, I bought a shaving kit consisting of disposable razor and small tube of shaving cream out the vending machines adjoining the changing room, stripped, crossed through the door leading to the baths and sat down at one of the rows of

177

little wooden stools inside the bathhouse, each with a knee-high shower unit in front. I looked at myself in the mirror in front of me—bearded, hair grown all out of control, cheek bones jutting out, neck no thicker than a goose's, rib cage showing, fingers as slender as lollipop sticks. Although my face was almost red in all the heat and steam coming up from the baths, my body was pale white reflected in the glass. I washed all over with soap, covering my entire skin with bubbles and foam and scrubbing my back with one of the white washrags provided. I lathered my hair three or four times with shampoo and asperged it with water from the shower faucet. Next I plastered shaving cream from my palms onto my face, took the plastic razor out its sheath, and tried to drag it down my jaw. Nothing came off. The thick beard was made of hard strands like copper wires. I stretched the skin of my bony right cheek with my right hand and tried again to depilate the area. With chops and scrapes of the razor, tufts began to dislodge. I had to attack the fronds as a woodcutter takes blows to clear the stumps of trees, yanking the blade through. When I had gone over my face completely I saw that patches of golden stubble remained in snippets and threads all round the corners of my jaw, so once again I recommenced work with the razor till finally by increments my face was clean of hair.

When I finished shaving and had soaked in the large communal bath for a while, I dried myself and got dressed. Back outside the station I cycled toward the Imperial Hotel—the haven to where Yumi and I had first eloped with our purloined money—located nearby down the road. My skin tingled and cheeks glowed. I found it symbolic that with the last of the remaining money I had left in the world, I had used it to cleanse myself, had washed my hands of it. It was time for a fresh beginning. At the hotel I entered the lobby. People milled around, sat on armchairs and had conversations over tea. The Christmas display that had been in the middle of the floor the last time I was there was nowhere to be seen, only yards of beige carpet and ample displays of flowers. I approached the reception desk and asked the pretty girl in Disney-style majorette's buttoned-up red tunic if she would call up to Captain Skip Atwater's room and say that he has a visitor, Tommy, the man who always makes people leave the room. The cute receptionist smiled and asked me to wait in one of the chairs in the lobby, and a few minutes later came over and said that Captain Atwater would see me in the place where we had met on the first occasion.

Once ensconced inside the bar on the first floor, as nearly as I could remember in the exact same seat where I had met Skip, I bided my time looking around me at the assortment of customers and smartly presented bar staff. One of the waiters tried to offer me a drinks menu but I waived it away saying that I was waiting for someone to join me. A few minutes passed, then into the room entered Skip Atwater, once again wearing a jumble of traditional costumes—this time in a sky-blue kimono to go with the same cowboy hat as he was wearing before. With his long white hair he was quite unmistakable—immediately the lined facial features came back to me as he walked over.

"So it is you after all," said Skip, recognizing me in turn. "I couldn't really remember the name, but I had a memory of someone showing me a trick of making a fella leave the room just by using psychic energy down here in the bar one evening, so to see whether you were the same person I just said I would meet you in the same place."

"I thought so," I said. "See what I mean—we're all psychic."

"What brings you to see me?" said Skip, sitting down. "But wait, first we need a drink before we can talk."

"Not for me thanks," I said. "I don't drink."

Skip frowned. "Well you were certainly knocking them back the last time I saw you. I had to leave you to it in case I got shitfaced." When he said that last word, he chuckled.

I told Skip that I had decided not to drink any alcohol some while previously and why I had made the ruling, explaining about alcohol's effects on people and how it changed them for the worst and how I did not want to be a worse person than I was already.

With each word of my confession, Skip laughed his head off. "What a load of crap," he sputtered between guffaws, when I had finished explaining. "Don't be so serious. C'mon let's have a drink. I don't want to sit here drinking alone, so if you want to tell me or ask me something, let's do it with a drink. Otherwise I'm going back to bed. I come here for one or two beers every day with all my friends." Skip waved his arm around so as to include all the people sitting in the bar area within the scope of its sweep.

"Okay I'll have a beer," I resigned.

"That's good." Skip held up two fingers to the nearest waiter, who interpreted the sign as two beers and got moving. Then Skip rummaged inside the folds of his kimono with his right hand, and pulled out a pack of cigars. "Help yourself," he remarked, putting the pack on the counter as he lit one. I took one out and ignited it as well. As we waited for the beers, Skip turned to me. "Alcohol doesn't change anybody, it only brings out what we are already. If you are an asshole after drinking, it just means that you are one before drinking as well; only you can keep it concealed when you are sober. But you don't look like an asshole to me. I've seen plenty of those in the past. Don't be so serious."

The beers arrived on the counter in front of us, two tall glasses on a rotund paper napkin each. As Skip lifted his glass to his lips, he said: "Alcohol is a botanical drug just as much as marijuana, ayahuasca, mushrooms, peyote and what-not, it is synthesized by plant cells alone and not expressed in animals. But, we humans produce an enzyme that breaks it down. Why do you think that that should be? Why did we evolve the capability to process this drug? It seems that there is some grand design at work, which foresaw that in the age of civilization we would want to drink alcohol. And like so-called psychedelics, alcohol brings us certain messages from the natural world. Good advice is only good to those who heed it, and is wasted on those who are insouciant, right? Those who experience mind-bending insights from herbal drugs feel pretty convinced that these plants are telling us something. As for alcohol, I find that I do a lot of my most creative thinking after one drink. Beyond that, not much more than a drunken mist. If I drink one beer, words and ideas course through my mind; much more than that and it turns to gibberish then I collapse in a heap—the next day I recollect nothing: the drug takes it back. So that should be the recommended dose of alcohol—one drink. All the unwanted effects of it are a result of going beyond that amount—antisocial strife, fighting, hangovers and messed-up livers. Not taken to excess, alcohol can teach us a thing or two. We often embarrass ourselves and make erroneous mistakes when drunk, so we learn from those mistakes. Alcohol teaches us what not to do. That's my theory, anyway. Don't forget, Tommy, beer and wine were a gift to the human race from the gods—every ancient culture contains a myth attesting to that. To the Romans, it was the harvest goddess Ceres who taught men how to brew beer from barley, which is why we now call barley a cereal crop, derived from her name, and the Spanish call beer *cerveza*, in her honor as well. So it would be sacrilege to the gods for us not to drink beer, after they endowed it to us as a gift."

"That depends on whether you believe in myths and the ancient gods," I replied, sniffing my beer, and simultaneously seeing the word *cerveza* written on the glass.

"I do," said Skip. "Do you want to know something? Look at the back of your hands."

I placed my hands palm-down flat on the counter.

"Have a good close look at them. What do you see?" said Skip.

"Knuckles, the nails, branching veins under the skin, crisscrossing swirls of tiny wrinkles…."

"Now look between each of your fingers and thumb at the base. There are four flaps of skin. Do you see them?—remnants of webbed fingers. So there you have it, we are all descended from Atlantis, the city underneath the sea that was built by Poseidon, the god of the waves."

"Okay, I believe you," I said. "Thanks for the beer." I took a sip. After a minute I added, "Now I bet there's something you didn't know."

"What's that?" said Skip.

It was a fragment that I had just remembered when surveying the backs of my hands close up. Manually demonstrating what to do, I said, "Hold your thumbs out like this, and place them one under each nostril. Okay, now breathe out through your nose."

Skip exhaled. "What am I supposed to learn here?" he asked.

"Didn't you feel it? You only expelled air out of one nostril. Try again."

"No I didn't! No wait, yes I do. That's funny. How did you know that?"

"We all do. The nostril we use changes left right left right every ten or fifteen minutes. Check in fifteen minutes' time, it will have changed from the one you are now breathing out with to the opposite side." I told Skip that no matter how many people I had demonstrated this to over many years since I had made the discovery, I had not met anyone who was aware that we only breathe out through one nostril at a time, and that this sole nostril alternates between left and right about every quarter hour.

I took another swig of my beer and as I swallowed it I looked around at the customers. "What did you mean by saying that these people are all your friends?" I asked Skip. "Do they all live here in the hotel as well and do you know everybody?"

"Never seen them before in my life," said Skip, surveying the people around us. "But I like to think of people generally as my friends, unless of course they turn out to be an asshole." At this he chuckled as well. "I prefer friends who come and go in this bar to having constant friends. I find that I get just as much if not more help and insights from making new friends than I might from a friend who is always the same person."

Skip finished his cigar and stubbed the end out on an ashtray, then opened the pack and lit another. He offered me one which I declined. "You smoke too much," I told him.

"No, I don't actually smoke them," was the reply. "I just take a puff then blow it out. I don't inhale the smoke. I'm like Winston Churchill, who always had a cigar going, but really only 'smoked matches.'"

This seemed like a good chance to ask Skip about what I had visited him to say, while he was feeling friendly and beneficent to all. I started by asking him, talking of Winston Churchill, whether he had time to tell me more about his experiences in the army and the atomic detonations he had seen. I wanted to know what that was like—it seemed quite unreal to me to meet someone who had actually witnessed an atomic bomb exploding.

"Lots of people saw them, not just army personnel," replied Skip. "From nearby Las Vegas, which was only forty miles away from Camp Desert Rock, or Atom Camp as it was known, tourists used to drive down to watch the mushroom clouds expanding to the top of the sky while sipping cocktails from their casino hotel rooms on the Strip. The representatives of the AEC, that is, the Atomic Energy Commission, used to give a media release to the local people just before a series of bomb tests was about to commence, so that anyone could get ready to view them. In those days it was not like now, with the army's impenetrable military secrets and immersed isolation. Camp Desert Rock in the 1950s and '60s was relatively open, with families and the press coming in and out. President Kennedy visited us once, going round in an open car with a big smile on his face, as was his wont. Now on the same site there is Area 51—nobody on the outside knows what they do in there, not even Bill Clinton."

Skip sipped his beer and lit another cigar from out the pack on the counter. Smoke lifted and expanded from the smoldering tip. "Let me tell you a bit of background to that time in history," he continued. "Back in the '50s, it wasn't thought much of a big deal to have nuclear weapons tests going off near to your town. Everyone was convinced that modern mankind was obsolete and that we were all going to be blown up imminently. The public quite cheerfully drank a toast to the idea of its own destruction. We were all resigned to the belief that nuclear war was inevitable.

"The U.S. Joint Intelligence Committee had declared that the Soviet Union was building up its nuclear arsenal to attack the United States at the earliest possible moment. The military had entered a sinister contest of speed, a nuclear armaments race with the Soviet Union. And in order to test whether soldiers could fight in a nuclear war, they drilled us boys with maneuvers and exercises close to where they set off the bombs. We were practically right underneath them most of the time—usually about three thousand yards away, which is two miles—not very far—standing in trenches or sitting in a tank, and the blasts went over us like sudden storms. A hot blast of dusty desert sirocco—then a depth of chaotic noise, rumbling and shaking the ground, gradually getting louder and louder and more and more tremendous. And then, up they went in red and orange and gray, slowly a steeple of fire and smoke and polluted poisonous debris enormous, a rolling doughball puffing and lifting and dragging its long stalk high over the scorched sands up into the burning sky. All we could do was stand at a predetermined distance that was just beyond its flames and watch.

"The army and the government thus concluded that with a few basic precautions, troops were able to fight and survive an atomic attack."

Skip found these recollections highly amusing and kept chuckling throughout the account. "The two atom bombs dropped on Japan in 1945 were puny compared with the 'super' bombs that followed in their wake," he continued. "Those first atomic bombs worked on the principle of fission, which is bombarding a small quantity of uranium or plutonium with an avalanche of neutrons so as to start a chain reaction, splitting the atom into smaller elements. Now when you measure the combined mass of the smaller nuclei resulting from fission plus that of all the released neutrons, it does not quite add up to the mass of the original atomic element. The missing mass is converted to energy by a factor of the speed of light squared, a colossal multiplier: $E = mc^2$. This energy released is the tremendous nuclear energy of fission reactions.

"But the atomic fission bombs that flattened Hiroshima and Nagasaki had only something like one thousandth the destructive potency of the next generation of weapons, which reproduced the powerful natural processes that are taking place in the interior of the sun—nuclear fusion. Fusion is the opposite process of fission, crushing together light elements to make heavier ones. Hydrogen is the lightest element, pounded together with such force by the sun's internal gravity that it is compressed into helium and heavier nuclei, releasing the immense quantities of energy that heat and light the earth and all the solar system. The forces liberated by hydrogen fusion are incomparably more powerful than those let loose by uranium fission. And both we and the Russians were stockpiling masses of nuclear weapons ready to fire at each other at any time.

"During the Cold War period, there was no limit to the destructive capability of the latest armaments. And the missiles were accurate enough to reach any target, anywhere in the world. Arms build-up was declared America's highest national priority. The more terrible the prospect of a nuclear war continued to appear, the more deterred the Soviets must be from ever beginning one—so it was gambled. One plan called for the launch of more than three thousand nuclear weapons, including hundreds of hydrogen bombs, to attack one thousand separate targets in the Communist bloc. This strike was estimated by our military planners to kill two hundred eighty-five million people, give or take a few. The population of a whole continent. Not much restraint was placed on when this attack might be launched either. It was an American Schlieffen Plan, an ultimate strategy for war winning under all circumstances of war initiation, regardless of political and military realities."

As we sat in the bar for the next few hours of the afternoon Skip related to me his tale of life in the Atomic Maneuver Battalion. He joined the Sixth Army straight from college, where he had received cadet training in the reserves. He had won a college scholarship from the army—it was the only way available for him to receive an education. The army and the navy infiltrated and provided funding for every school, every laboratory and every department of advanced education. "The United States is a military nation, make no mistake about that," said Skip. "The army rules. So I enlisted as a second lieutenant at the Presidio of San Francisco, and that's how I found myself working at the NTS, or

Nevada Test Site."

Skip's army duties mostly involved overseeing erecting tents and building living quarters, temporary sumps for garbage disposal, sanitary fill areas, and knocking together mess tables, kitchen areas and towers holding water tanks for showers. He was responsible for electrical work, carpenter work and placing signage at the camp, as well as establishing a command post and constructing emplacements at the Forward Area on Yucca Flat where the nuclear tests were conducted. Activities at the Forward Area included work orders for theater seats, a hospital area, chapel benches and sundry other items. Skip's unit built roads and prepared the instigation of a water point to meet the needs of Camp Desert Rock.

In all, Skip spent four years at the Nevada Test Site eventually winning promotion to captain. After being discharged from the army in 1963 he went on to start up his own construction business, S. P. Atwater Construction Co. The army had taught him a lot. His new business began by building homes and farms, and got its first big project building dams outside Las Vegas in the late sixties. From then, S. P. Atwater became known as a leading general contractor in the area, building schools, hospitals, retail stores, sewers, water lines and utilities. Skip's military expertise was called into action for the construction of an underground ballistic missile launching facility at Nellis AFB, Nevada, which eventually became the prototype for nuclear missile installations. The 1970s were explosive years for the company with hundreds of projects completed in the decade, including the relocation of London Bridge to Lake Havasu, Arizona. The antique bridge was disassembled where it had stood over the River Thames since 1831 and each of its granite stones numbered then shipped ten thousand miles to the Arizona desert, where the reassembled structure served as a tourist attraction. S. P. Atwater Construction Co. also expanded its operations by forming and acquiring subsidiary companies and opening branch offices throughout the western states. The company was eventually acquired as a wholly owned subsidiary and Skip retired on the day of his sixtieth birthday—February 18th, 1993—a very rich and successful man.

It was back in the 1960s, while still in the early days when Skip headed S.P. Atwater, that he met his soon-to-be wife, Nora Kitaoka. One warm evening, one of Skip's friends and partners in the company, Rob A.

Storry, called him on the phone with a request. Rob had become enchanted with a beautiful local girl of Korean background, named Gina, and had asked her for a date that night. Gina's answer was yes so long as she could bring a girlfriend of hers along with her, and that Rob likewise bring someone as well for a double date. Rob was desperate to go out with Gina, so over the crackly telephone line he begged Skip to accompany him because he was, in Rob's words, "The only good friend I have and the sole person I know who can make me look like my associates are successful people." When Skip asked who this other girl was, Rob said that he did not know, but added, "She's Japanese I think."

Skip was feeling worn out by a long day spent on a building site but agreed anyway out of intrigue. "Double date?" he thought out loud on the phone to Rob. "Okay, why not."

That night the two buddies were sitting in the restaurant where they had agreed to meet Gina and her accomplice, when in walked the two most beautiful women Skip had ever before seen or even imagined. The woman who turned out to be Gina was tall with dark brown hair done up in a pile of loose curls. Her friend, who wore her dark, shining hair let loose over her shoulders, was the woman who was to become his future bride, Nora Kitaoka. Both women wore white dresses with a small shiny handbag dangling from an elbow. Both were daughters of wealthy local farmers whose East Asian descendents had migrated to and prospered in the early days of settlement in Nevada. Gina's grandfather had long ago entered the United States on a Japanese passport, because Korea was under Japanese occupation at that time, to work as a laborer, first crossing the sea to the Hawaiian Islands then to California and finally settling in Nevada. And Nora's background story, it turned out as the two couples sat and got to know one another that evening, was almost exactly the same as Gina's.

Nora and her twin sister Esmeralda were the granddaughters of a Japanese-born immigrant local farmer, Masa "Kit" Kitaoka, who had trekked to the States many decades ago with a dream to enact. As a sixteen-year-old youth, Kit had moved to Nevada with the specific intention of owning and operating a ranch—which people of Japanese origin were not permitted to do, at that time, in neighboring California where he, like Gina's grandfather, had been living since he first arrived in America. Kit made his way by long voyage from Nagasaki to California, first settling in Sacramento, making ends meet by picking fruit or else by working as a cook in whatever places would hire him. For a while he drifted around taking jobs in gardening and plant nursery work, saving up all the money he earned.

Then one night, while he was sitting in the hot confines of his favorite Chinese diner, Ariake Chop Suey, eating a bowl of vegetable soup, (the cheapest item on the menu), by chance Kit found himself talking with the man sitting next to him, an American who had insisted to the Chinese waiter on wanting to eat using chopsticks, not a spoon, but, having had his wish granted, was evidently having trouble in handling the slender armless utensils. Kit offered to teach the man how to hold chopsticks and having successfully done so got to talking with the fellow, who happened to be a real estate agent and had just returned from a visit to Las Vegas to sell lots. When Kit told the man that his long-time dream was to own and operate a ranch, the trader advised him to go to Las Vegas immediately. "It's hot and gets fairly cold in the winter," he said, "but if you can stand the weather conditions you just might make a living out there."

That was August 1914. At a time when the population in the greater Las Vegas area was less than one thousand souls, Kit traveled to that remote place and bought forty acres of desert land in Clark County.

Kit soon discovered that farming in southern Nevada was not as simple as reproducing the methods that he had used in his days as a grower in fertile California. So he began by planting alfalfa, a valuable forage plant for horses, as his main money crop. Since all the planting guides he had with him were worthless, he began conducting experiments. He planted crops every two-to-three weeks so as to find the best schedule, and after a few years of empirical investigation and much back-breaking hard work succeeded in developing planting timetables for a cornucopia of produce: broccoli, green onions, dandelion greens, beets, parsley, gumbo, okra, endive, bell peppers, snap beans, butter beans, navy beans and pea beans. Soon, Kit found himself becoming famous in the area for supplying his goods several weeks ahead of the California market—and they were fresher, tasted better and were cheaper too. Kit supplied restaurants throughout the region, in Indian Springs, Sandy Valley, Henderson and Gene. The little family—he, his wife and son—helped harvest, clean and bundle their produce and together they accompanied him on his delivery rounds in their trusty truck.

As time passed, Kit's son grew up and aspired to become an architect. The young man was accepted as an apprentice to Frank Lloyd Wright, the revered philosopher and famous creator of organic architecture, and had nearly completed his degree at Berkeley when his career was derailed because of the Second World War. In 1942, months after Japan had attacked Pearl Harbor in Hawaii and thus plunged the United States into war, he was forced to return to Kit's farm in faraway Nevada. At that time, President Roosevelt signed into effect Executive Order 9066, giving families of Japanese descent ten days to sell their businesses, homes and belongings before they were rounded up and sent to internment camps. California was not a safe place for Japanese Americans, but Nevada was largely unaffected by the military's panic over security and anti-Japanese sentiment in the national press. So, the young man went home and decided to abandon his goal of becoming an architect. He worked his father's ranch over the years, marrying his childhood sweetheart, who was also a child of Japanese immigrant farm workers, and Nora and her twin sister, Esmeralda, were born to them as a consolatory gift in the years after the bloody world war had ended and its replacement, the Cold War, was getting under way.

Nora and Esmeralda were raised as happy farm girls. Their early years were spent playing among fields and fruit trees watching the town of Las Vegas grow up nearby. Their education was given them by their parents at home and was guided by instilling in the twin girls an awareness of the four principles: truth, deeds, loyalty and courage; and the three disciplinary measures: knowledge, virtue and health. Although the children were overtly strong-bodied and happy, only one consideration quietly harried the Kitaoka family's elders—the commonly held Japanese notion that among twins one will always thrive while the other must wither. As the twins were reared through their childhood and into adolescence this fearful supposition constantly haunted their close-knit kin.

Eventually, the twins reached maturity, twenty years of age according to Japanese custom, and within weeks Nora was heard to be in love with and getting engaged to an American ex-soldier and construction engineer. Skip went to the Kitaoka family ranch often and always was kind and polite, which endeared him to the folks, and when he asked the family to give him their permission to wed Nora, they agreed, her frustrated would-be-architect father especially pleased to have a construction engineer in the family, although in secret he later admitted that he could not sleep for a month due to concern about the decision to allow his daughter to marry a non-Japanese American.

Both couples, Nora with Skip and their friends Gina with Rob, had fallen in love on the night they met and were quickly married not long after their providential double date. Nora and Skip tied the knot at the Little White Wedding Chapel on the booming Las Vegas Strip, with her identical double Esmeralda as sole witness and bridesmaid. For fun, in their white wedding outfits Skip kept pretending that he did not know which sister he was marrying, and had to hold Nora's hand firmly all the way up the aisle so as to make sure his bride was not Esmeralda by mistke.

Once they were married, Skip, who despite being a rich businessman had been living in a trailer till then, and his new bride built for themselves a beautiful home on land they bought on the outskirts of Las Vegas, in a valley with abundant wild grasses growing and plentiful water supplies. Nora designed the house down to every last detail. Although she was an American woman of Japanese origin, habitually shod in riding boots and clad in jodhpurs and a brown suede motorcycle jacket, her tastes were decidedly European: the house she built was a desultory assortment of buildings of different styles—Provence country estate made of fieldstone, shallow-pitched clay tile roof and windows accented with colorful shutters; Tuscan stone villa interspersed with brick at door and window openings and building corners, frieze cornices and Roman pan clay tiled roof; Spanish resort with expansive stucco walls, deeply recessed windows and towers capturing views of the surrounding terrain; English cottage with thatched roof overhanging leaded glass windows, low wooden beam ceilings, dark carved wainscoting and flagstone floors. A ruby-red asphodel-strewn lawn and stone courtyard surrounded by clipped hedges, climbing roses, forget-me-nots and bluebells and an arch clothed by clematis featured in the heart of this caprice of constructions; in the center of the courtyard was erected a lofty brownstone folly. Whatever took Nora's fancy Skip had ordered from its local source and shipped to their land for adding to the expanding warren's geometry. In all, work on their homestead took three years to complete, and when at last it was finished the buildings and grounds occupied an area the size of a football field, an isolated valley of dwellings and multifarious colored pastures, hurdled over by a steady canopy of clouds wagon-trailing 'cross the desert.

Skip briefly paused from telling me all this so as to contemplate the intense happiness that he had known in those days; of his and Nora's youth and their freedom and power they had had to build their castle. "Then one morning," he went on, "I stepped outside the cottage and noticed that the red asphodels in the garden had wilted and shrunk away, and in their place bloomed uncountable proliferations of white daisies. I went inside and found Nora, who in tears cried that the brief life that she had led among the flowers was coming to an end."

"I'm not with you," I said. "What do you mean?"

"She died."

"Died—how?"

"Tranquilly, not many days afterwards. She had leukemia."

"I'm sorry to hear that," I said, not sure of what words to utter. "What did you do?" I asked.

"I kept working," said Skip, a long look of sadness in his face. "I went back to work with a vengeance. I had employees to look after, contracts to honor, much to do. It felt better to go back to work, cured me a little bit, over the ensuing years. But, in all that time I was bugged by stray feelings, unanswered questions and longing."

"Do you mean about why Nora died?" I inquired. "And her family's prophecy about the twins? One must thrive and one wither?"

"I was convinced that her sickness was caused by the A-bomb tests that I had taken part in. The only known cause of leukemia, of acute myelogenous leukemia, is high doses of ionizing radiation. Nora had grown up in the shadow of the Nevada bomb tests. I couldn't stop thinking about them, about the two bombs that the U.S. had dropped on Japan, that the distinctive insignia of my Sixth Army unit I had worn on my sleeve contained the device of red enamel rays suggestive of Japan, with the motto 'Born of War,' denoting that the Sixth Army was created to fight in the Pacific Theater of World War Two; that the Nevada state motto is 'Battle Born'; that Nora's sister's name, Esmeralda, is also Nevada's nickname; that Nora's Japanese descendents wandered to America from Nagasaki, once obliterated by an atom bomb, and that once they got there they discovered little more than toil, discrimination, segregation, incarceration and death. So I knew that I had to come to Japan," said Skip. "To make personal atonement."

Skip then related to me an account of his travels on arriving in Japan, tracking down the local origins of the Kitaoka clan as best he could, using an old map discovered among Nora's belongings, and praying for her soul at a shrine near the place where her grandfather was born, meeting all kinds of people at every stop of the way, learning local customs and trying new foods and drinks, always being as friendly as he could to everyone he encountered. His adopted rule was derived from the Japanese creed of "*ichizoku ichizen*"—for each day, a deed of kindness. He was impressed by Meiji-period Japan's historical feat of transforming itself from an immaterial and famine-struck secluded island made up of warring feudal domains rapidly into a modern patriotic nation-state with a constitution, over the course of a few short years of self-programmed "civilization and enlightenment" at the end of the nineteenth century, by the people's combining to exercise pointed determination and willpower to reform—and with that determination managed to avoid being carved up by European maritime powers, as was witnessed simultaneously in China and other parts of East Asia—allowing Japan to become the one and only nation in the history of Western expansionism to escape predation by the white folk.

Instead, so as to meet the North Americans and Europeans on their own terms, the Japanese "resurrected themselves as Europeans," said Skip—and could keep their Japanesy intact. Having taken that step, they set about a process of modernization and industrialization using the only resources they had available: brainpower and many hands. Unfettered by any conservative dogmas, and armed only with logic, the people set about rebuilding. There followed on the barren rock of Japan, with its year-round horrible weather consisting of winter snow, baking humid heat in summer and barrel-loads of rain in between, and no resources like petroleum, lead, tin, rubber, aluminum, iron ore, copper, cotton or coal to call its own, the building of an infrastructure based on manufactures, construction, transportation and communications and a highly efficient and intensive use of scarce agricultural land, from which was spewed an incalculable series of inventions, patents, ideas, information, innovations, and improvements and modifications of creations large and small, all a synthesis of Japanese concepts and handiwork.

"To us outsiders, the Japanese may seem pretty crazy by many appearances," said Skip, "but what these people know is the equal of any nation's learning and erudition, and Japan is, I believe, a plausible contender for the most advanced nation there is, if that were possible to adjudicate. And that's all the more remarkable because unlike Europe, the Americas, Russia, the Middle East, China, Africa, even Antarctica, this is a very asset-poor country. It has the most inclement weather, useless land, and there are no natural resources here; nothing is formed underground, or grows abundantly of its own accord, there are no green meadows, beautiful beaches and paradisiacal getaways, beasts of burden and places of adventure. Japan's is an unenviable natural flora and fauna consisting of coarse grass, pine trees that exude tons of allergic pollen and animals that scavenge—scrawny wildcats, jungle crows and big insects, and not much else. There is nothing by which the people can profit from the land. So while other peoples can enjoy the fruits of their own garden, or market the baubles sprung up from the bowels of the earth below their feet, Japan was built only on dreams, an illusion, an illusion held in place by constantly working at it. The quality of life of the people in Japan must rank as the worst in the whole wide world, because there is no break allowed from the chain gang, lest the dream is dispelled."

"Well that's a very glamorous description of Japan you have there Skip," I replied, "but it lacks a few imperfections that I can think of, such as Japan as a nation has never stood up for any good cause as far as I am aware, and there has not been much great art from here either—I mean music and so forth."

"That's not true. Japan has produced great literature. But there is very little passion or anger here, and those are what are needed to inspire music, poetry and films. On the other hand, the Japanese do appreciate the best of these made by other peoples. Again, that is how their cleverness comes in—by eliminating all the dissatisfaction and dissent in society they created peaceful harmony at the expense of much creative edge, so instead they merely import art from abroad—music, exhibitions and so on—a bit like employing cheap foreign labor to assemble factory products from overseas."

The day passed with Skip and I sitting in the bar of the Imperial Hotel exchanging opinions and talking away. We had been sitting there quite a few hours while he had been telling me his life-story. I asked Skip whether he intended to stay for long in Japan and he replied that he was undecided—he might stay or go on elsewhere, or return to the States at some point. Meanwhile he was sufficiently wealthy to reside in Japan indefinitely. "I'm retired," he told me. "If I stayed put in one place now, I would just be looking forward to death. It's better to keep moving."

When at last Skip grew tired of talking, he asked me again why I had come to see him. I began by relating what had happened to me since our previous encounter, altering the account only slightly by saying that, back then, I had a mass of savings that I had accrued by putting money away as a nest-egg every month while I was at work in Nimsan, till finally I had saved enough to quit my job and travel around Japan with Yumi, but apart from that untruth about how I obtained my money I kept to the facts by saying that when we were at the seaside we had been robbed by a stranger and I lost everything including Yumi, and had returned to Tokyo alone on foot.

And now, I added, I did not have a penny left, and could Skip think of a way to help me? I was not asking him for money, but to help me think of a way to survive because I had been living on the streets and sleeping in a park for the last several weeks and was going crazy. I had even gone berserk and taken it out on someone in the street, pouncing on him for no good reason. I needed an occupation of some sort, but there was nothing available that I knew about, I was in Japan and did not have any connections. Could Skip help me? I had formulated an idea and proffered it to Skip: "Why don't I write your life story?" I asked him, "as an amanuensis, a scribe, a secretary, a scrivener? I'm pretty good with words. If you can dictate your life's tale just as you told it to me today, I will write it all down—your memoirs of being in the army and the A-bomb tests you witnessed. They make an interesting story, which will otherwise just be lost when you go. None of us is getting any younger you know. I can type, and have plenty of experience as an editor. As a matter of fact, I had a crash course in editing in my last job—my mentor at Nimsan was quite a taskmaster, and in her own way she goaded me into being diligent.

"And when you have finished narrating each section," I continued to Skip, "I can brush it up as well. It needn't take very long each day, or

193

whenever you have time to do it. If you let me write your biography, in return I just need a place to stay, under a real roof, on the floor would be fine, and perhaps a bite to eat every day, till I can get back on my feet again."

When I finished saying this, I looked up at Skip, who appeared to be soaking it in.

Or was he? Then he erupted into laughter. "You're going to have to come up with something a bit better than that!" he hooted. "What if I don't want my story told? It's nothing special. Who wants to read about what I did? And in any case, my story isn't over yet, so how can I tell it? Do I look all that old to you?" he asked me, pointing at his face, "Well these wrinkles round my eyes, they're not due to old age, sun or tobacco, no, I got those from listening to music."

"I've got nowhere else to go," I told Skip.

"You can try getting a job," was the reply. "That's your weakness, you just don't want to work. You spent a few weeks going to an office, and now you consider that you've had enough of it. You should try taking army orders for a living, as I did, and being A-bombed into the bargain."

Seeing that I looked dejected, Skip lowered his tone a little. "Okay listen," he said. "Instead of you making me an offer, why don't I make you one, since I'm the person here with all the incentives. I can put you up with a room in this hotel, while you write not my life story, but *yours*. Why don't you write down what happened to you in Japan, make a book out of it, detailing your impressions and all the incidents that befell you. Work at it and teach yourself to become a writer. Then when you're done, if you are any good you will be able to consider yourself a writer, a writer with a finished book on your hands to prove it. After that you will be on your own. But an offer of a place to stay without having to pay any rent while you can just write is a better deal than any that I ever heard some other writer tell having had when getting started. If you are interested in doing that, you are welcome to stay here as my guest for the time it takes.

"And besides," added Skip, "I can't let you back out on the streets to go around attacking people, you're a menace to society."

To this marvelous godsend I agreed immediately. I started writing my story that afternoon, casting my mind back to the moment I set foot in Japan and my meeting with Dr. Gunji in Narita Airport, and continuing from there. Skip lived in the portion of the Imperial Hotel known as the

"Tower" annex, a high-rise building overlooking the gardens of the Imperial Palace, the Emperor's residence. Skip occupied not a room or suite but one floor of the Tower; that is, he had the use of all seven rooms on the twentieth floor. Each of these rooms had a name of a color instead of a number: the Blue Room, the Purple Room, the Green Room and so on for orange, white, violet and black. Within each of these rooms, though, I was disappointed to find out, the decor was standard hotel fare and not what I was hoping would be inside—ornaments and tapestries in each respective color with casements of stained glass in those same colors throwing tinted light into the interiors. Instead, each room had a neatly made bed, bureau table with a telephone, shelves and wardrobes. Skip mainly occupied the Blue Room, which was spacious and had the best view of the gardens below, and reserved the other rooms for putting up guests, visitors and "people he liked," although there was no one staying in any of the rooms at that particular time. When Skip asked me what room I wanted to use, I instinctively opted to stay in the White Room, which shared the name of the song by Cream, and was also round a corner of the corridor from Skip's Blue Room, which I thought would negate the chances of my getting under Skip's feet and allow him to forget that I was there. Skip himself had given the rooms their names and had requested the hotel management to take off the old room numbers. Since he was a permanent resident, he did not want to feel like he was living in a prison, he told me.

This story ends here. Over the next few weeks I did little but sit in the White Room and write, using a small Dell computer that Skip set up for me. Every morning I took my breakfast in the help-yourself dining area of the Imperial Hotel, then returned to my room or at first took a walk outside, then went back up to my computer. I spent hours at it. There is not much else to report from that time. Nothing happened. Out of habitually being confined there, I spoonerized my room name and began to call it the Write Womb. Sometimes I raced through my manuscript, producing pages and pages of word after word in an hour—other times I sat looking at the ivory computer screen and could not write a single syllable all day. I often considered whether to spruce up my story with unsubstantiated flights of fancy, to make it more interesting. After all, a book's contents ought to be more intriguing than the everyday world around us. I toyed with the idea of making Yumi come back to me. I wondered how I could retrieve the money I had lost simply by writing that it was returned to me somehow. Or that perhaps I could be given a second chance and collect another huge sum. In one version of my story, I typed that when The Cadaver drove off with Yumi in the black taxi at Ino Point, leaving me beached by the roadside, I watched through the rear window as she valiantly grappled with him, causing him to brake, and that Yumi scrambled out the stopped cab door with our bag of money and ran to meet me as I sprinted over to the scene. As we embraced, kissing and vowing never to leave one another again, abruptly The Cadaver barged in, pounced on us and tried to seize the bag; I squared up to the bastard and socked him on the jaw with a single, Clint Eastwood-style punch that sent him sprawling on his back like a starfish spread out on the sand. Taking Yumi by her hand, we ran toward the dunes as The Cadaver followed on our heels—now brandishing a shiny metal handgun. We dove from one position of cover to the next as we evaded our dangerous predator. With each sprint we made for fresh cover, gunshots fired at us from our rear. I heard one tobogganing bullet gasp an inch past my ear—from a hundred yards behind to the same distance ahead in a second….

But I deleted all the flights of fancy. I stuck to actual events as I remembered them, knowing that memories at length become imaginary anyway.

I was also aware as I wrote down the story of what happened to me, that since I could describe the involved events of an entire day in a fraction of that time, therefore with each paragraph completed I was catching up with the present. At some point, where I was in my account and where I was while sitting down chronicling it were going to converge. From that moment, then, what further I wrote about myself may as well continue into the future. Was it possible to write a doomsday of predictions that pans out as written? Or one that influences what might happen? It was a tempting prospect, except that I knew that to try to force my will on destiny is condemned from the start. All my expectations and attempts to envision the future in glimpses and foretastes have always fallen flat. When the moment arrived, it looked nothing like how I had imagined it.

There was only one satisfactory way to write my story. Since what we imagine ahead is all wrong, and then what really happens instead becomes imaginary as it recedes further into the past, because our memory is just as faulty as our precognitions, I could see that what I had to do was rethink recent events clearly and record them as closely as possible to the truth without embellishment. And when I got to now, I must stop. So I did just that. In time, the story of my Japanese adventure, starting from when I arrived at the office of Nimsan, to riches briefly, and finally back to my customary penury, was written. It was a story in three parts, each in different dire straits: a trilogy. *Sanbusaku*. The results are the book you are holding in your hands. More followed afterwards, more adventures and mishaps, but those are for another book.